Praise for THE JAGUAR'S CHILDREN

"*The Jaguar's Children* is extraordinarily powerful."   *National Post*

"Applause for John Vaillant, please. He is masterful in creating literary suspense and methodically doling out insights into the many aspects of Héctor's life. The novel forces you to be still, to take small sips and to count down the pages."   *The Vancouver Sun*

"As he demonstrated in his non-fiction, Vaillant has a way of seeing stories where others see inevitabilities, and his work, here, as always, shows a tremendous respect for life—human and otherwise."
Robert Wiersema, *The Georgia Straight*

"Vaillant's novel is irresistible."
Melanie Jackson, *Edmonton Journal*

"Urgent and compelling."   *The Walrus*

"*The Jaguar's Children* feels just as real as *The Golden Spruce* or *The Tiger*, perhaps more so, considering that the subject matter isn't just fodder for a plot but someone's life. The book is labelled as fiction, yet Vaillant's work remains firmly rooted in fact."
The Globe and Mail

"A heart-wrenching literary thriller . . . a complicated, generations-spanning tale that offers a distressing yet often beautiful depiction of life in modern Mexico. . . . But for all the vibrancy and colour of the backdrop, it's that horrifying main hook of a group of desperate migrants slowly dying of thirst, heat and hunger that will no doubt haunt the reader long after the last page is turned."

Calgary Herald

"A vibrant portrait of life and nation. . . . *The Jaguar's Children* confirms Vaillant . . . is equally skilled in the telling of stories both true and imagined. . . . The novel unfurls at the pace of a geopolitical thriller, with the gravitas of allegory."

National Post

"Gripping. . . . Vaillant's moving novel shows a deep understanding of how societies are changed by events they cannot control, and the impact of those changes on the fate of individuals."

Winnipeg Free Press

"Vaillant's triumph is the way he invites readers to know Héctor so intimately as he waits for salvation or death. . . . This is what novels can do—illuminate shadowed lives, enable us to contemplate our own depths of kindness, challenge our beliefs about fate."

Amanda Eyre Ward, *The New York Times Book Review*

"A woozy heartbreaker of a novel."

The Boston Globe

"*The Jaguar's Children* is devastating. It's at once a literary mystery, an engrossing tour de force, and a brilliant commentary on humanity's role in the physical world. The voice that echoes out from that abandoned place Vaillant so masterfully creates won't leave me."

Joseph Boyden

THE JAGUAR'S CHILDREN

John Vaillant

Vintage Canada

VINTAGE CANADA EDITION, 2015

Copyright © 2015 John Vaillant

Published in Canada by Vintage Canada, a division of Penguin Random House Canada Limited, Toronto, in 2015. Originally published in hardcover in Canada by Knopf Canada, a division of Penguin Random House Canada Limited, in 2015. Distributed in Canada by Penguin Random House Canada Limited.

Vintage Canada with colophon is a registered trademark.

www.penguinrandomhouse.ca

This book is a work of fiction. Names, characters, places and incidents either are the product of the author's imagination or are used fictitiously. Any resemblance to actual persons, living or dead, events or locales is entirely coincidental.

Library and Archives Canada Cataloguing in Publication

Vaillant, John (John H.). author
The jaguar's children : a novel / John Vaillant.

ISBN 978-0-307-39717-1
eBook ISBN 978-0-307-36694-8

I. Title.

PS8643.I364J33 2016   C813'.6   C2014-901537-2

Text design by Chrissy Kurpeski
Cover design by CS Richardson
Image credits: (fence) John Moore/Getty Images,
(tire tracks) Ken Kistler/Shutterstock.com

Printed and bound in the United States of America

2 4 6 8 9 7 5 3 1

Penguin
Random
House

*For my family
passed and present*

Anyone attempting to classify Olmec figures will be borne imperceptibly into those of the jaguar. Gradually, human faces will acquire feline features, blending one into the other before turning, finally, into jaguars. What is important is the intimate connection between the man and the animal.

— IGNACIO BERNAL, *THE OLMEC WORLD*

1

Thu Apr 5 — 08:31 [text]
hello i am sorry to bother you but i need your assistance —
i am hector — cesars friend — its an emergency now for
cesar — are you in el norte? i think we are also — arizona near
nogales or sonoita — since yesterday we are in this truck with
no one coming — we need water and a doctor — and a torch
for cutting metal

Thu Apr 5 — 08:48
please text me annimac — we need help

Thu Apr 5 — 08:59

are you there annimac? it's hector — please text me

Thu Apr 5 — 09:52

there was a storm — 1 bar only now — ARE YOU THERE???

Thu Apr 5 — 10:09

1 bar — something's broken — maybe from the lightning — the helicopter came again but doesn't stop — how do they not see us? nothing going now

Thu Apr 5 — 10:26 [soundfile]

Hello? I hope this works. Still one bar only but I'm recording now and when the signal comes back I will send it in a soundfile with all the details and the information from César. He is badly hurt, AnniMac — unconscious. I looked in his contacts for someone else, but the Mexican numbers won't work now, and you are the only one with an American code. I hope you are his friend. I know him from school, but I haven't seen him in many years. We've been together only a short time now to cross the border and already he gave me so many things. I have been telling him he's not alone, that I sent you messages and you're coming soon, that you will save us. I don't know if he hears, but in this darkness how will he know to live without a voice — some sign of life? So I talk to him, and to you also.

AnniMac, if you get these messages and come to look for us what you are looking for is a water truck — an old Dina. The tank is a big one — ten thousand liters and you will know it when you see an adobe-color truck that says on the side AGUA PARA USO

HUMANO — Water for Human Use. But that doesn't mean you can drink it. This one is different because someone has painted J and R so it says now JAGUAR PARA USO HUMANO. I saw this in the garage before we loaded and I didn't know if it was graffiti or some kind of code, the secret language of coyotes, but then I was nervous to ask and later it was too late.

Thu Apr 5 — 10:34

It works. I made a soundfile. I will send it when the bars come back, and this one also. The coyotes told us it was a good idea to fill a water truck with people. A good way to get across. No one will know we are here because there is no way into the tank besides two small pipes in the back. The door on top is too small for a person, and they put a box inside with water so if the truck is stopped and searched by la Migra it will not look suspicious. This is what the coyotes told us, like they were describing special features on a new car. It is expensive to do it they said, and this is why we must pay extra, but only un poquito. They were talking fast all the time, but not as fast as their eyes.

Some things you want to know about coyotes — just like in the wild nature there are no fat ones and no old ones. They are young machos hoping one day to be something more — a heavy, a real chingón. But first they must do this thing — this taking across the border, and this is where they learn to be hard. Coyotes have another name also. Polleros. A pollero is a man who herds the chickens. There is no such thing really because chickens go where they want, but this is the name for these men. And we — the ones who want to cross — are the pollos. Maybe you know *pollo* is not a chicken running in the yard — *gallina* is the name for that. *Pollo* is chicken cooked on a plate — a dinner for coyotes. This is who is speaking to you now.

Besides me and César in here are thirteen others — nine men and four women, all of us from the south. Two are even from Nicaragua. I don't know how they can pay unless they are pandilleros because it is expensive to be in here. To fit us all in, a mechanic with a torch cut a hole in the belly of the tank. Then we climbed in, and with a welder he closed the hole again and painted it over. Inside is dark like you're blind with only the cold metal to sit on and so crowded you are always touching someone. There is a smell of rust and old water and the walls are alive with something that likes to grow in the wet and dark, something that needs much less air than a man.

I can touch the ceiling if I stand, but the tank is slippery from whatever is growing in here and I could hear people falling when they got in. Unless you are in the very back or the front, the walls are round so it is hard to sit. César and me were the last ones so we are in the back by the pipes and we have a straight wall. It is a good position and we must protect it, the same as the shoeshine man must protect his puesto on the plaza.

The promise made to us for thirty thousand pesos each — *pesitos* Lupo called them, like they were only small — the promise was to cross the border quickly between Sonoita and Nogales — no more than three hours, garantizado. Then drive straight to a warehouse where a compadre will cut the hole again and let us out. We will be safe there, he said, with water and gringo clothes and time to call our contacts. In the warehouse there is some kind of secret door with a place to meet the vans so we can leave invisible. These were the promises made to us.

All of us agreed to wait until this morning, until it got hot again, and then if the coyotes did not come back we would use the phones to call for help. No one wanted to do this. No one wants to see la Migra and be deported. We have traveled so far and paid so much. So we waited as long as we could — all day and all the night, but people are afraid now because we can die in here you know, and it is difficult to breathe.

There are four phones I know about — mine, César's, Naldo's and another guy from Veracruz with no more minutes who will not speak now. Naldo is a Mixtec kid from Puebla, maybe sixteen years old. He had some minutes, but he couldn't get a signal and then he used up his battery reading old text messages from his girlfriend, even though the Veracruzano told him not to. He has been crying a lot and this is bad for water conservation. Talking is not so good either, but to only wait is worse. Already it is more than thirty hours.

Thu Apr 5 — 10:41

We didn't know what side of the border we were on so first I tried Emergencias 066. I had two bars and a tone, but it would not go so I tried your 911 and it was the same. Then I tried to call my tío in L.A. who is expecting me to come there, but it made a sound I never heard in a phone and the text would not go either. Maybe it is all the metal around us, or maybe la Migra is jamming the signal from Mexican phones. Who knows. I didn't want to worry my mother so after this I tried to call my father's cell, but it didn't work. Only then I called my home in Oaxaca, and it was terrible — the call goes through — and it is my mother who answers, but for some reason she cannot hear me. It is like a dream and I am yelling but she says only "¿Bueno? ¿Bueno? ¿Quién es?"— she even guesses it is me —"¡Hectorcito!" she says — I can hear how worried she is —"¿Tito? ¿Eres tú? ¿Dónde estás?"— and I'm shouting "¡Mamá!" and the others in the truck are so quiet, listening so hard I can feel it because they think I'm connected. They think they're saved. But it's only me hearing her, and then she says to someone — my father, or my sister, "Nadie está allí," and she was gone.

Es una gran chingadera, a knife in my heart, but people were shouting at me to call again. In that moment there was so much hope. I must tell you it was hard to lose my mother like that, but not as hard as losing my minutes because when I tried again I got the message from Telcel saying my minutes were finished. I had so many but they went so fast. That's how I knew we'd crossed the border. After this, I had despair. Maybe you saw that movie where the spaceman's cable is cut and he floats away smaller and smaller, and there is nothing in the world he can do.

Naldo was trying to call then also, but his phone is old and nothing was going. The Veracruzano couldn't even get any bars. Of course I tried César's phone. His phone is a good one — a Nokia 95, but he must be on a different network — when I called my home, the voice was so strange and far I couldn't recognize it. I tried again to call my tío in L.A., also 066 and 911, and then I tried Sofía from my Customer Service class, and Dani, another friend from the university, but nothing would go. That's when I looked in César's directory. Maybe you know César has been living in D.F. for five or six years now, going to the university — to UNAM, and working there also, so he has many numbers from the Mexico City code. I looked through them all — what else is there to do? That's when I found your American code together with an email address. The call wouldn't go so I tried a text. There were two bars then — strong, and I said the texts are going, and people cheered. But I was afraid of losing César's minutes too — we should wait, I told them, to see if anything comes back. That's when we heard the thunder, beating us like a drum. And a woman near me praying, "Dios salvanos," over and over, like those are the only words she knows. Already it was smelling very strong in the tank — sweat and fear and other bad body odors, and the heat inside was growing.

Most of us have only a liter of water because it is such a short trip. That is all I have too, but I didn't forget that feeling I had yesterday morning when the truck stopped and we thought we were there and César said, "Dios, espero que sí." That little prayer, maybe it's his premonition, I don't know, but after it I was careful with my water. The others are saying this also — Save your water. But now it's too late. Some people finished their water already and the food they brought is no good — Mars bars and lollipops and chicharrones con salsa — I know it by the smell. We are like children in here. Locked in a dark room.

2

I don't think anyone in here speaks English besides me and César, but I can see with the phone a baby-face man sitting near us, a mestizo, who is suspicious. Him and some others, they were asking what I'm saying. They want to know if the bars came back, if I'm talking to a real person. I said to them, People send messages to God and the saints all the time and mine is not the only voice in here. Others are praying too, but not like last night when there were so many calls going out: *Virgencita ayúdame . . . Jesús mío, misericordia . . . Adorada Guadalupe llena de gracia . . . Ave María, santísima . . .*

¡Señor, por favor! And I knew by their words that some of them have not been to the church in a long time.

How much can I tell you about what is happening in here? It is hard to see it, but even harder to say it. These are things no one wants to know. The son of the praying woman is moaning now and will not stop. It is not a normal moaning but the same sound every time in a rhythm. His mother is holding his head and begging him to be quiet, to rest, but he will not, or cannot. Maybe his ears don't work anymore, or his mind. It is harder to think good thoughts in the dark.

The only other voices now besides them and me is an older man in front who is also praying sometimes. Everyone else is only breathing, saving themselves. I don't know if anyone is dying and I don't want to know. I am only looking at the screen, at the battery and at your name.

¡Chingada madre! Still one bar only. So many messages I wrote and all of it is saved for later.

So I tell you because this waiting is a torture.

When the sun came up this morning, we knew it only by the sounds the tank was making as the walls got warm and then hot. It is a desert all around us, but in here the air is thick like the jungle and with the heat comes the smell of everyone, a thick blanket you can feel but cannot see. On the left side of the tank, two people down from me, is a woman from Michoacán, a baker, who left her home because of so many threats from the narcos if she doesn't pay them every month. They killed her husband for this already and I heard her ask the praying woman, "What is better, to leave your home or stay in a place so heavy with fear and hate not even bread can rise?"

"God knows," said the praying woman.

"I think He left already," said the baker.

She is the one who said we should make a toilet at one end of the tank, in a bag, but no one wanted to give up their place and no one wanted to be near the bag and some others could not wait so now the whole tank is a toilet. People are ashamed to talk about it so they are doing what they have to just anywhere, maybe in their water bottle, maybe in a plastic bag or their backpack, but it is bad anyway — the smell crowding around you with nowhere to go so you must breathe through your shirt, a sock, whatever you have. More than one person threw up already. With this and the heat and the thirst, people aren't thinking right. I know this from the things they say. Some ask for empty bottles, but in return others ask for water. Some are begging even. No one wants to say what they have. In the dark, you can keep some things a secret, but not the sound or the smell.

¡Ay, estamos jodidos! This situation is fucked, no? When those Greeks were hiding in that horse they wanted to attack the city, and when the terrorists were hiding in those planes they wanted to attack the country, but when Mexicanos hide in a truck, what do they want to do? They want to pick the lettuce. And cut your grass.

There are brave fighters in my country, I swear, but most of them are dead or working for the narcos.

Thu Apr 5 — 11:10

I gave César some water. He cannot take more than a little without choking so I must drip it in with the cap. Then I take a capful for myself.

Did you ever find yourself in a situation that you cannot believe is happening — to you? That last part is important. Maybe you had dreams like this, but in the end you are permitted to wake up. I am talking about la realidad — the dream without end, a dream you would refuse to believe if only your power to refuse was so strong. Of course there are many sad situations — more and more all the time. All our newspapers have la página roja with its narco murders and terrible accidents, and I think we are like the bulls in la corrida, always distracted by the red. But since your NAFTA and the narcos, people have lost interest in the bulls, and why not? We are sacrificing humans now, just like in the old times. We are used to such things in the news, but it is different when it is happening to you, no? It is hard in this moment to believe I am actually awake and alive.

It is so dark I jumped at the touch of my own hand.

Thu Apr 5 — 11:22

César's phone gives me hope — his strong battery and his minutes. I am amazed no one stole it before he got in the truck, but he hid it very well I can tell you. On our way to meet the coyotes, the bus was stopped outside Santa Ana and the police went through everything, made us empty our pockets. Searching for drugs and weapons they said, but of course they sell them also. To migrantes, everyone always says, Don't bring anything valuable because they will take it — if not the police, then the soldiers or some other cabrones. Maybe you must pay a mordida, maybe they look in your bag and find something they like. Whenever they want they can do this, and each time is like those screens they use to sort the rocks for cement — smaller and smaller until you have left only sand. That is about all we had when we got to the border.

We got off the bus in Altar, which is in the state of Sonora, eighty kilometers from the border. This is where my father instructed me to go. Altar is a little town only for migrantes and narcos and you pay extra to get off there. There is a lot of extra between Oaxaca and el Norte. From the bus I saw a sign saying ÉXODO 1:12. I was half asleep, tired from traveling three days, and I thought it was the time until we reached that place. But then there was another one — ÉXODO 3:17 and then MATEO 5:5 and more after that. Maybe you have a Bible and you can tell me what this means.

The moment we stepped off the bus we were surrounded by coyotes, some on foot and some in vans with dark windows. They were working that place like pimps and all their girls had sexy American names —

"Yo, chapo, you want L.A., Atlanta, Nueva York? I got 'em right now."

"Oye, esé, you like Miami — you get a job in a country club ten dollars an hour como mi hermano. Todo es posible. We go tonight."

"¡Chis, Oaxaca! Over here. Where you want to go, güey? Tacoma? I got a good price for you."

In the north, Oaxaca is an insult and many times that first day I heard it — "Heyyyy, Oaxaquito!" What they are really saying is, "Heyyyy, stupid poor indio from the south, let me take your money!"

I just looked away because everyone knows there are many pandilleros up here. But in my mind I was saying, "Chinga tu madre y chupa mi verga oaxaqueña, pinche pendejo."

Besides the church which is old from the days of the missions, there is nothing in Altar, barely a tree, just a few blocks of houses, some hotels and restaurants, a gas station, the Western Union, some little tiendas and many rooms and beds for rent. Always on the plaza was an old man sweeping with his broom made of branches — sweeping and sweeping even when there was nothing to sweep. There are stalls there with things to buy, but there is nothing for the house or the milpa, nothing nice to eat or to wear. Besides expensive water, it is mostly clothes and almost all of them are black or gray—T-shirts, jackets, balaclavas and gloves, even the bags—so you can be invisible in the desert, in the dark, because that is what a migrante needs to be to make it in el Norte.

Altar is the same I think in English—where you go to make an offering, a sacrifice. You can tell by the faces and the bodies that people come from everywhere to do this—not only from Mexico, but Guatemala, Nicaragua, Panama, some guëros and chinos too. There were so many—hundreds, thousands even—almost all men, wandering around the bus stop, the plaza, the streets. It was like the corrals at the matadero where they keep the cattle waiting. There were more around the church of Our Lady of Guadalupe and inside also, praying for the journey. In Altar, la Virgen de Guadalupe is everywhere—on the men's jackets, on their pants, tattooed on their skin and painted on the walls, rising up over the mountains of el Norte to guide and comfort her dark children—los migrantes, los peregrinos, los hijos de la chingada.

Most of them are walking. It is a long trip, two or three days from the Sásabe crossing, and it is easy to get lost in the desert, easy to die. Along the border there are signs from the government saying, ¡CUIDADO! IT'S NOT WORTH IT, with pictures of snakes and scorpions and skulls. But when you look north, past the sand and rock and mesquite, toward that wall of mountains with only cactus growing, you still believe you can do it because who wants to turn back now when you came so far? What is there to go back to? Your family is depending on you. And if you are still not sure, there is the voice of the coyote—"¡Ándale! Stay together. If you fall behind we cannot wait for you." This is the message of Progress in the New World, and coyotes are the messengers. But some of us do fall behind. In Altar, by the church, I saw a map with red dots marking all the places migrantes have died. Everywhere north of Sásabe was covered in red dots, all the way to Tucson. If they ever make a *Guinness Book of Third World Records,* this border will be in there for sure.

It was César's idea to go in the truck. I was going to walk across because it is cheaper, but César told me about his older brother, Goyo, who walked into California from Tecate and nearly died. "He had a good coyote who stayed with them," said César, "but they got lost anyway. It was only when one of them climbed a small mountain and saw the lights that they knew where to go. By the time they got to the place on the highway to meet the van, they'd had no water for a whole day and they were almost crazy. He said their saliva was like glue, their tongues so thick they couldn't speak. And that was in January."

"Goyo saw some things out there," said César. "At the end of the first day they found a body. He told me it was like the ones you see in las catacumbas where the mouth is open screaming and screaming and the skin is tight like a drum. The face of this one, he said it was full of cactus spines. Because this is what happens when you go crazy from the thirst — you will try to eat a cactus and the pain will not stop you. Nothing will stop you and anything is possible," said César. "Goyo told me that face stays with him — como un fantasma oscuro — visiting him in the night. There is another thing my brother saw out there and that was the diapers. Goyo is a father, you know, and to think of babies and small children out there in such an infierno —'Who can do this with a child?' he said."

César's brother told him there are thousands of bodies out there, thousands of red dots. When I was young in the pueblo the padre read to us about the Valley of Dry Bones, but then I did not know it was real, or that those bones were ours. César said his brother made him swear on their mother he would never try to walk across, but it wasn't until we got to Altar and met Lupo that César told me of this promise.

We found Lupo in his garage across from el Mercado Coyote Blanco. He was tall and thin with rings in both ears and a mustache so short and fine you can count the hairs. There was some kind of tattoo animal crawling out of his collar. I couldn't see what it was, but its claws were in his neck. When Lupo gave us the choice to walk for twenty thousand or ride for thirty, César is the one who said to me, "There is some risk with a vehicle of getting discovered at the border, but I'm telling you, man, three hours in a truck beats the shit out of three days in the desert."

I could have left him then. I had the chance, but I was afraid to go alone. I called my father and told him about the truck and how it was more expensive but safer than walking. He called back soon. Don Serafín would permit this, he said, but I must pay the difference and if I don't make the payments every month there will be a problem between him and Don Serafín — so I must not fail. I know my father was afraid for me, but he is also afraid of Don Serafín and how I might cause him shame and other problems if I don't pay back the money. That was the last time I talked to my father, and after it I felt like I was carrying one of his buckets of cement.

César made his own bargain with Lupo, but he did not speak of it to me and I did not ask. Once this was done there was only the waiting for the truck to be ready. Behind the garage where Lupo and his compadres were working, there was a little choza with some old mattresses and pieces of foam on the floor and this is where he told us to sleep. "If you go out," he said, "be careful. You can be kidnapped here. It doesn't matter if you have nothing, they will get it from your family no matter where you live. And if they can't, they can make you carry a gun for them or maybe la mota. Or maybe they just kill you for your liver and kidneys—there is a market for that here too—and when they finish there are many holes in the desert filled with Oaxacas just like you."

He wasn't lying about this. "My brother Goyo made this trip many times," said César, "but five years ago was the last time. Before, it was different—you could go back and forth, no problems. You might get robbed, but you wouldn't be kidnapped and killed. Now the whole situation is changing—many times they move the people and the drugs together. I think now he can never come back to Mexico."

It is the same for my tío in L.A. who has no papers. He hasn't been home in ten years. That part of the family is broken off now, like they went to China.

The last thing Lupo said to us before they closed up the hole—"Whatever happens, don't make a sound."

Well, something happened. First the road was smooth for maybe an hour like we were on the highway to Sonoita, and then it wasn't. I thought, Oh, it is construction, because in Mexico the road is always under construction. I said this to César. And this is when he said, "Dios, espero que sí." That is when I began to be afraid. There was something in his voice and I was thinking then I must save my water. I don't know these other people except for César and I said nothing after that, only to curse when my head hit the wall of the tank. The road was never smooth again, only rough and more rough, and we were banging around inside here like turkeys in the back of my father's truck. People were becoming frightened and angry and the air was getting bad. Our clothes were wet from the rusty water and the things growing and this was mixing with our dried sweat and sour clothes from all the days traveling to be here and it smelled like food going bad. It was the end of the night and because most of us are from the south it was cold for us. Whatever clothes we had, we were wearing them. For me it was only jeans, a polo and my sweatshirt with the hood.

We drove like this, slow, in a low gear, for another hour — maybe more, it is difficult to say. Something happens to your sense of time in the dark. Then we stopped like we hit a wall. I heard heads and bodies hitting the front of the tank. There was crying and cursing and some little pieces of prayers, even though we were supposed to be quiet. The truck was leaning to one side and I knew something had happened to the front wheel — maybe it was flat or in a hole. But the motor was still running and we were still hoping that this was the border and that soon we would be moving again because to imagine something else was intolerable. Es demasiado.

Someone whispered, "¿La frontera?" Another said, "¡Gracias a Dios!" Then César said a prayer to la Virgen María de Juquila who is not only César's protector but a great help to travelers, especially Zapotecos. Of course we have many virgins in Mexico and most of them are güeras — white, like you maybe, but Juquila es una morena, dark like us. Like me. We look into her small face and see someone we know and many people, including César, believe she really understands. For her my family has made the pilgrimage. Our Juquila is the smallest virgin of them all — the size of a Barbie with long black hair, and I was thinking then, Yes, Juquilita is the right virgin for this situation. She is small enough to fit in here. After the truck stopped everything was still, everyone holding their breath and listening, except for César who prayed for all of us quiet and quick —

Dear Mother, Virgin of Juquila, Virgin of our life,
*   please intercede in all misfortunes that may befall us.*
If, in this world of injustice, of misery and sin,
*   you see that our lives are turbulent, don't abandon us.*

Dear Mother, protect the travelers and pilgrims.
Guide the poor who have nothing and those whose bread has been
    taken from them.
Accompany us throughout our journey, liberate us from sin,
    and please — deliver us home.

There was whispering and soft words as some others followed along, and at the end in many voices, "Amén."

There were small sounds in the dark then as some people crossed themselves, kissed a crucifix, a medallion, their crossed fingers, counted off their rosaries. I had nothing but the little clay head my abuelo gave me and I held this tight in my fist. I will tell you, it is not the head of a saint or a virgin, it is the head of a jaguar made a long time ago when men and jaguars lived much closer together. My grandfather knew this animal well. Never was this an easy thing to do, now it is harder.

After César's prayer, we did like Lupo told us — we stayed silent as water in a tank. For an hour we waited like this with the motor running. Outside, there was no other sound, no voices or birds, no other cars or trucks. I wondered to myself if this was a special crossing point in the desert. Maybe we were waiting for someone to come and read the words on the truck — the secret coyote code. César was sitting next to me and I felt him moving in the dark. "Where are we?" he whispered. "What the fuck are they doing out there?"

Right after that I felt him stand up. I don't know why he did this, maybe he was impatient, but in that same moment the engine roared and the truck jumped forward and then stopped dead — the motor and everything. It was a surprise for everyone and it threw us all backward. I hit my head hard on the back wall and I felt César falling over me. There was so much shouting and cursing it took a moment to understand what was happening, but soon I knew there was a problem with César. He wasn't moving, he was only lying on me, very heavy. I said his name, but there was no answer. I was feeling for his face, and when I found him his forehead was wet and I knew it wasn't water. Right there near his head is a place on the back wall where the pipes come in — only a few centimeters, but the edges are sharp and it was enough to hurt César. I rolled him off me and put my ear to his face. He was breathing, but not in the normal way.

I was telling the people around me that a man is hurt, but a woman in front started banging on the tank and screaming. Others were telling her to stop. "¡Chis, cállate!" they hissed. "You will give us away!" There was some kind of fighting then, it moved through the tank in a wave and I was kicked in the face. That was the third time I wished I never left Oaxaca. I heard the door of the truck and someone outside hit the tank hard with a pipe or a stone, shouting, "Shut the fuck up or you will all be discovered and shot!"

This is what they say can happen on the border now — maybe your Minutemen, maybe agents from la Migra take you in the green truck, and no one ever sees you again. So we were quiet then because no one wants to die or disappear, and César, my only friend in here, lying next to me just breathing and breathing like a broken machine.

3

It is hard to say this, AnniMac, because I am ashamed to be in such a situation. But what reason to hide it now? Who knows, maybe you would do the same in my place. I must tell you so that somebody knows what happened to César and all of us. Maybe you can find the people who did this.

Luego, it happens like this —

The truck is stopped, we don't know where, and César is lying beside me somewhere between death and sleeping. Outside, I can hear the coyotes talking to themselves. They are coyotes so of course they are hard to understand, but it sounds like they are looking at the truck, trying to figure out what to do. I whisper once more that someone is hurt but no one notices because they are trying to hear the coyotes. So I feel César's face again and his forehead, and there is the cut, right on the line where the hair is growing and it is pushed in a little bit, the skin and bone together. I open my water bottle and pour some drops on his forehead to wash the blood away, but it keeps coming so with my phone I look around for something to stop it and that's when I see the little cotton dress sticking out of his jacket pocket, the one he bought for the Virgin Juquila when we were still in Oaxaca. The blood is coming fast and there isn't time to think so I put the dress on there and push on it.

This is when I hear one of the coyotes climbing on the hood, on top of the cab. There is a scraping noise at the front of the tank, near the top, and then comes a blade of light so sharp we all cry out and cover our eyes. We are mostly grown men and women in there but the way we hide and cover ourselves is like when your father comes at you with the belt. A moment comes and goes like this and then carefully I look through my fingers. The light is still there blinding, screaming in over our heads — como la Anunciación — and I understand it is a flashlight coming through a small hole. Then a shadow comes across it and I see only teeth.

"¡Amigos! ¿Qué tal?" says the shadow with its teeth. "Tenemos un pequeño problema aquí. It is the front wheel — this is broken. Everything else is OK but we must bring our mechanic to fix it. We tried many times to call but he will not answer so now we must go to find him. We are close — only ten kilometers so it won't take long. We will bring back some water too because maybe you are getting thirsty."

"¿Cuando?" asks a man in the front.

"Not until the night. Because of la Migra."

"How long is that?"

There is a moment, another blade of light is stabbing us and then the shadow again. "Not long — a few hours."

This of course cannot be true because we left only a few hours ago and a man in front with a Zapotec accent says, "What are you talking about? It's six in the morning! We can't wait here all day!"

"¡Cabrón!" says the coyote. "Be quiet or you will make big problems for us and for you. La pinche Migra has powerful sensors all over the desert and they can hear everything you say. Oye, we want to help you, but we are going to need some money to do it."

"We already paid our money," says the Zapotec man.

"Yes, but that is different money, only for Don Serafín. It is untouchable. We are just the guides, amigo, and now we have this little problem so we must work together to fix it, no?"

"How much?" asks another man. He sounds old and tired and I wonder if he has done this before.

"To buy the parts and pay the mechanic to come here — five hundred," says the coyote. "Five-fifty with the water."

"Five hundred and fifty pesos," says the Zapotec man.

The coyote makes a disgusting noise and spits. "¡No más pesitos! You're in America now, bro —"

"Then let us out!" shouts the baker from Michoacán.

"Tranquilo," says the coyote. "It isn't safe here. And we have no torch." There is a silence in the truck. "The mechanic has one, but he won't take pesos. Solamente dólares gringos."

"Who has five hundred and fifty dollars?" says the Zapotec man.

"If you want to get delivered," says the coyote, "you do."

"A man is badly hurt," I say. "We need some help in here."

Outside, away from the truck, I hear the other coyote saying, "¡Flaco! A la chingada. Let's get out of here."

There is another silence because we are turning a corner now and the Zapotec man whispers, "Does anyone have dollars?"

No one will answer, but the truth is most of us have some. But this is our only money for getting where we need to go on the other side. Without it we are trapped. The older man says, "How do we know you won't just take the money and leave us here?"

Then, very quiet, like he is sharing with us a special secret, the coyote says, "You hear my compa — what he says? He is ready to leave right now. I want to help you, amigos, but I don't have all day. We need to hurry if we're going to find the mechanic and get you out of here."

The people talk between themselves. "What do you think? Do we pay? Can we trust him?"

But what choice do we have?

The older man is old enough to be the coyote's father and he says to him, "Son, we paid so much already. Call Don Serafín and explain the situation."

This was a mistake.

"Listen to my words, Señor Oaxaca. I am not your fucking son and Don Serafín doesn't give a fuck about you or me or this truck. My compa is walking away now and all he is thinking about is cold beer and la conchita. If you want we can keep chatting until the Minutemen find us and burn the truck, or if Migra finds you first they'll kick your country asses right back over the border. Either way you lose your money. I'm offering you a chance to make it. You have one minute."

How can we know what is true and what is not? So now people are taking their clothes off to get their secret money. I can hear seams ripping and the sound of Velcro and because we are getting used to the light it is embarrassing for the women. I have forty dollars my father sent me through the Western Union. It is in my sneaker and to get it I must move my hands from César's head. I take off my sneaker and pass the money up to the front. After this I pull out the shoelace and tie Juquila's dress to César's head. I try to make the knot over the cut to make more pressure because the blood is still coming and there is a smell of metal more than all the rust in here. My hands are slippery with it and I wipe them on his jacket.

The men in front are taking the money and pushing it through the slot. I can hear the coyote counting and then shouting, "No more fucking pesos!" But he doesn't give them back. He stops counting at three hundred and fifty-five. "Doscientos más," he says. "¡Pronto, pronto!"

We are moving fast and we are afraid and no one knows exactly how much money we have given already. When it's done the men in front look back at us to see if there is more. I hold up my empty hands and I am surprised how red they are. We look at each other then and the Zapotec man says, "That's all we have."

"It's not enough," says the coyote.

The older man claps his hands. "For the love of God, we're not donating to the church here. Give it if you have it!"

This is difficult because no one wants to confess that they are holding back. The baby-face man looks over at César. He is about twenty-five with a goatee and lots of gel in his hair. "What about him?" he says.

"What about him?" I say.

"His money. We need it now."

"You're going to rob him?"

"We're not robbing him, we're helping him."

Everyone is watching and I don't know what to do, but I can't let them touch him. "I'll look for it," I say.

And I do this, go through César's pockets, but there is nothing there, only some pesos and his bus ticket.

"He's got money, look at his shoes," says the baby-face man. They are new ones, Pumas, and he pulls one off.

"Don't touch him!" I shout, and I kick his hands away, but he still has the shoe, shaking it and peeling out the inside. "Keep your hands off him!"

He throws the shoe back.

"Maybe he took it already," says the baby-face man's friend, looking at me, "when it was dark."

"Fuck off," I say.

"Maybe it's in his chones," says the baby-face man.

"Look at him!" I say, and I put my phone screen by César's face which is still wet with the blood. "He has enough trouble already. Leave him alone."

In that moment, the coyote hits the tank again with the metal thing and it rings like a broken church bell making everybody jump. "¡Ahora!" he shouts.

Sitting near me is a young Maya from Chiapas and she reaches into her skirt then and pulls out a little pouch. She is crying as she passes it up to the older man. All of us are feeling this. He opens it, takes out the bills and pushes them through.

"Four hundred and seventeen," says the coyote.

Everyone is staring at everyone else now, very suspicious. But no more money is coming. "That's really all," says the older man. "You cleaned us out."

"It's too bad," says the coyote. "With this I can't promise anything."

"We need water," says the man.

"You're going to need more than that," says the coyote.

"When are you coming back?"

"It depends on the mechanic. If it's not enough for him there's nothing I can do."

"Let us out, motherfucker!" shouts one of the Nicas.

"Listen!" I say again. "A man is badly hurt in here. We need help now!"

"You can't just leave us!" shouts the older man.

Then there is the scraping noise and the tank goes black.

"Open it! Open it!" screams a woman in the front. "¡No nos abandones!" Another woman is crying now and I can hear the voice of the older man: "¡Por el amor de Dios!" There is more shouting and cursing, and all of us who can are pounding on the walls of the tank.

"¡Vámonos!" says the other coyote. Already he was walking.

Vámonos was the last human word we heard out there, but even with the shouting I could hear the coyotes' feet grinding past us over the rocks and sand, heading back from where we came. Some in the tank followed the sound, calling out and chasing after it until they were on top of me and César, pounding on the back wall and screaming. I stayed in my place, my back against the wall and my legs across César with my hands up, trying to keep people from stepping on him. I couldn't hear the coyotes anymore, only one bird outside warning the others, because the sound in here was terrible, a frenzy. I was trying to get them off, shouting, pushing and kicking them away, but we were like a bucket of crabs with the lid on and no place to go. So many trying to get out in every direction — stepping on anyone in their way, trying to open the money hole, others praying or crying or trying not to be hurt. I heard the baker from Michoacán shouting, "Don't panic! They'll come back. They have to come back!" Naldo and the man from Veracruz had their phones on, using them for the light, looking everywhere for some way out. Faces came and went and the walls flickered with blue fire. Never have I seen so much fear in one small place, the eyes so wide and the pupils so big they looked like from another animal. I saw the young woman from Chiapas and she was holding her ears and rocking back and forth, saying something in Maya that sounded like a man was talking. Then, somewhere in the middle of the tank, the boy

Naldo was sick. It was a loud and desperate sound, crying and gagging with everything coming out of him at once. This and the high sharp smell of it filled the truck and made everyone stop like they'd been slapped. Somehow I think it helped people to understand the situation — that panic would not save them.

But that was yesterday and it is different now — more quiet — because everyone understands there is no escaping. In an ordinary truck we could maybe find a way, but because this is a water truck there are no cracks or bolts or pieces that can be lifted or broken. It is the perfect prison, smooth inside like an egg. When I looked for the false water box the coyotes told us about, there was nothing up there — only a small round hatch, locked from the outside. The hole where we came in is welded all the way around. The baby-face man and his friend tried jumping on it after the coyotes left — many of us did, but it is too strong. The woman from Chiapas is sitting on it now with the older one who is always praying.

The screen on César's phone makes everything look cold and blue like we are underwater, or dead already — cruel jokes in here — and to save the battery I turned it down. Nobody has a flashlight or a lighter or even a match because who is planning for this? There is nothing to see now anyway and not a lot to talk about because here we are, you know, and what is there to say? No one has the spirit for Hola, where you from, how is your family? — only for crying and praying and cursing the coyotes. *¡Pinches coyotes!* All the questions like Does anybody have a knife or some tool? are finished already. We know what everybody has and it is very little and not helping. The Zapoteco in the front with the older man had a knife, but he broke it trying to get through the money hole, trying to open the little door. He cut himself doing this and he is having problems now. I gave him my phone so he could look at the cut — to clean it and wrap it up. I know from his accent he is from the Sierra Juárez same as me. I've heard of his pueblo, but it is far from the highway and hard to get to.

They say coyotes have their own name for a truck full of migrantes — they call it a coffin load. Before now, I thought this might be another story from the government to scare us, but not after seeing those faces all around me. They were the faces of people being buried alive. I tried not to look at them anymore because I knew none of them could help me. This is also when I became confused — between thanking God for pushing me to the back by the pipes and cursing Him for my misfortune. Es una blasfemia, I know, to say this, but you can also say a truck full of people who are tired of working and working, barely making enough to live while a man sits and watches from behind the dark glass of a BMW car es una blasfemia. Yes, and you can say the same of coyotes, no? Is it not a blasfemia to put our faith in these men who are criminals and even killers? And why do we do this? Does the Bible teach us this — to put our money and our lives into the hands of one we cannot see and cannot know? To pray that he will do as we wish or as he promised? The moment you climb into the truck the coyote becomes your god just as he was before the Spanish came. Your fate is in his hands, but Coyote does not know what a promise is. Maybe he speaks your language, but for him the words have no meaning, they are only so much barking — empty as a bowl of smoke. And he does not offer refunds. No, he does what Coyote has done for all time — plays tricks, eats as much pollo as he can and disappears into the hills until he is hungry again. I would prefer to trust a jaguar.

My god, it is too hot to speak.

I must give César some water.

4

It is better now — cooler, but the heat of the day is like a fever and all
of us are feeling it. People's clothes have been wet so long now they
are having problems with their skin. It is impossible to be comfortable. The bottom of the tank is wet and the metal is so hard — in
the night it pulls all the heat out of you and in the day some parts
are too hot to touch. My pants are wet so I took them off and put
them on my bag to dry. I am sitting on my shoes with my feet on
my bag. I rolled César onto his side because the baker said it's not

healthy for him to stay in one position so long. I tried to make a bed for him from his backpack and a sweatshirt he had in there. I made him a pillow with his socks, trying to keep his skin away from the hot metal.

Now it is only César's phone that has minutes and a good battery together, and I am waiting for the deep night when maybe reception will be better. But I hope you can find us before then.

It was an accident how we came here, César and me, and if it hadn't happened we would still be in Oaxaca now, which can be its own prison. I wonder if you even know where Oaxaca is, because it is far — two thousand kilometers from the border. Maybe you heard of Puerto Escondido and the surfers who go there? That is in Oaxaca. Maybe you know Monte Albán, the great Zapotec city with the pyramids all around? Once I went up there with my school. My favorite part was the planes flying out of the airport — so close you can look in the windows, but when I waved no one waved back. If you never heard of Monte Albán and do not surf and are afraid to go to Mexico, I can tell you something about it. They say Oaxaca is the second-poorest state. We have fifteen indio languages and a hundred dialects. There are people in my pueblo — my Abuela Zeferina was one — who never learned Spanish. Not in five hundred years. But it doesn't matter, the same Spanish families control Oaxaca now who controlled it since Cortés came. You don't see them much, but when they come out for a wedding at the botanical garden in el centro, you can spy them through that gate on the corner of Reforma and Constitución. Very tall and beautiful women in there — blondes sometimes even — with the leg muscles shaped like diamonds and heels sharp enough to kill a man.

Our capital — wait — there is a plane —

Thu Apr 5 — 17:49

The plane is gone. It never came close. But to hear such sounds is a reason for hope, no? If you want to live, there is no choice in here but to think this way.

I was telling you about my home, where I lived until last week. Oaxaca de Juárez is a famous colonial city with many churches and busy markets and quiet plazas. It is named for Benito Juárez, our hero and liberator who stands on the Llano with the crown of Spain broken at his feet. Benito Juárez was a Zapoteco — one of us, and he took the power and the lands from the Spanish Church and gave them back to the Mexican people. At the same time you had slaves in el Norte, here was this dark-skin indio in charge of a country where power and white skin go together like beans and rice. He was even the friend of your Abraham Lincoln. Hard to believe it, no? It didn't last because in my country we have learned to enslave ourselves.

After Benito we had a dictator again — Porfirio Díaz, and he was the cause of our great revolution one hundred years ago. Porfirio Díaz was a Oaxaqueño too, and he was also part indio — mestizo — so his skin was dark. He put white powder on it trying to look like a güero, but it didn't work, everybody knew what he was so he only looked like an ugly Michael Jackson. Of course many indios and mestizos wish their skin was more white. There are powders and creams you can buy just for this and they have been selling here a long time, but my mother will not do it, and she is even darker than me. One time we were looking at pictures of Michael Jackson in a magazine and she hit his face with the back of her hand, saying, "Look at him there — like a clown! Doing such things to yourself is an insult to God."

From the capital it is a day of driving through the mountains to Puerto Escondido and the Pacific Ocean. The road is not old, younger than my father, but so steep and winding it makes the tourists sick and always you will see an accident. When someone goes over the side it is so far down you find them only by the smoke. You never drive that road at night because you can be robbed. Even in the daytime you might come to a pueblo — dust, cement, banana trees and indio girls in la moda jeans that never fit right and their fathers in sombreros with machetes hanging from their shoulders and all of them standing on the roadside while two hard men draw a chain across to block your way and someone's mother comes to your window with a bucket for money or you cannot pass. But if you are a pilgrim and your truck is decorated with flowers and a picture of the Virgin you will not be stopped, except by the police.

If you keep going south you will get to Puerto Escondido and then to Juchitán where they have the windmills now and iguanas in the hair and those ladyboys dressing up like Frida Kahlo. It happens down there where the country is most thin and the wind blows from ocean to ocean so hard it will make you crazy. Maybe that is why they do it. And just past there is Chiapas — you know Subcomandante Marcos and his Zapatistas? Cigars and balaclavas in the jungle? It is a fashion now. Those are our neighbors too, and then you're in Guatemala. Purgatorio.

If you ever come to Oaxaca I don't think you want to visit my neighborhood. I think you would prefer to stay in el centro, on the Zócalo with the fountains and the bandstand and our enormous cathedral. You can have coffee and ice cream there in the shade of the laurel trees, and you will see everyone — the balloon seller, the millionaire, the tourist, and the campesina with a sign demanding justice for her murdered son. And you will see artists, many of them, coming from everywhere, not to see the magical realism but to witness the marvelous real.

This is where me and César are from — different pueblos a couple hours driving from el centro. For one year we went to the same school, but back then I watched him more than I knew him. On the bus north he would not even sit with me but hid himself behind a new hat and sunglasses. Only waiting for the coyotes would he talk to me and that is when I told him my mother came from Santa Magdalena Tlapazetla, which is where they make the red pots shaped like animals. He said this was also the home of his grandfather and for a few moments we thought we might be cousins. We drank to this possibility and to our good luck in el Norte, but still he would not tell me the whole reason he must leave Mexico right now with a coyote and no passport.

Thu Apr 5 — 18:09

I hope to God, AnniMac, that you are the right person. I am putting my faith in you because it must go somewhere, no? And God has not been so helpful lately. I'm just telling you anything, I know, but what else can I do? There is a saying we have down here when things go bad — *Canta y no llores.* Sing, don't cry. I hope you understand why I must try to make the connection, why I must keep singing. Besides the coyotes, no one knows we're here, unless that one is you.

If I have just *one* more bar I know I can reach you. One more fucking bar and we are saved! ¡No es *justo!*

¡CHINGAOCHINGAOCHINGAOCHINGAOCHINGAO!

5

Thu Apr 5 — 18:47

It's getting cold again. I put my pants back on and look at César who is the same — like a dead man breathing. On the phone only one bar showing, and nothing from you. People are angry with me for talking so much — for shouting at nothing. I heard the baby-face man's friend say he thinks I'm going crazy, but I'm not the only one and I can't hear him now.

Are you by any chance a Catholic? Do you have la velada — the vigil for the dead? There is always a certain odor in that room because death has its own smell, you know — close and wet and sour-sweet like strange meat, and you can't hide it — not behind the food or the flowers or your own sweat. Not even behind all the shit and piss and puke in this truck because I'm smelling it now, AnniMac. We have a saint for the hopeless situations, but praying to her is not helping anyone in here. Oye, I need your help. I need something more than the dream of water and another bar for the phone. It is almost two days and there has been enough patience and praying in here for a convent, but who is answering us? *Who* is coming? Nobody. ¡Nadie! *¡Nunca!*

Estamos jodidos.

Because I will tell you something about us, AnniMac. El catolicismo is the official religion of Mexico, but chingar is the official verb. Chingar is "to fuck," y es un concepto complicado y muy importante para los Mexicanos. If you don't believe me, ask Octavio Paz who is the expert on this — a real chingón of Mexican letters. There are so many forms of chingar because there are so many ways to do it, but of all the forms there are only two you must remember. One is the kind of chingar you do to someone else and the other is the kind someone else does to you — el Chingón y la Chingada, the Fucker and the Fucked. Papá y Mamá. El Chingón is the one with the power who does things to other people if they like it or not. He is the one who controls the money, gives the permission and orders the killing. It is the dream of every drug lord since he was a little boy, and the dream of Don Serafín also. It is Cortés and King Herod and the Godfather. And, if you ask Abraham, it is God.

Here is a riddle from Octavio Paz —

How does a chingón cure his friend's headache?

He shoots him in the head.

There is a darkness, no? And not just in here. These days, of course, a woman can be a chingona too — like the famous luchadora La Diabólica or our own minister of agriculture who can buy you, sell you or have you killed. But more often in Mexico the women are chingadas like the rest of us — the ones getting fucked. And I must tell you, there is a lot of this going on in Mexico today.

Of all the chingadas, man or woman, of course Jesus is the most famous — el Chingón de las Chingadas. Every nail, every hole from the thorn and the spear is a chingadera — a kind of fucking. Jesus is our mirror and so is Cuauhtémoc — Falling Eagle, who was brought down and tortured by Cortés. There is a saying we have here, a war cry — *¡Viva Mexico! ¡Hijos de la chingada!* Long live Mexico! Children of the fucked! And it goes very well with that crazy mestizo sound that only a Mexicano can make — that cry at the end of the verse or after a shot of mezcal — joy and sorrow and madness and murder all coming together and tearing apart in the same moment. Down here it is an honor, this cry, a sign of your toughness, of how many chingaderas you can take, how many wounds you can suffer and keep going — keep singing. Because in Mexico suffering is an art and there are many opportunities to practice. Maybe you know our great singer Vicente Fernández? He is a favorite of my father and an expert on this. "My veins want to burst," he sings, "from the pain you cause inside me!" Now that is some kind of chingadera. That is how it is to suffer like a Mexicano. Have you ever had such a feeling in your veins?

Maybe now you can understand why we have so many virgins and why we love them so much. Because we need someone in our lives who hasn't been fucked and someone to watch over the rest of us who have. Because the vagina is the source of all of us and all of this. It is the wound that will not heal — and so is the border between us. If you don't believe me, ask Octavio Paz or Vicente Fernández. Or look inside this truck.

Thu Apr 5 — 19:15

I am not so friendly with God these days, but I am praying too. All this time we believed the coyotes would come back. Because how can they just leave us? They are partly human too, yes? But no. The answer is no. They are only coyotes. Who knows what they told Lupo or Don Serafín, or if they really went to find a mechanic, but still we hope and wait. Such pretty pictures we make with our minds in here — maybe the mechanic will drive up in a little truck with a shiny red box of tools. "¡Hola, amigos! ¿Como están? So sorry to be late. It will only take a minute. ¿Prefieren Corona o Pepsi?"

I will admit even I hold such a dream — and so together we hear the mechanic in every bird and passing jet. When the tank was cooling in the night, clicking and popping, we thought he was coming, and when the helicopter passed over this morning, we whispered, "It's him. We're saved!" But this is how it is when you have nothing and no power — you make the meaning you want from any little thing.

Thu Apr 5 — 19:23

This time now and in the morning are the only mercy for us. You cannot know until you are in here how much it takes to make these words. This is how people relax in the café, no? Talking, sending messages, but let me tell you — in here, where your head is pounding like with dengue, where the day is too hot to do anything but breathe and the night too cold to do anything but hold yourself — it is difficult.

But it is worse to only wait.

Thu Apr 5 — 19:37

Hello, AnniMac. I stay as close as I can with César to keep us both warm. I am talking to him — everything I say to you. Who knows what he hears, but what else is there besides the comfort of words and heat? Because I think he must live, not only for himself but for what he carries.

If you know César, you know already he is too smart to need a coyote, that something in his life must be broken for him to be in such a situation. Even a stranger can hear this in the way he talks — like he is making the words himself with a hammer and pieces of iron — and so many. How can such a young man be so sure of what he is saying? But he was always this way since we first met in school. Even this time, when he looked at me there is something about his eyes — I cannot hold them and must look away. It is not only because he is older, it is because his mind is stronger, his soul. I can feel it, like a powerful animal. I admit I am a bit angry about this because we are not so different, César and me, we come from the same place — from the same mountains named for Benito Juárez. It is in these steep forests that all of us began — speaking the same language, eating the same corn, working in the same high milpas. But Benito was a president, and César is a scientist, and I am a — what?

It is this question that put me in the truck.

In the pueblos, if you are a good student and the teacher or the padre notices you, maybe you go to secondary school. If you pay them a mordida your chances will be better and this is what my abuelo did for me. He had some artifacts he found when he was a young man, and he sold them so I could go to school. For this I was sent to Guelatao, the birthplace of Benito Juárez. The biggest difference from my home pueblo, besides the school and a bigger church, is the Internet café and more girls. These and the basketball court. Even if there's no phone in the pueblo, even if there's no priest and no road, there's a basketball court, but the one in Guelatao is the first I saw with a roof on it. We have gods for corn and rain and clouds and lightning, and we have Jesus and Mary in all her manifestations, but Michael Jordan is our patron saint of basketballs. That picture of him leaping — it is painted on every backboard in the Sierra como un retablo, and we know it like the cross. Most of us boys worshiped at that altar every day, and some girls also. When I turned fifteen, my tío sent me a Bulls jacket from L.A., and I wore it all the time until it was stolen.

But besides these things and the giant statue of Benito, Guelatao is only another pueblo. In the people's yards there is still corn and beans and calla lilies growing, a couple guayaba and nispero trees, always some chickens and maybe a pair of oxen or an old Vocho. In the mountains all around is the same forest with the same orchids and bromeliads growing in the trees, and by the streams and road-sides the same butterflies in every color you can imagine — some with wings like silver coins and others clear as glass so you can see right through. It is here I met César Ramírez when I was fourteen years old.

Everyone called him Cheche and the first time I saw him he was floating in the air. Even the kids with no English knew what hang-time was, but César was the only one of us who had any. The girls noticed this and some of them would come down to the court and watch, not only because he was handsome but because it is some-thing different to see a person fly. I watched him too, and it was a couple of days before I was brave enough to play. César was eight-een then so already he was taking exams for the university. Many students go to the church to pray for this — to pray they will pass, and César did this also, but not in the church. He went outside town to a shrine for Juquila built into a cliff by the road where the roots of an old oak tree made a little cave. It is normal for students to leave offerings of money or Pepsi or mezcal along with a note and a candle, but César left his prayers to Juquila under a little pile of corn that was all the colors of the rainbow. Back then I thought he did it because he was so poor and had nothing else to offer, but I was wrong. He did it because corn is the center of everything in the Sierra, and he is its apostle.

Everyone in Guelatao knows how César's exam scores were the highest ever for our school and that he won scholarships to UABJO in Oaxaca and then UNAM in D.F. where he took a job in a big lab to study the corn. César is a bit famous in the Sierra now — not just because he is so smart, but because he made it in Mexico and that is hard for an indio to do.

The school in Guelatao is small so everyone knows everyone, and César and me both studied English and liked to read so he would talk to me sometimes, even though I was four years younger. He said I was the only chico he knew who had heard of Charles Dickens or Roberto Bolaño, and I felt proud when he noticed me. César had the first copy of *The Savage Detectives* in Guelatao. He let me borrow it and I kept that book because what he had I wanted also. "We should move up to D.F.," he said when he gave it to me, "because no one around here is getting conchita like those guys are." He was laughing and I tried to laugh also, but it was hard because my voice was barely changed and I'd never had a girlfriend. Another time we talked about Borges — there was a teacher at the school who loved him and who read to all of us "The Writing of the God." We were talking about it after and I said, "I think the priest is going crazy after all that time in the cell, and that's why he thinks he can read the spots on the jaguar," but César said, "No, it's because all that time alone cleared his mind so he can understand the older language. The patterns on the jaguar, on the wings of the butterfly, in the kernels of the corn — those are pages from the original codex."

That's how it is with César — if he pays attention to you, you remember the details, even when you don't know what he's talking about.

I take some water now and put some drops in César's mouth, but only a little because I must make it last.

Thu Apr 5 — 20:11

I am so tired, but it is not possible to sleep. The tank is cold now and the bottom is wet with everything so you must sit or lie on your shoes, your bag, whatever you have, but how long can you do that? You have to move, but where do you move when everyone else is right there? Once, my friend's brother hid under a car seat for three days with only water and tortillas. It was a Mitsubishi Pajero and they didn't let him out until Virginia because they said that even far from the border the police will see a car of Mexicanos and stop you for nothing. He couldn't walk for two days after, but then he got a job killing chickens. You can live with the pain, he said, but you can't live without the money. I think about that and how he never complained. Also it is Lent. We are giving up a lot in here already, but I will try to give up complaining also. The anger will be harder.

Do you know how many Oaxaqueños do this — go up to el Norte to work and to live? I have read in the newspaper one out of three. So Oaxaca, you can say, is bleeding men. All over your country. There are Zapotec barrios in L.A. where my mother's brother lives. Mixtec too. Strange things happen to us up there. A friend of mine from secondary school called Blanquito for his pale skin was gone four years — three months picking apples and the rest in a jail outside Spokane for la mota. He swears he only smoked and didn't sell, but they put him in there anyway. Now he's back in Oaxaca teaching English because he had so much time in the jail to practice.

I understand there are some in your country who hate Mexicanos and even try to kill them. There are vigilantes and your Minutemen hunting us on the border. My tío told me that besides some indios there is no one else in el Norte except immigrants — es puro migrante. So how do they decide who to hunt? But maybe it is like in Mexico — the more white you are, the more rich and free, the less you are hated or need to hate yourself. And the longer you will live.

Before NAFTA it was not so hard to get into your country and many of us did it — a few months up there working and then home again every year in time for the village fiesta. When I was young, my tío worked like this on a ranch in Arizona. It was next to a big military base and he told me about the planes they have there, especially the one called el Cerdo — the Pig — a jet with cannons on it that is so crazy fast that all the noise — guns, jets, exploding — comes only after the plane is gone. So the sound is roaring by itself like thunder in the empty sky, and you are dead before you know it. He said not even God can save you from such a thing. There were bombers too and some of them are as big as the cathedral in el centro, but those didn't worry him so much. You can see them coming, he said, you still have time to pray.

One time, my tío came back to the pueblo for our fiesta and when a vulture flew over he said, "Look! There goes the Mexican Air Force." He was smiling like it was funny. Before that day I never thought much about the Mexican Air Force, but that vulture with its tattered wings and shaking flight — that is how my tío saw himself, saw all of us, after working in el Norte. Along with the used Ford Bronco, Air Jordans almost new and the Sony CD player, this joke is what he brought home with him. This and the feeling that he was a halfman among princes and magicians. I asked him one time if the Pig is used to hunt mojados on the border, and he said maybe. I don't always know when he is joking, but he told me back then never try to cross. Too dangerous, he said, and someone has to look after Abuelita Clara who is the mother of my mother. My tío is her only living son and when he stopped coming home it made the sadness from her husband even bigger.

6

Thu Apr 5 — 20:33

It is a strange thing — how one day you can be praying no one will find you but on the next you are praying anyone will, and I can tell you it doesn't take long in the dark to stop caring about the money. All we want now is water and light. Like plants. And soon — tomorrow — I think it will be water only — like the algae on these walls. You see then what a decoration our life is, una ilusión — the money, the clothes, the talking, the gods. It is all just a thin layer of paint — gone in a few hours. It is the same that makes a truck red or blue or brown, but underneath is only metal coming from the mountain. In the end, this truck is just a rock driving around pretending for a little while to be a truck. And here we are in the desert, AnniMac, breaking down.

Thu Apr 5 — 20:39

All this time I believed César will wake up because how can this be his fate — to stand up at the wrong moment? In school, you could not stop him. He was always thinking and moving faster than the rest of us and when he left I didn't see him again until last week — seven years, más o menos. At home we talk a lot about Fate and God's Will because not a lot of people believe in coincidence. Maybe in el Norte you have a name for it when you come out of the Club KittiLoco drunk with no girl and no money for a taxi but one stops in front of you and you get in anyway just because it's there. Maybe you got a name for it also when the driver says, Where to? And you say, Mártires de Río Blanco. And he says, OK if I go up Suárez? Chapultepec is torn up at Venus.

Well, it's two in the morning after three mezcals and so many beers and what do you care about lost battles or other planets or black holes in the street? But there's something familiar about the taxista's voice and you look in the mirror and even through the glasses you notice his eyes because they are looking right back at you and in that moment there is a connection, a knowing, and you're thinking, I've seen this guy before.

That's when I say, "Cheche?"

His eyes get big and he looks away. So I lean forward over the seat. He's wearing a beard and mustache, but this is like putting a coffee sack on a beautiful girl — some things you can't hide. I'm sure it's César under there and I'm drunk and I say, "¡Vato! What you doing back here? Driving a taxi?"

"You got the wrong guy."

"The fuck I do! I *know* you, man. You're Cheche Ramírez — from Guelatao. ¡Qué *paso!*"

He pulls over hard and stops, and turns around fast and says to my face, "Listen. You think it's me, but it's not. You know what I'm saying? You did not see me here, and you don't tell anyone. If you do, I'm fucked. And so are you."

Then he turns back and starts driving again. His words are moving slow through the beer and mezcal like bullets underwater, and I don't look in the mirror again. I put my hands in my pockets because it's cool out and then I remember that all I have besides my phone is a ten-peso coin and that little clay head from my abuelo. It's not enough to pay for a taxi and I wonder if I should tell him this, but I'm having trouble thinking so I say nothing. This is how it is driving down Calle Independencia — no one looking, no one talking. This is how it is when we're hit by the truck.

It is the last thing you expect after midnight in Oaxaca because it is quiet then, the streets are empty and you can drive how you like — the traffic signals are there, but red or green, no one is caring so much and to run the red is no sin. This is what César is doing on Independencia near the Zócalo — not fast, just normal. Our misfortune is that there is a truck of federales coming down Juárez at the same time — fast, and they have the green. Well, you can imagine a military Ford 250 hitting a little Nissan Tsuru — it is a disaster for the Nissan. We are mostly OK, but the taxi is not — the front is finished and the engine is not where it is supposed to be. It will never be fixed, but that is only the beginning for César and me.

These federale trucks are a special kind that came to Oaxaca with all our troubles last year. They are painted black like skin so there is no reflection and they have a machine gun standing in the back, the kind that can stop a bus or empty a plaza. The men in these trucks are all in black too — helmets, boots, gloves, and their bodies are thick with the armor. There is only one thing with color and that is the bandolera hanging from the gun, each bullet the size of a dog's dick and shining as bright as the gold in church. Every man in the truck has also his own powerful guns and they are ready to shoot at all times — you can see this by their fingers. Pues, it is the dead hour of the night and we are in it — César with the broken taxi, me in the back with ten pesos, and five federales who can make their own war.

The first problem for us is that we have frightened the federales because it is by this same method that narcos are killing police in Mexico — they block them with a car in some lonely place and then compadres who are hiding shoot them all. So as soon as the truck is stopped, all the men in the back and in the cab are shouting and pointing their guns in different directions — doors, windows, roofs, and one of them is pointing his gun out the window right at César who is only a meter away. In that moment something like ice is pouring through my body and I cannot move, even to open my mouth. I think it is the same for César because he is just sitting there, his hands on the steering wheel like he will never let it go. I can tell you, I never got sober so fast. There is nothing else in the street, no other cars or people, only low buildings because it is a neighborhood sleeping. Some who hear the crash open their shutters to look, but close them right away. No one wants to be a witness to this kind of thing.

By now the federales understand it is an accident, not an ambush, but when they get out of the truck and come over to the taxi they still have their guns to their shoulders ready to shoot. The officer by César signals him with the barrel to get out of the car. César's door won't open anymore so he must leave by the other side. He is moving slow and when he gets out the officer is shouting, "What's in your hand! Drop it!"

Every gun is pointing and I am afraid they're going to shoot us right now, but I hear only the sound of César's keys falling in the street. One of the officers shines a light on them and I see the medallion there. It is the one for Juquila — I know it by the shape. I am still in the back when the first officer turns to me. "Show your hands!" When I get out, he points behind the taxi. "Over there!" My knees are shaking and when I look at César the same officer shouts, "No contact!" So I look at the ground where I can see the taxi bleeding its fluids black and green between the cobblestones. Two federales are now studying the dead taxi and the truck, which has only a flat tire and a broken light. One of them gets back in the truck and picks up the radio. Another puts his rifle over his shoulder and walks over to César who stands with his head turned, trying not to be blinded by the flashlight. The officer pats him down, but he misses César's phone.

"Where's your wallet."

"Stolen," mumbles César.

"Really," says the officer. "Your license too?"

César looks down at his shirt pocket. As the officer reaches in to get it, the officer standing behind him with the flashlight says, "Search the car." It sounds like a woman talking, but it's hard to know with the helmet and goggles. An officer standing guard comes over to the passenger side of the taxi and starts looking through the glove compartment and under the seats, pulling up the mats.

"César Ramírez Santiago," says the officer by César, comparing the picture on the license to his face. "All the way from D.F. What brings you down here?" He looks over his shoulder and calls out César's name and license number to his partner in the truck who repeats it into the radio. At that moment, the officer searching the car climbs out and hands something to the man questioning César.

"Stolen?" he says, holding up César's wallet. He opens it, pulls out some bills and puts them in his pocket. "You'll need a bigger reward than that to get it back." Then he punches César in the stomach and I can hear the air come out. "What's a bullshitter like you doing in Oaxaca? Coming to start more trouble? The strike is finished, maricón. We finished it." César is bent over with his elbows on his knees. He coughs and mumbles something about his father. "This isn't his taxi," says the officer. "I thought you said you live in D.F." César lifts himself up, shakes his head and looks at the ground. The officer pulls some cards from his wallet. "Madre, what's a campesino like you doing at UNAM? I thought you were a taxi driver." He looks at another card. "And what the hell is *SantaMaize*?"

"Probably fake," says the officer with the flashlight. I see César look from side to side like he is trying to see where this voice is coming from, but the light is too bright. Female federales are not common, but when this one turns her head I can see the tail of hair coming out of her helmet. "Are you color-blind?" she asks, pretending to study César's squinting eyes. "Or does everyone in D.F. run the lights like you?"

César is standing there like he can't understand what she's saying and I wonder if his head is injured. Then, very soft, he says, "¿Mande?"

"Your eyes," she says. "Maybe you should have them checked." Another car turns onto the street, but as soon as the driver sees the federales he turns around and drives away. The woman takes a step forward so she is shoulder to shoulder with the other officer and without a warning she knocks César in the forehead with the flashlight hard enough that his head jerks back. "What are you doing in this taxi!" She puts the light right in his face, she's close enough to kiss him now. "I asked you a question, puto."

For César the answer will change everything that comes after. But then I didn't know how, and it is why I must tell you about the traffic signals. In Oaxaca there are two kinds, those for cars and those for people. The ones for people are made of many little lights that together make a moving picture of a man — a green man walking, but when the time to walk is almost finished, the green man begins to run, faster and faster until he turns suddenly red and stops, like a man waiting, or maybe if you look at it, like a man lying in the street. In the corner of my eye I can see these signals changing one into the other. I know already César is in some kind of trouble and now it is like a choice he must make — a test — and his answer will decide if he is the green man or the red man.

I hear a siren and I'm holding my breath, wondering what César will say and what the federales will do, when I see the officer with César's wallet turn to look at the truck. His partner in the cab holds up the radio and nods toward César. The officer puts César's wallet into his shirt pocket and reaches for his handcuffs. I can see César shifting his feet, turning his head toward the taxi. At first I think he's looking for me, but he's not, he's looking for his keys with the medallion of Juquila. Maybe he's saying a prayer, I don't know, but in this moment there comes an interceding.

It begins with a screaming sound and then, farther down Juárez, an explosion. All the federales — who do not forget the possibility of an ambush — drop to one knee with their guns up and pointing around. César is too scared to move and so am I when around the corner of Hidalgo, one block down, comes a giant puppet — a lady with enormous chichis and yellow hair, and then another one looking like Benito Juárez, and another with a big bandana and long hair like Axl Rose, and each one is tall as a house and dancing all around. Behind them is the sound of a band starting to play and this comes around the corner too — ten musicians with trumpets and trombones and drums, also a tuba, and they are playing dance music. There is another scream and another explosion and now it is clear it is only the coheteros with their skyrockets for waking the gods. "¡Otra calenda!" shouts the woman federale, and all of them can see it now because this is what is coming up the street — una calenda por Santa María, por la Fiesta de la Anunciación. It was the congregation from a local church so it wasn't a big procession, but along with them and the giant monos and the band and the coheteros are las chinas oaxaqueñas—ladies dancing in their fiesta clothes—long skirts and ribbons in the hair with sexy blusas and red red lips, each one with a big basket on her head filled with flowers and special decorations. But in their baskets are also secret things you cannot see—bricks and stones—because the heavier your basket and the longer you dance, the greater your devotion to the Virgin. My mother does this also, especially por la Virgen de la Soledad. You will not believe what she carries—and for so long because most calendas start at eight or nine at night and don't stop until the morning. In between, they go all over the city in a big circle that finishes only when they come back to the home church. All this time, the monos and the ladies are dancing and the band is playing and the coheteros are sending up rockets like flares from a sinking ship. To you it might look like a party, but really it is the dance of hope in the darkness, our way of saying, "¡Virgen, Santo, DIOS, por favor! We are down HERE! Can't you SEE us? Can't you HEAR us? Please do not FORGET us!"

It is the same what César prays to la Virgen de Juquila by the broken taxi.

But the calenda can't go all night without a little rest and some food, and this is what happened—around the corner from us is where they stopped for some time on Hidalgo with no music or dancing or rockets. Of course they are tired by now, and all along the way there are friends and family, maybe other churches, who know this and feed them tortas con queso y frijoles, also beer and soda, to keep them going. And always there is mezcal.

Maybe you can imagine it—a hundred people, sometimes many more, drinking mezcal and dancing half the night already. Zapotecs have been praying this way for two thousand years, and this is maybe why, when they finish resting, they turn north on Juárez to meet the federales. They can see now what is happening there, and it is a story they know very well — everyone has a brother or a father or an uncle who has troubles with the police. No one likes them, especially this kind — and don't forget these are Zapotecos. Some of their pueblos were never conquered by the Aztecs. Now, with Santa María and Señor Mezcal by their side who can stop them? Like this, all together, they come up Juárez, filling the street, the sound of them getting louder and the federales getting nervous, looking at each other, not sure where to put their fingers until two of them come forward with their guns by their hips. "This street is closed," says one. "Go back!"

It is a dangerous moment. The federales are outnumbered and the people are not stopping. The woman officer is watching César, but she must also watch the calenda and her men. Everyone is watching the monos too because not to watch is impossible. They are giants, six meters tall and very colorful, also very particular because many people make their own how they want. Mister Peanut is my favorite, and when you're inside that mono loaded with mezcal you are not really you anymore. You are something else because what is the mono really but a kind of spirit — nothing more than empty clothes on a bamboo frame. To such a one the bullet can do no more damage than to a ghost or a cloud. So the monos keep coming, spinning in circles with their long arms flapping and their giant heads nodding this way and that like they are saying hello to everyone in the houses along the street where the shutters are now opening, to the birds in the trees and the stars in the sky, to the radio towers blinking across town on Cerro del Fortín.

The lady mono with the yellow hair is still in front and her chichis are even more wonderful up close, bouncing around in her red dress, balloons of helium filled with so much love by the mono dancer. At the same time, Benito Juárez — our great hero and liberator, el Mono MaxiMex — is bending over like he is inspecting the two federales below him and asking them some question like, Do you know whose street you're on?

In between the monos comes now the mezcal man with his big bottle and who knows where the top is? Over his shoulder is a string bag and in this are some tubes of bamboo about as long as your finger. These are the cups for the mezcal and he is taking some out to offer the federales who are serious men, but they are also young and even la policía can be believers — maybe some are even Zapotec. It is hard to be completely angry in such a situation — after all, the nights in the truck can be so long and boring. But these are thoughts happening inside and their guns are happening outside, still on their hips and pointing into the heart of the calenda. This is how they confront the monos and the mezcal man, who stop now about twenty meters down the block from César and me. From behind are still coming las chinas oaxaqueñas and the musicians, and now everyone is bunching up behind the monos and spreading onto the sidewalks and the air is getting thick and loud with the smoke and music and rockets launching with loud screams that are imitated by some of the men so it sounds like twenty rockets going up at once.

César is standing by the side of the taxi, watching all this like a man in a trance and I am a couple meters behind him. There is a soft wind blowing and with it comes the smell of smoke and sweat and lilies and mezcal. It is at this moment that Axl Rose, who is still spinning in circles, trips on the sidewalk. He is a tall one and he goes down slow like a big tree falling. When finally he hits the ground, he blocks almost the whole street like a barricade, and his giant papier-mâché bandana rolls away leaving only those crazy eyes made of broken mirror glass staring through a mess of orange yarn. Everyone is cheering for the fallen mono and another rocket goes up. Then, one more time, the lights change — the red man turns into the green man and, very loud, someone starts singing "Sweet Child o' Mine."

This is the signal for César. Juquila has heard him.

The green man is running and now César is running too — for his life — down the sidewalk and into the calenda. The female federale brings up her gun, but there are too many people so she is shouting instead. The two federales in front go after him, but Axl Rose is still rolling around and the mess of bamboo and giant clothes slows them down — only for a moment, but it is sufficient. Everyone is looking at César now, pointing and shouting, and then I am running too, behind the taxi and the truck to the other side of the street and into the crowd. By the time the two federales get through, César is down at the corner and I am past the calenda, maybe twenty meters behind. César takes a last look over his shoulder and one of the federales stops to aim his gun. There is the scream of a rocket and then a shot. There is the puff of smoke as the rocket explodes above the street and a cloud of dust as the bullet hits the adobe wall by César's shoulder. But César doesn't notice and he is faster than he looks. Juquila is with him, and around the corner he goes. All the federales are chasing us now, but the band is going crazy, playing many songs at once, and the dancers are getting in their way. The shooter in front turns and sees me on the other side of the street, but fear makes you faster and I make it to the corner. There is one more shot and then only shouting, music and rockets.

César is ahead of me running and he seems to know where he is going. He disappears through an open gate, and I follow him — across a courtyard, up a fig tree, over the wall of an abandoned house. I am trying to keep up with him, but he is fast and I am still half a block behind. We make it to Guerrero, heading for Bustamante and the market on 20 de Noviembre. I hear more sirens, but César has wings on his feet and — he told me later he can feel this — Juquila is guarding him with her tiny cloak. Police cars speed past a block away and all the time we are moving — south and west because already César knows where he must go. For ten blocks we travel like this — invisible — until César sees a taxi. I can tell by how he whistles and waves it down that he knows the driver, and he jumps in the back. He's pulling the door closed when I catch up to him and pull it open again.

"What the fuck are you doing here?" he says.

Well, this is my question also.

"Get out!" he shouts.

"No!" I say. "You can't leave me here!"

He tries to push me out the door but I grab on to the headrest in front and will not let go and now the driver is shouting, "No fighting in my taxi or you both get out!"

Well, César wants to get away more than he wants to fight. "¡Abastos!" he says. "¡Pronto! But for God's sake don't run any lights."

And then we are driving with me closing the door and both of us breathing hard. I turn around to look for the police, but César pushes my head down. After maybe one minute with no sirens César lets out a long breath and looks over at me. "I can't believe we got away from those chingados."

"Why did you run?"

"Because it's worse if I don't. It's dangerous to be near me right now. When we get to the market you must leave."

Jesucristo — qué demonios —

1

Thu Apr 5 — 22:08

There was some fighting in the front of the tank. By their accent it is the Nicas who started it. I think they had only one bottle of water for the two of them and when they tried to get some from la Michoacana — the baker — she would not give it. They insulted her then and the baby-face man and his friend said they are also from Michoacán, and they threatened the Nicas. No one can see anything in here, but one of the Nicas followed their voices, punching into the darkness. I heard grunting and swearing and I think the baby-face man or his friend caught the Nica's arm and did something to it — I heard the sound of wet sticks breaking, and the Nica screamed and cursed for a long time after.

How can Hell be worse than this?

But it is quiet now and I can't think about them. Only César and the story —

We are going to the part of the city where no tourist wants to go. There are no cafés or pretty plazas around Abastos market, only broken cement and sheet metal, dead cars and sex clubs and shops of Chinese clothes with not a tree in sight. Es una Oaxaca paralela where people like me live when we move to the city. Very hot there in the day. But now it is dark and the night is growing damp and old around us. Even down on the floor of the taxi, which is tight for the two of us, we know where we are. We know it by the smells coming in the windows — yesterday's chocolate from the mills on Calle Mina — and by the rattle of the wheels crossing the rail lines on Mier y Terán, that wide right turn onto Mercaderes, and the next one, left onto Cosijopi. I can see César smiling to himself.

"You drive like a professional," he says to the back of the seat.

"Por supuesto," says his friend. He does not ask us why we are back there hiding. He knows as much as he needs to know. Sometimes these things happen.

In this moment, César told me later, he felt more free than any other time he could remember — floating almost. Who knows what los pinches federales will do to him if they catch him and find out who he is, but thanks be to la Virgen de Juquila bendecida he escaped from those pendejos. It was sooner than he planned, but he knew what he must do.

The taxi stops on the west side of Abastos near the river, what is left of it. It is not even four, but already the first trucks are coming in from the coast with fish and oranges, seashells and coconuts, maybe a special order of turtle eggs hiding in the belly of a tuna, or a crocodile skull with all its teeth. And from the south they come with coffee and mangoes, chocolate, iguanas and velvet huipils, and from the Sierra with calla lilies, beef, pots in all sizes still scarred by the fire that made them, maybe even the skin of a jaguar, and from the north with a saddle for the horse, or a yoke for the plow hecho a mano from the trunk of a tree. Maybe you need an ox to go with it, a burro, a goat, some turkey chicks or birds that sing. Maybe corn, mole, mezcal, vanilla, worms or chapulines — sí, those are grasshoppers, amiga — big or small as you like. The ladies from the pueblos catch them in the grass — my abuelas did this. And if you're lucky there will be huitlacoche — that fungus in the corn that makes the seed explode — con la bisteca es perfecto. All the things that make Oaxaca famous, you can find them in this market and most other things too, even la última cena — the last supper — not the holy picture for the wall but a poison for the rats. Not even the big box stores in Gringolandia have such things, and the prices are better, but only if you bargain.

Abastos es una paradoja — here you can find anything, but you can also lose anyone, and this is why César comes here. Abastos is the biggest market in the state of Oaxaca and it is a labyrinth — who knows what's at the center or even where the center is. You can live your whole life in here and some people do. It can be frightening for a güero or a campesino who is not used to so many people and so many things all in one place together. Because every kind of person is here from every tribe — Zapotec, Mixtec, Mazatec, Trique, Huave, Chinanteco — so many different faces and clothes and dialects and so many ancient products — copal, cochineal and bark paper for medicine bundles, herbs and seeds, mushrooms and magic ingredients and witch supplies — mango-color beaks from the toucan and black hands from the monkey. All this you can find next to action figures for the Undertaker and the Blue Demon, or a statue of Santa Muerte, or blades for the fighting cock, and every kind of mezcal. There is magic here for everyone.

For César, it is the magic of disappearing. Because running from the federales is a serious thing. These ones will not forget you, they will hunt you like dogs, and if they can't find you they will find your family. The taxista pulls into the market, past the delivery trucks, nosing in as deep as he can go under the patchwork roof of plastic and canvas and old Sol and Corona banners. There, he stops with the engine running. "Arriba."

César lifts his head to see where he is and with his messy hair and careful eyes he looks like he did some mornings at school when he came in late for class. But the moment passes quickly and when he reaches into the top of his sock and pulls out a bill the driver shakes his head. "Next time."

César pats his shoulder. "Claro, caballero."

Then he gets out of the taxi and disappears into the maze. I follow him — I'm not sure why exactly, but I know I will need to hide for a while also. "Where are you going?" I ask his back.

"To find a gown for Juquila," he says without turning around. "She saved me tonight. It is a miracle to get away like that. She saved you too, which is interesting."

"You think so?"

"Maybe she has a plan for you."

"What kind of a plan?"

"How should I know?" he said. "You must go away now."

"Where?"

"That's not my problem."

I am running to keep up with him as he twists and turns through the dark market, down tight walkways between covered stalls and tables, ducking to miss things hanging overhead — piñatas and baskets and leather bags, a plastic tricycle, communion dresses. "It wasn't me driving the taxi," I say. "And you ran away. They saw both of us. I can't stay around here now."

I never knew César to be without an answer, but he was quiet after this, just walking fast and swearing to himself. "Nothing's open. I'm going to have to wait."

This is a dangerous thing to do, but César does it because Juquila is a local virgin and he won't find a gown her size — made only for her — anywhere else in Mexico. When he comes under a light in the market, he notices dust on his right shoulder, the kind that comes from adobe bricks mixed with plaster, and he brushes it away. "Un otro milagro," he says, shaking his head and crossing himself. Then he looks into a dark corner, finds a table with a cloth over it and crawls under. I crawl under the table next to it. I'm thinking César is bad luck for me, but I don't know what else to do.

"After you find her gown," I whisper, "where are you going then?"

"It's no concern of yours. Now leave me alone."

I don't know how he does it, but he's asleep in five minutes. I can hear him breathing one meter away, deep and steady in the dark, and it makes me more calm.

Sometime after sunrise, I am kicked awake. At first I am confused and afraid, but then I am happy because the foot that is kicking me has no boot on it and belongs to an old lady. But she is not happy and kicks César also. "This is not a hotel," she says. "Get up."

"Lo siento, doña," says César. "I need to buy a gown for the Virgin Juquila."

"No you don't," she says. "You need to go home and sober up. Now get away from here. I'm busy."

We crawl out from under the tables and are surrounded by flowers — roses, birds of paradise, gladioli and bundles of orchids from the Sierra. The sight of them there so many and so close makes me think of my abuelo and I feel it hard in my chest. All these flowers we put on his grave. César is already moving away deeper into the market, which is wide awake now. He does not look back but I follow him. I hear him asking for the ladies from Juquila who make special clothes for the Virgin. I smell meat and realize I am hungry when a man in a bloody jacket pushes past me and then César with the leg of a cow on his shoulder. In a moment we are among the butchers. It's early, so the meat is piled high on the shelves and hanging thick on the hooks — rags of carne asada, strings of sausages round as beads, heavy blankets of tripe, piles of goat heads staring blind over pyramids of chickens with their marigold feet hanging in the walkway. When César passes a juice stand, he buys a liter and takes it with him through the heart of the market and over to the far side, closer to the rail line and el centro. We are in a clothing section now so he asks again for the ladies from Juquila and is sent over to a young Zapoteca in bluejeans and a T-shirt with fake diamonds who is reading a fashion magazine and listening to an MP3 player with tiny headphones.

"Excuse me," says César. "Is your mother here?"

The girl pulls out one of the headphones. "¿Mande?"

"Your mother, is she here?"

"Who are you?"

"Nobody. I need a gown for Juquilita."

"Why don't you say so?"

The girl's stall is made of light metal bars going up and across all around her, like a giant cage. On every bar are hangers with colored shirts and blouses covered in fine flowers all from sewing. The girl points behind her with her thumb and high in the back is a row of tiny gowns too small even for a baby, covered in a layer of brown dust. "That's all we got left," says the girl. "No more until November."

César chooses the brightest one, light green with gold threads. The girl takes it down with a long pole, gives it a shake and hands it to César. "Quinientos," she says.

You can buy five shirts for this kind of money, but César doesn't bother to bargain. He kneels down, pulls some bills from his sock and pays her. Then he folds the gown into his jacket pocket and makes his way back through the market toward the river, making sure to go a different way. It is harder to find a taxi on the back side of the market, but it is dangerous to be near the entrance. Always the police are there. I follow César outside where he is asking people about colectivos going north. I stand apart from him and he ignores me. After some minutes waiting, a minivan comes and he squeezes in the back with three hundred kilos of nuns going to Nochixtlán. I get the last seat behind the driver. I can see that César is angry, but what can he say with all these nuns?

The driver waits to collect the money until he is out of the city traffic and on the highway. This is a difficult moment for me because I have only the ten pesos. I am also hungry like the devil. I am hoping the driver will not notice me with all the nuns, but he does, and after everyone has paid he looks at me in his mirror and raises his eyebrows. "Didn't he pay for us already?" I say, and point back to César with my thumb. I turn around and César gives me a look like, What the fuck are you doing?

"I would be home sleeping now if it wasn't for you," I say. César is furious, but the nuns are turning to look at us and he doesn't want to attract any more attention.

"Cincuenta y cinco," says the driver.

"I'll pay you back," I say to César.

Without looking at me, César passes the money forward to the driver and then turns his head to the gray rocks and bare brown hills of the Mixteca, a desert compared to our green Sierra.

When we got off in Nochixtlán on the edge of town both of us were watching for federales and police, but there was nothing — only freight trucks and cars. We were deep in the Mixteca, two hours north of el centro, and on the hills around us there was barely a tree. The road here was wide with many holes and little shade and on both sides were tire repair shops with cars and trucks up on jacks or piles of stones with the wheels off. It was only ten in the morning but the wind was hot already and smelled of rubber and garbage and cooking meat. César crossed the road to a taquería and from the lady there he ordered memelitas al pastor, something I wished to eat myself. There were two metal tables with folding chairs around them and this is where César sat and waited in the full sun with no hat. When the lady's young son brought the memelitas to the table, three of them, I waited until César had eaten one. Then I crossed the road, sat down next to him and thanked him for paying my fare, but he wouldn't look at me. "Why are you dogging me, man? I have enough trouble as it is."

"What did you expect me to do," I said, "wait for another taxi?

César didn't answer but took a bite of the second memelita. There was sweat on his forehead. On the table was a plate of napkins and two clay dishes of red and green salsa as bright and round as traffic signals. Flies circled, landing on the rims and spoons. When they landed on César's plate, he didn't wave them away.

"Do you remember who I am?" I asked.

César was looking south, toward the city. "You're the chico who borrowed my copy of *The Savage Detectives* and never gave it back. Tino? Nico?"

"Tito. I still have it."

"No shit. Slow reader?" He finished the second memelita. They were small and he saw me watching. He looked at the last one and pushed his plate toward me. "And you're still mooching."

"In this moment, yes, but I have some money at home. I have been saving it."

"For what? Taxis and memelitas?"

My mouth was too full to talk so I shook my head. "For university," I said. "But my father says I should go to el Norte."

César waved the serving boy over and ordered two Cokes. I

pulled out my ten-peso coin and put it on the table, but César ignored it. The boy brought two bottles, opened them and set them in front of us. César took a long drink, then he leaned forward in his chair and looked me in the eyes. It was the first time I saw fear in there and also how tired he was. "I need to leave the country," he said. "Immediately."

When I heard this, I felt more worried for César than for myself. "What has happened?" I asked.

"It's not just the taxi. That's all I can tell you."

"I'll go with you."

The words surprised me how quick they came. They surprised César too and he sat back in his chair. "Well," I said, "they saw both of us, didn't they? And both of us ran." César dropped his head, swinging it back and forth like a burro trying to find its way under a fence. "You don't understand," I said. "My father has been on my ass for years to do this — to go up there. Most of my friends are gone already. It will make him happy to see me go."

César took another sip of his Coke and rubbed his eyes.

"I could help you," I said.

He raised his eyebrows and looked me up and down. "I don't think so."

"My father has a connection."

"Everybody has a connection."

"To Don Serafín."

César made a snorting sound. "*Your* father knows Don Serafín?"

"He works for him all the time," I said.

César sat up in his chair. "Can Don Serafín get you a good coyote?"

"If my father asks him, yes."

Don Serafín is what we call a cacique, a rich and powerful chingón with a lot of property and influence who can make war if he wants. Caciques were here before the Spanish came, and they're still here. Don Serafín is Zapoteco, but his great-grandfather was half Spanish, un hacendado with a lot of land to the east of el centro. Now his family grows agave there for the mezcal and makes it also. For people like my father, Don Serafín can do many things — find work, loan money, grant favors, offer advice. In return my father gives him loyalty and must do whatever he asks.

"If you're going to call your father," said César, "I guess you'll want to borrow my phone"— he smiled a little bit —"along with my books and money and food?"

"I have my own phone," I said.

He laughed then, and it was the first time I heard him do that since we were in school. "Just don't mention my name."

When my father answered he was mixing cement. At first he was irritated, and when I told him I was ready to go to el Norte he was surprised. I told him as much of the truth as I could — that I have a small problem with the police, but I swear on the Virgin it wasn't my fault and this is why I cannot come home to say goodbye. I think he knew I was not saying everything, but he has done this himself and he did not press me. You must understand, to go north is my father's dream since I was young, and more than anything he wants to believe it will come true, not only for me but for him.

César found a patio with some shade near the bus stop and we waited there with a beer for my father to call back. César never once took out his phone, but when mine played "Back in Black" in the middle of the afternoon he jumped. "Bueno," my father said. "I have consulted Don Serafín and he has agreed to help us. But you must understand, this is a special favor he is doing, loaning us so much money. You must promise me you will pay it back as quickly as you can, and you cannot forget the interest. It will be bad for me — for the family — if he must come looking for it."

"I promise, Papá, as soon as I find work. Tío will help me."

My father was nervous and I could hear it. "He let me sit in his car, Tito. It's the first time in all these years."

I have seen Don Serafín's cars before in el centro. His new one is the BMW 760. In all of Oaxaca there are only two or three like this. For someone like my father it is an honor to sit in such a car, but it is also a burden. The problem with the favor is that there will always come the day when you must repay it. You cannot know when or for what you will be asked, but when it comes from a heavy chingón like Don Serafín it will hurt and you can never say no. I was afraid for my father then and I didn't know what to say so I asked him what it was like.

"If Pancho Villa was alive today," he said, "his car would be like this one. Every seat is a throne. And when he called his man Lupo? The car turned into a telephone!"

After this, Papá told me where to go and how to find this Lupo. I thanked him, but it wasn't enough.

"I hope you will come back," he said, "but not until there is a reason for hope. L.A. is best for you, I think. I'll tell Tío you're coming. Your mother will be worried so call when you can. Suerte. Vaya con Dios."

8

Thu Apr 5 — 23:14

Time, you know. Minutes. When my abuelo was young he didn't
know what a minute was because in Zapotec there aren't any minutes, only days and seasons and harvests. I'm not sure I know what
minutes are myself now. But I know they matter, especially when
you're trying to count how many you have left. And this I do not
know. There are many of us, AnniMac, but there was never a plan
for something like this so everyone is just reacting to themselves,
giving up or holding on to some private hope the way they hold on
to their crucifixes or water bottles or cell phones.

With no water we can go maybe two more days in here if we stay quiet and don't get the heat stroke, maybe longer if we drink our urine. Someone has to find us by then. I have to believe this because my water is almost gone. More than forty hours I made it last. It is easier when you are not moving, when you are breathing air that is so wet, even if it smells like the sewer. And when I imagine it is my abuelo holding the bottle, saying, Only one taste every hour. The heat makes you stupid and angry, and the thirst can make you crazy so you must fill your mind with something else — something stronger. For me it is my abuelo, the father of my father who was no blood to him or me but who always felt closer than blood.

The only way out is into your mind so that is where I go, trying to rest, trying to breathe only through my nose so I don't lose too much water. When I drink now it is only a cap at a time and I hold it in my mouth as long as I can. Then I imagine Abuelo's voice and it carries me out of here. I don't think I slept last night, but I dreamed so many things and my abuelo was there also. He was called Hilario Lázaro after a saint and the Spanish family that once owned the land around our pueblo. To this my abuelo said, "¡Hilario! ¡El Dios español es un bromista cósmico!" My abuelo was a bromista too — a funny guy, and when I hold this little jaguar head, I feel that he is with me.

In my dream he was sharpening his machete. It is something he did many times a day, right up until he died last year. I cannot say he was a good Christian, but this sharpening was for him a telling of the beads and it worked very well. He ground that blade so fine he could take the hairs off his face with it, and cut an ox bone in the air. "Throw it this way," he says to me in Zapotec, and he shows me how to do it so the bone is floating there in front of him. Then he takes his machete in two hands and says, *"Lédá!"* I throw the bone up and one moment there is a bone floating and that blade is only light, singing in the air and *Ya!* — there are two bones falling on the ground.

"Abuelo!" I say. "You can play for the Guerreros!"

He laughs and makes his machete sing again. "Only if they want to have two baseballs."

Abuelo was a real campesino, a kind of workingman that maybe you don't have in el Norte. He was even shorter than me and his feet were thick like a car tire. The lines in his face were so deep you couldn't see the bottom and his nose was a dark mountain standing by itself. He always looked old to me, but when I was little if his hand got hold of you, you could never get away no matter how you twisted. He worked his whole life in the milpa that he cleared himself from the forest and planted with corn and beans, squash and chiles and many other plants. It looks simple from the outside because you see only the corn growing, or maybe the beans climbing the dead stalks, doubled over, but inside there is a small jungle — a world of plants all connected. Es un sistema complicado and it takes a long time to learn. I know only part of it.

The pueblo where I was born is built on a ridge and you get to it by a dirt road off the highway. On a clear day you can see off both sides into different river valleys with the green mountains all around. When I was young and my father was away, I would go with my abuelo into the milpa after he burned off the old crop of corn and beans and we would plant the new crop together. Abuelo went first with his machete, stabbing it into the ground to make the hole, and I would follow, taking the seeds from the little sack my abuela made for me, dropping them in there and mounding the dirt over. It was a good job for small hands and we made a steady rhythm together, back and forth along the rows from the bottom of the milpa all the way to the top — and ours were steep up there, almost too steep for a plow.

In the heat of the day we would sit under the palapa with the soup and tortillas, and all around us the smell of smoke and chicken and burned earth. If we were lucky maybe we would see a rainbow or an eagle down below. On such a day I asked my abuelo how can something so small as a kernel of corn grow so big and feed so many, and he said to me, "It is the god inside doing this — *Pitao*. Some say that long ago, *Pitao* made us from the corn. I don't know if that is so, but what I do know is this — without it we would not exist, and without us there would be no corn. And if we become separated? We will turn into different things. We will lose our strength, our understanding of what and who we are."

Abuelo liked the nighttime and even after a long day of work he would stay up after everyone else went to sleep. He liked to smoke a little yerba, listen to the night sounds and watch the stars — I think there were more of them back then. He could talk like a gecko and he tried to teach me — put the side of your tongue against your teeth, left side, and suck in hard. You hear that hollow clicking sound? But I could never get it right. I'd try and Abuelo would say, "Oh no, now you're insulting him! It's like this." And they'd call right back. He always liked the darkness best.

Once my mother brought him a kilo of oranges from el centro. Oranges don't grow in the mountains where we live and he ate them all with the skin and everything. This is not because he was ignorant. It is because he grew up in the time of la Revolución with no father and he never forgot what it was to be hungry.

At least once a week my abuelo would take his burro into the mountains to cut the wood for cooking. That burro is still alive and she's older than me. When you live close with such animals for a long time they become your family. You learn all the little ways they have, and they learn yours too because in the campo there is a lot of time for watching. One of Isabel's little tricks is to bite your ass when you aren't looking. It is a game with her, but it hurts like hell. My abuelo was smart about this and she almost never got him, but one time she did — and bad, so he grabbed her by the lower lip, twisted it up and very close to her he said, "What, you bad burro!

You think you are a wolf now? Well, look out then. I am a jaguar."
And his eyes were sparkling. She always worked hard for him and
he never made her carry him on the steep trails as many others do.

One Sunday, long before I was born, the priest called on my
abuelo for a tithe. Abuelo refused to give him the money and said
right there in the church that the gods he serves are not asking him
for pesos. Many disapproved of this and the mayordomo's wife accused him of being a witch. There is a brujo in our pueblo, but it
is not my abuelo. It didn't matter. Since that time, when the village
council was deciding who gets to cut wood, or who is getting the
water for the milpa, Abuelo was at the end of the line, and it was the
same for my father. In the pueblo, you carry the sins of your family
before you, and my father's burden was heavier than most.

If you go to visit my pueblo today and ask someone what time it
is, they might hold their hand to the sky and point to the angle of
the sun. If you tell them they have the wrong time they might say to
you, "We follow the hours of God, not the hours of the devil." Maybe
they smile when they say this and maybe they don't. When I was
young and living there we didn't see gringos very much, and when
we did it was only hallelujahs — evangelistas. Like we needed more
gods. The hallelujahs were enormous and white with dog-color hair
and glass eyes and my sister and me would watch them only from
a distance. Sometimes they would bring us bags of old clothes and
shoes. One of the T-shirts Mamá got said "Jesus Hates the Yankees."
Whenever we were bad or didn't listen she would say, "Look out,
or the gringos will come in the night and take you away!" And you
know, AnniMac, mi madre was right. Look how many Mexicanos
you got up there now.

But not my abuelo and abuela. They stayed in the Sierra all the
way to the end. Always my abuelo worked with the burro, he never
had a truck, and you know a burro is not like a horse — a burro
is one uncomfortable ride. The packsaddle is wood and hard, but

without it the backbone will break you in two. Riding on one for a long time, your kidneys hurt after, your tailbone — other things too. And at the end of the day when they came back to the pueblo, him and that burro were both so heavy with the firewood that from behind you could not tell who was the animal and who was the man. That's how it is in the pueblos — a lot of times it's hard to tell.

And that is why, when I was five years old, Papá took me to el Norte.

9

We crossed at Presidio in Texas. Back then, there was just the small bridge and around a bend in the river a boat waiting in the tall grass, but Papá did not have enough money for a coyote so we had to swim. My tío in L.A. did this also and he told Papá where to go and how to do it. In a market on the border, Papá bought a box of plastic garbage bags. Then we walked out of town for a long time to a quiet place where there were no people. There, under a tree, we took off all our clothes and put them in one of the garbage bags. Papá blew up the bag then like a balloon and tied it up. After this he put it inside another bag, and more after that, and each time he tied the bag again. Then we walked to the water with only our chones. The Río Bravo was bigger and slower than the rivers I knew at home and it was the color of sand, even ankle-deep you couldn't see your feet. Papá held the bag in his arms like a sack of corn and walked into the water. He crouched down there and said, "Get on my back and hold on."

But it was December, the sun was going down and the water was cold. I was afraid and I remember saying, "I want to go home."

"That's where we're going," said Papá, "to a new home. Hold tight to me now and the river will take us where we need to go."

I did as he said and I gasped when we went under. The bag was big, but it was already full of our clothes and it sank. When we came up only my father's head was above the water. My arms were wrapped around his neck like vines and I could hear him choking as we were pulled into the current. "Easy," he whispered. "We're just going for a little swim."

I climbed up higher, tucking my nose in behind his ear, and the smell of his hair calmed me. I loosened my grip then, but only a little. I could feel him kicking under us — not hard but steady — and like this we left Mexico behind. Drifting down and slowly across, we made our way toward a line of willows on the far bank. By the time my feet touched the bottom I could smell the mud of el Norte. Between my toes it was as soft and slippery as the inside of my mouth.

Papá took my hand and we ran into the trees. We sat down in the leaves and he tore open the bags. "Bienvenidos al Norte," he said, pulling off my wet chones and rubbing me down with his T-shirt. "Maybe one day you will be a real Americano."

Papá threw the garbage bags and our wet chones into the bushes and gave me a tortilla to eat. When I asked him why he wasn't eating, he said he ate already. For a while we sat there with the wind blowing us dry, watching the sun drop through the branches. Out on the riverbank, standing in the sand as tall as my father, was a rusty metal cage. I remember this cage was so orange in the low sun it was like fire, like that cage was burning, and I asked my father if this was some special kind from the circus. "No," he said. "Es para criminales y migrantes."

"¿Qué es un migrante?"

"It is a good man trying to do better."

"Why is there a cage for him?"

"There are many cages, m'hijo, all shapes and sizes. Come now, we will go and find Tío Martín."

Tío Martín was four thousand kilometers away. He is my father's older cousin and he was always lucky. For many years he worked in a hotel in Massachusetts out in the country and he told my father to come — again and again he told him this. There is work, he said — in the kitchen, cutting the grass — many things to do. It is safe and quiet there, he said, and far from the city so la Migra will not find you. For us it was almost true.

After we crossed, we walked for a long time in the dark, down a dirt road where the trees were low and made a tunnel. It was cold and damp in there like winter in the Sierra. You could smell the river — muddy and full of rotting things and you knew even without seeing that it was big. I think my father carried me for most of the night. He is almost as big as a gringo and strong like a machine. He can lift a twenty-liter bucket full of cement with one hand, put it on his shoulder, then do the same with another bucket and walk as far as he needs to walk. Since he was young he was called el Biche for his green eyes. His mother, my Abuela Zeferina, called him Ezequiel because Ezequiel saw the future and was not afraid. Also because God told him in the Bible, "Son of Man, I will send you to a fighting nation that is fighting me. They and their fathers are going against me, even now."

Always I think Abuela believed her son would go to el Norte.

I remember sleeping in the woods with Papá, wrapped in his jacket, and I remember the tortillas. At home we ate only corn tortillas and these white ones were like eating the side of a box. I did it only because I was so hungry. We traveled this way for maybe three days until we got to a town with cement on the streets. It was just morning and Papá said to look for a white dog running. Every corner we turned I remember leaning around, hanging off his hand and I was proud because I saw it first. "¡El perro blanco!" I shouted. "¡El perro blanco!" He was there running up the side of a low building and he looked so thin and fast. My father took a deep breath then, like you do when you're stepping into a cold river. I couldn't understand why that dog was so important, but now of course I do. That dog took us all the way to Tío Martín.

In the bus station nobody was glad to see us. Some fanned their faces when we passed by. My father cannot read so well — all his life there is something between his eyes and the words — so he went to the wrong window and I am glad now that we didn't understand what the man there told us to do. He looked down at us like we were bringing him a plate of shit. His lip twisted as he talked and then he waved us away, sliding shut his little door. Through the thick glass I watched him turn his back and light a cigarette. After that, my father and me stood over by the pay phones, watching. There was another window on another wall and people were coming and going from there. I watched closely this one man who came away with a ticket in his hand. He was old in a jean jacket and he was dark like me, but his hair was white and woolly as a sheep. I had never seen a negrito before and I stared at his nose and lips until my father growled, "Basta," and pushed my head away.

We went to the window where the negrito came from and my father said, "Espreenfill." Then he held up two fingers. The lady in the window looked down at us, her eyes squeezed together like the sun was too bright. Her eyelids were silvery blue and sparkling the same as some butterflies you see around our pueblo. The hair above her forehead was yellow. It stood up by itself and I wondered how.

"*Espreen*feel," my father says again, a little louder. "Mossa-*shoo*sis."

"*Sprang*fail?" she says back. "Massa*tooch*its?"

My father bit his lip and nodded, hoping they were talking about the same thing. The lady looked at a list she had and said some things my father couldn't understand.

"¿Cuánto cuesta?" he said, but the lady only looked at him. He made a writing motion and she wrote something down. He looked at it and nodded. "Ven," he said to me, and we left the window. The lady said something else and my father waved and then he took my hand and led me into the toilet. He took me into a stall with him and pulled his pants down. There, sewn on the inside of his pants leg, was one of my baby sister's socks and inside it was the money — dólares. He counted some out, put these in his pocket, put the rest — not much — back into my sister's sock and tied up his pants. Then he put the seat of the toilet down and told me to go. He left me there and went out and I could hear him washing at the sink. I had never sat on a toilet seat. The walls were stone and everything echoed and smelled of chemicals and pine trees. It was a palace in there, but when someone in the next stall flushed the toilet I ran out so fast I tripped on my pants.

We left the bathroom and went back to the ticket window. My father pushed the money through and said, "*Espran*fail."

The lady looked at the dirty, wrinkled bills, shook her head and blew air out through her lips so they flapped. This made her cheeks puff out and with her sparkling eyes and tall yellow hair she looked like a puppet I saw once at a fiesta in Tlacolula. My father was getting nervous, his eyes going fast from her hands to her face and back to her hands. The lady said something to someone we couldn't see, shook her head again, and counted the money, holding the bills only by the corner. She didn't put them in the drawer but set them to the side. She pushed a single bill and some coins back through the window along with the tickets. Then she held up a little map with the white dog on it and started talking slow and loud and we had no idea what she was saying. She pointed to a red dot on the map, then to my father and then to the inside of the bus station. Then she made a line to a bigger red dot and said "Dallas!" about five times like it was something very important. Then she made a long line past many other red dots and said "New York."

"Nueva York?" said my father.

"*New* York," she said again. Then she made another line to a smaller dot and said the magic word—"*Sprang*fail."

This was the first time I saw my father smile since we crossed the river. When we got on the bus that afternoon, he patted the wall and said, "Perro bravo." He slapped my knee. "¡Perro bravo! ¡Vámonos!"

We were on that bus so long I turned six. Tío Martín picked us up at the bus station and he laughed when he embraced my father. "¡Híjole! Biche, you smell even worse than usual!" We walked out into the parking lot and what I remember most was the cold and Tío Martín's Chevy truck. It was a model we didn't have in Oaxaca, dark green with a cap on the back, and it looked new. I was never inside a new truck before and I couldn't believe how clean it was. The moment Tío Martín opened the door you could smell it—como la farmacia—perfecto, inmaculado. I was so cold, but I was afraid to get in and I went around to the back like I did at home. My tío opened the back window of the cap and threw my father's bag in there. I started to climb in too, but he stopped me. "You can ride on your papá's lap," he said.

All this time, Papá was only staring at the truck. "This is yours?"

I had never heard his voice sound like that—amazed and sad all at once like he was saying, "You? In this? How is it possible?"

Tío Martín said the truck belonged to him and his boss and the bank, and he was laughing, but I didn't care if he had to share it, that Chevy was the most beautiful thing I'd ever seen. "¡Bienvenidos a El Dorado!" he said. "Where you can have everything but own nothing."

"This is not Esprangfail?" I whispered, but Papá didn't answer.

It was December and I had never seen snow before that day. We drove through the tall stone city and out onto a highway with the windows up. Our truck at home was an old Chevy Apache that didn't even have all its windows, but this one was so new and quiet it seemed to float above the road. While Papá and Tío Martín hurried to fill in the missing years, I stared at the blinking radio, at the shiny paint outside and at the great green road signs growing bigger and bigger until they disappeared.

The place Tío Martín worked was in the forest and except for some tall pines all the trees around there looked like they were dead. The hotel was big and gray and made of wood with black windows and a stone roof. Everything inside it was made of wood also—the floors, the stairs, the toilet seat. It was nothing like Oaxaca, and I couldn't understand why anyone would want to stay in such a dark, cold place. Across the road was a field, but there was no sign of corn or flowers anywhere. Everything had died from the cold. In their place were lights—in the windows, in the trees, on the roof, all blinking day and night like fireworks that never ended. I knew it was for la Navidad, but where was the nacimiento? The camels and the kings? This did not look like a fiesta por el niño, it looked like a fiesta for lightbulbs.

We stayed in a room above the garage. Papá worked for Tío Martín and I followed him around in a pair of red rubber boots that were cold and heavy on my feet. There were some gringo kids there and they liked to stare at me. They waved and said things, but they made no sense. "Why do all these gringos talk like babies?" I asked.

"It is their own language," Papá said. "English, and you will have to learn it. That is your job here, that is why I brought you."

This made me feel scared and proud all at once. I was small and young but I wanted to work because that is what we do. Always in the pueblo I helped my parents. This work, given to me by my father who can go for days without speaking, filled me with a reason. *That is your job here.* So I worked hard. At night I told him all my new words, and he nodded and said, "Say them again." When he was working, shoveling the snow or taking out the trash or cutting firewood, I could see his lips moving, trying to make these new sounds himself, but it was so hard for him. He'd try and then shake his head, hawk up a big one from deep in his throat and spit into a snowbank. It was like those words were fishbones stuck in there.

There was a lady and her name was Señora Ellen. She ran the hotel with her husband, Señor Ron. Señora Ellen was the opposite of my mother — so tall and thin and white you could see through her skin to her blue veins. Have you seen some small plant trying to grow under a pot or in a dark place? They will look like this and I thought, even then, This pobrecita needs more sun and tortillas. I was afraid of her at first because she looked like la Catrina, the tall fine skeleton lady who comes out por el Día de los Muertos. She does not have her own lotería card, but she is famous in Oaxaca and before last year, when the tourists stopped coming, you could buy her in any form. Some of the workers at the hotel called Señora Ellen "Catrina" behind her back, but she was kind to me — she gave me cookies and taught me little songs. This is when I discovered I had special powers. Somehow I could remember her songs perfectly, without understanding the words.

The peace of Christ makes fresh my heart,
A fountain ever springing.
All things are mine since I am His.
How can I keep from singing?

Is a gift to be simple, is a gift to be free,
Is a gift to come down where you want to be.
And when you find yourself in a place just right,
It will be in the valley of love and the light.

And I could sing them like she did, even the tunes — all stayed perfect in my head. I could see this made her happy because she smiled and gave me more cookies. When you are six, Oreos Americanos can help you forget almost any sadness, at least for a while. She gave me many hugs also, and this was something I knew how to do so I gave them back, pushing my cheek into her chest which was all bones like an old man — so different from mi mamá, from any Mexicana I knew, and I wondered to myself, What kind of a woman is this? Where are her chichis? Sometimes she would hold me for a long time and I would get a strange feeling — you know when you shake someone's hand and they don't let go so you have to shake it more, even when the moment is really finished? But it made her happy and I wanted her to be happy — needed her to be. She had so many cookies.

"You are a very bright little fellow," she said. "¡Y muy guapo! What I would give for a boy just like you."

And I said it right back. Like a parrot — her pet parrot.

"You need to be in school," she said.

Señora Ellen talked to Papá. He was nervous about la Migra, but Señora said, No, not at this school. It is small, she said, and she is the friend of the boss. All of them belonged to the same church, a strange one with no color and no padre. Papá was also worrying about the money, but Señora said, No, the church will pay it, because she thinks I am some kind of special boy and she wants to help. It was hard for my father to accept, but this is why he brought me to el Norte — to learn so I could come back later to work and to live, and bring him and Mamá and my sister Vera also. Then Señora Ellen took me to the doctor who gave me three shots and medicine for my worms. After this she bought me some new clothes and a handsome backpack with so many zippers, and I went to the school which was in a house of wood like the hotel and the church. It was all gringos in there except for me, but already I could speak some English and the words came easy, even though it was so hard for Papá. It went like this for more than one year and I was speaking a lot, learning my letters and numbers, learning the games those kids played, but I never learned to like the snow. La maestra, Miss Morris, was nice to me and very pretty and many times during Story I sat on her lap. It was there, in the warmth and softness of her, that I started forgetting I was different from them. I started forgetting where I was from, what Mamá and Vera and my abuelos looked like. There was one photo Papá had, but it was hard to know after a while who those people were.

I can feel it happening again now and it is dangerous because when you forget, you can disappear. Besides César, there is nothing and no one in here to remind me who I am. So I must do it, tell it.

10

On the day la Migra came to the hotel, the snow was finally gone and so was Tío Martín. Where did he go? To buy goldfish for Señora Ellen's pond. How often did that happen? Only one time, but I told you Tío Martín was lucky. La Migra caught Papá and me and two others, but they never caught Tío Martín. I don't know if there is a virgin for goldfish, but that is my tío's protector. We heard the story later from his parents — my father's tío and tía — about the lucky goldfish and how after we were deported Señor Ron helped him apply for the amnesty because he was in el Norte so long already. He is still there and always he sends money to his wife and his parents, but he never comes home. Maybe he has his own pond of goldfish now.

Papá never forgave Tío Martín for that—for his good luck of getting away. And he never forgave himself for not going up there when Tío Martín first asked him. But how could he know that the amnesty was only for Mexicanos who were there before 1986? I was just a baby then and if Papá had gone maybe I would never know him. Maybe I would never even exist. But here we are and there is mi papá. Envy is the dog and Papá is the bone. Or maybe it is the other way around because he can never put it down. I think life is always complicated for him, but there are reasons for it.

After they caught us, la Migra sent us to Brownsville, Texas, on a bus with other migrantes from all over the place. We were only allowed to get off once a day and the toilet was broken so the smell was terrible. My father was silent for most of the trip—three days, but one thing I remember he said was, "It is because of your school they found us." I don't know if it's true or not, but when we returned to Oaxaca there was nowhere for us to go but back to the pueblo and for Papá this was a humiliation. "Why do they deport *me*," he said to Abuelo, "when half of those pendejos up there can't even mix cement? I have a right to work as much as that pinche Martín."

"Maybe," said Abuelo. "But how can they know it when you talk like such a mojado and can't even read?"

That was the last time my father sat down in his stepfather's house, which is the house where he was born. It was also the first time I saw him hit my mother. He was drunk and shouting in her face, saying he wasn't going to live his life behind the oxen staring at their culos. "Walking all day behind them," he yelled, "every time they shit, it's like they're shitting in your face!"

The next morning, Papá drove away in the Chevy Apache and from that day he lived most of his time in el centro, coming back only once in a month. Because he grew up making adobe bricks with Abuelo and his uncles, my father was good with plaster and cement and he worked on roads and buildings and made deliveries in the Apache. Often he did these jobs for Don Serafín, the same man who paid for our bus tickets home from the border. It was around that time el cacique Don Serafín tried to put a McDonald's on the Zócalo, which is the heart of el centro and also a UNESCO site. There were protests and he did not succeed, but Don Serafín got his revenge. Now, at night, if you look out over the Valley of Oaxaca, cradle of the Zapotec civilization, you will see stars above the dark and ancient mountains, shadows of pyramids on the ridges, maybe the moon rising behind — and down by the baseball stadium, the great golden chichis of Santa McDoña. It is the biggest sign in Oaxaca — as tall as a church and bright like the sun, and it marks the only McDonald's in south Mexico with the playground and the tunnel slide. My father told me this — it was him who built the walls around the flower beds.

We left the pueblo — my home — when I was thirteen. That's when Papá had enough money to move all of us into a two-room cement house he rented in Mártires de Río Blanco under the Milenio Cross, thirty minutes walking from the Zócalo and la Basílica de la Soledad. The only water we had came in the garrafón, the electricity we took with a wire from the transformer down the hill and the same with the phone.

I never liked it there and I was glad to go away to secondary school because I had my own plan, you know — to go to university. I am smart enough for it. I did not win the scholarship like César, but the tuition is not terrible. For two years I studied at UABJO in Oaxaca — Tourism and Hospitality because of my English, and also Literature because of my abuelo who taught me to read. But then comes the strike last year, first the teachers' union and then so many others joining — students, campesinos, all kinds of people from many other unions and tribes — until the whole city stopped functioning because so many were protesting our terrible governor. For months there was a big camp on the Zócalo, people were arrested and killed — people I know, and many things were broken. After all this trouble my father would not help me anymore. "Show me your tourists now," he said. "You are wasting your time and my money. Look at your cousin Efraín — five years in university and still he is riding a bicycle!"

Last December, a month after the strike was broken, me and Papá and his mother-in-law, my Abuelita Clara, went to el centro so Papá could go to the market and Abuelita could sell some of her pots in the Zócalo. We had to go on the bus because the motor in the Chevy Apache will not hold oil anymore. Papá was in a bad mood about this and some other things and when we were unpacking my abuelita's jugs and dishes he dropped one and it broke. "Look what you've done!" she said. "I haven't sold a thing today and I'm already down forty pesos."

"And what is forty pesos?" he said. "A liter of motor oil?" He kicked the broken pieces then and my abuelita flinched like he was kicking her. "And how many of these will you sell today with no tourists — two? Three? None? What difference does it make?"

It is not common for Zapotecos to shout in public, but Papá was doing it now and I wondered if he'd been drinking. "We're trapped in the past!" he said. "All of us!" With his hand he swept past my abuelita's pots and over to the French iron bandstand where they played music from a hundred years ago. "Who built that? Emperor Maximilian!" He pointed to the shoeshine man napping in his chair in his snakeskin boots. "Where is he going? Nowhere!"

Like this, his hand a compass needle, my father circled the Zócalo, pointing out the bird man by the fountain with the singing cages on his back, the blind organ grinder on the corner with his hat in his hand, the Maya candy seller with her long wool skirt and shiny blouse, the clowns with their white gloves and red noses, the woman selling sweets off a platter on her head, the young couple on the bench with their children eating ice cream, the Trique women protesting again with their bare feet and their banners. And watching all this — and him and us — like visitors to a human zoo, the handful of pale tourists in the empty cafés with their big black cameras, shooting everything in sight.

"Can't you see it?" my father said to me. "The world has moved on without us, and for a young man there is no worse fate. You are missing the future because the future isn't here." He looked at me hard with his angry eyes. "The future is there!"

Papá's compass needle swung again and he stabbed his finger to the north like he would poke a hole in it, like he would poke a hole in the bandstand with its bat-wing roof, in the central post office that hadn't been modern since before he was born, in the cathedral that was built when the Spanish came, in the hills and corn and oxen that hadn't changed in a thousand years, in the megacity of D.F. where he didn't stand a chance, in all the states conquered by the drug cartels, in the new steel border fence growing longer and higher with every passing year, in the pile of bones spreading across the American desert, in all the family, friends and neighbors who had lost their faith in Mexico and were never coming back.

"But we are still here," he said, dropping his hand to his side, too heavy to hold up any longer.

Fri Apr 6 —00:17

There are different ways to count success in Mexico and for campesinos it is mostly counted in trucks and cement. You know someone is doing good when they buy a Ford Lobo Lariat with the super cabina in racing red. And you know it when they build a house of cement. In my old pueblo the brother of the mayordomo has such a house with the garage and two doors that are electric. Maybe it's normal in California, but this house is in a little pueblo two hours from el centro on a road made of broken rock with chickens running and burro shit down the middle and all the neighbors in adobe. And who lives in that big house? Nobody. It is a palace for insects and mice. Everyone who can work in that family is in el Norte sending money home to pay for the house, and now it's so hard to come back maybe they're never going to live in there. Maybe their neighbor just sends them a video.

My abuelo could never understand why people want to give up adobe when it is so cool to live in and you can make it yourself. Cement is hot to live in and you must buy it from someone else. Cucarachas and spiders and scorpions still come in, and the cement patio holds water so mosquitoes can grow and these ones are carrying dengue now. But everyone wants it anyway because it looks so clean and modern and because it is what rich Americanos do. Más importante, it is what rich Mexicanos in America do. So of course we must do it too. Because adobe is for poor people — for Oaxacas. What does my father want more than anything? A new truck and his own house of cement — not to rent from someone else as we must do since leaving the Sierra. "Look at that shitbox you were born in," he says. "We're still living like the troglodytes. And your mother needs a gas range. You are young and strong. Go."

It is a tradition in the pueblo to bury your baby's placenta in the dirt floor of the house. It means you will always come back. For most of us it is a root into that place, but for my father I think it is a chain. That memory of Tío Martín with his goldfish and green card and shiny new truck — it chews on him, eating him alive. And you know, my young sister Vera is the same. After she turned thirteen, she would never touch Abuelita Clara's clay again. I asked her why and she said it's dirty. Now she is at the hairdresser school and her favorite T-shirt is a pink one saying with fake diamonds, "Is Not a Hobie — Is a Pasion." When someone takes her picture with the phone, she will flash some gang sign she learned, but only to show her fingernails because if you've got long fingernails it means you're not working in the milpa anymore, and if you're eighteen and trying to make it in el centro the first step is to look like you never saw a milpa in your life. Many times when I went to visit Abuelo, Vera would laugh and say, "Hey country boy, don't forget your *huaraches!*" Well, they are our traditional shoes with excellent ventilation, and the cactus spines will not go through the bottom. Even mi padre wears them. Once, Tío brought him some Nike Michael Jordans from L.A., but they are so big and white he saves them only for church. On him they look like shoes for a clown, but I never say this. Vera wears only el Converse, black with rainbow socks. Them, or las fuckmes.

Nothing is changing in five hundred years — more, even. Always there is a handful of chingones controlling everything and the rest of us chasing the crumbs. So many other young people have gone already — anyone who can make the trip north. I saw this with my own eyes, how the pueblo is a nut with a worm in it — the shell is there, but inside, out of sight, the meat is being eaten away. Many young people say that in Mexico to get ahead now the only way is to cheat and break some rule. But to do this you must have some connections or be very smart, or very hard. For the rest of us there is only el Norte y los dólares gringos.

In my pueblo, half are gone to the States. Almost four hundred people. You walk through there now and you think maybe there has been a war or some disease — just kids and old people and animals left. Abuelo told me it was like this also after la Revolución — a million Mexicanos died from that and many survivors went to el Norte,

maybe a million more. And you had half our country already—
Tejas, California, Arizona, Nuevo Mexico, Nevada, Colorado and
some others I can't remember, plus all those rivers. It was all once
Mexico—you can see it by the names. Mexicanos don't forget this
and there are many songs. Tijuana No! are rapping about it also, a
history lesson for gringos and a kind of promise too—la Recon-
quista . . . Because we are coming back.

Maybe this is our destiny—not for Mexico to lose her people or
for America to lose her soul, but for all of us to come together—the
United States of América. It will be a new superpower, but with better food.

Ever since I was young, my father talked of going back, but he never
did, and when I asked him why, he only made excuses until one day
last fall when we were arguing again about me going to university,
I got angry. "Why are you always telling me to go up there," I said,
"when it is you who wants it so much?"

It was the first time I spoke to him like a man and not like a son
or a boy. Instead of shouting or raising his hand, Papá looked away
out the window, took a sip of his beer and said nothing. We were in
the Chevy Apache on the road to Tlacolula, the nearest town to our
pueblo. I was driving and we had just come through Santa María
del Tule, past the giant cedar there, which rises like a green fountain from the valley floor—three thousand years old and wider
than the church. Outside of town, vultures circled over the road
waiting for something to die. Papá did not speak as we passed the
quarry where they cut a hill in half and the fallen blocks lie scat-
tered, almost yellow in the pale green brush. Or when three state
police cars raced up behind us with sirens and disappeared over a
hill. My heart was starting to settle and my hands relax again when
my father finally spoke.

"You may not remember this," he said, still looking out the window, "but when we got deported, they held us in Brownsville for two days. They put me with the men. You were the only child in our group and you went with the women. You didn't cry when they took you away and I was proud. Of course I protested — I said you were my only son and that we must stay together, but the agents said I had broken the law and had no right to make demands. They put us in barracks like in the army, it was hot as hell, the mosquitoes were terrible, and I hoped it was better where you were. On the second day, two agents from la Migra took me to another building. There, in a small room, they took my picture, my fingerprints, all my details, but it was not this that frightened me. It was their words. 'We will be watching for you,' they said. 'If you ever come back we will put you in prison, and where will your boy be then?'" My father finished his beer and threw the bottle out the window. "That is why."

"You believed them?" I said.

"If you had been in that room," he said, "you would have believed them too. Those chingados can take anything from you — your job, your freedom, your child. Without these, what is a man?"

11

If you are my witness, AnniMac, I am your invisible man. O su su-
plicante. Pues, I am saying all this because I cannot see or do anything else. Because remembering the past helps me forget the present. Because maybe right now someone is fixing the tower and these
messages will finally go. I tell myself that even if the mechanic never
comes, la Migra will find us. It is what your border army is for, no?
We hear all the time in Mexico about your modern technologies
for catching migrantes — the cactus microphones and the cameras
in space and the great engines under the desert that rumble in the

night, powering the whole machine. And we see the pictures of all your green men with their trucks and planes and helicopters, and their dogs and indios to follow the tracks. I know this truck is big and easy to see — it is an elephant out here. It even has a sign on it en español which is yelling now — DEPORT ME. Or maybe it is DRINK ME.

Even with César so close I'm freezing. I'm holding him as tight as I can. It is the only way I can stop my teeth from rattling. I'm not the only one doing this, but I'm glad no one can see it.

Fri Apr 6 — 08:36

The helicopter went over us so low we were sure they saw us, but that was half an hour ago. The truck is getting warmer, but I am so stiff from the cold and the metal. The viejo in front who was insulted by the coyote, I think he is hallucinating — talking to his wife, asking her for agua de jamaica. There are some in here who think I am hallucinating too, talking to people who aren't there. Sometimes the baby-face man and his friend told me to be quiet, but not for a while. I know people are in trouble now, I can hear it by how they breathe — like dogs and sick people. It is a big question — if all of us will live to be saved. My water is gone and I think it is the same for everyone.

Maybe César is the lucky one. Maybe his accident was Juquila's mercy protecting him from something worse. Because what are the chances of such an injury? César said Juquila saved me also — from the federales. He said she might have a plan for me, but a plan is not the same as protection. César didn't give me his phone because he is a nice guy or because he didn't want it anymore — he gave it to me because he wanted someone to keep it alive. In there are some files and documents about the corn and a company called SantaMaize.

I know this because of what I saw and what he told me on our last night in Altar. But this is not the only thing I have from César.

I did not say before how I came to have his phone because of what came with it, what I took. Two nights ago when the tank was cooling — for a short time before the cold it was better for us. This is when César started moving again — his hand. It was a surprise for me because it is the first time since he fell, and I said, "Cheche! Are you OK?"

But he only whispered, "Tito," his voice so quiet I must put my ear by his mouth to hear it, and I said, "Yes, I am here," and took his hand.

Luego, he pulled my hand over to his pants and they were wet. He pushed my hand down on the zipper. "Take it," he whispered. "Take it."

I didn't know what he was talking about and even in the dark it was embarrassing. I thought he must be delirious, so I'm pulling my hand away and saying, "What? What is it?" But he keeps pushing my hand down there so I can feel everything and he's saying, "Take it," and then I feel something hard that is not him. It is completely dark, but I'm looking around anyway because you don't want any-one to see you doing like this — it feels so wrong. And then I do it, AnniMac, reach my hand into his pants. I try to stay outside his chones, but that's not where it is. I have to go inside them all the way because this is where he hides his phone. It is a safe place there and it is the reason he still has it, but I think I am going to be sick, trying not to touch anything but the phone, and when I get it I wipe it on my pants, and that's when I feel it — his battery, the new Mugen that lasts for many days.

César took a big breath, and another, and then he lets go my hand. I am afraid he's dying, right in that moment, but when I listen he is still breathing the same way like before. When I touch his head

I can feel that the bleeding is finished which I hope is good. I try to give him some water, but he chokes on it and I don't know what else to do. No one can help me, and I can't help César.

But his water — when I found that in the pocket of his jacket, I put it in my backpack. All this time I saved it.

Fri Apr 6 — 10:01

I am finally warm and I was trying to rest, but there was a problem in the tank. The Zapotec man who cut himself still has my phone from before, and the baby-face man asked him to use it. "It's not my phone," said the Zapoteco. I could hear by his voice that he was having problems. He was gasping.

"Just give it to me," said the baby-face man whose voice didn't sound right either. "My feet are fucking killing me. They don't fit in my fucking shoes anymore."

"I can't," said the Zapoteco.

"What the fuck," said the baby-face man. "You down there, paisano, I need to use your phone."

I do not like this guy since he pulled off César's shoe, and before, when I passed my phone to the Zapoteco, I didn't want him to touch it so I sent it down the other side of the tank, from the Maya to the mother and her son to the baker from Michoacán to another young woman who didn't speak and then to the Veracruzano. "What do you need it for?" I asked.

"So I can call my motherfucking lifeline. ¡Güey! My fucking feet are swelling up. Something's not right with them. I need to look."

I did not have the energy to fight or argue. I was afraid of this guy, but I was also afraid of people turning against me, coming after the water. "You can use it for a minute," I said, "but don't waste the battery."

"Órale," says the baby-face man.

All of this was happening in the dark. The Zapoteco must have given him my phone then because when the screen came on the baby-face man had it. "¡Jesucristo!" he said. Even in that light I could see his feet—like someone blew them up with air, and dark red. The baker from Michoacán was sitting opposite him and when she saw them so close she pulled away. "You need to elevate them," she said. She was whispering because her voice didn't work anymore. "Put them over your head."

"How the fuck am I going to do that?"

"Is that the only word you know?" asked the baker who was more like a mayordomo than a baker. "I'm telling you—if you want the swelling to go down."

The baby-face man held up my phone and looked around the tank. To his right, in the glow of the screen, I saw the two Nicas and the injured one was pale and silent, his head on the other's shoulder, holding his hand which looked now like a purple glove. The way the light was in there, people's faces did not look like living faces anymore but like masks, the kind a witch would make if she wanted to curse you, and I wondered if I looked the same.

"Who has water?" croaked the baby-face man.

To ask this in here is like going to a cemetery and saying, Who's alive?

He went from face to face with the screen light, saying, "You? You? You?"

People covered their eyes or turned away. With his head down, the Veracruzano held up an empty bottle in one hand and wiggled two fingers in the sign for Fuck yourself.

"Turn the screen down," I said, but he ignored me.

"What about you?" he said to a young woman next to the Veracruzano who was kneeling on her bag, facing the wall of the tank. She was an india, but I couldn't tell where she was from. Her jeans were wet and her head was bowed over her hands. She looked like pictures I saw of people waiting to be executed. "What are you doing there?" he asked. "Praying for rain?" The woman didn't answer. The baby-face man looked around the tank again. "We'll be drinking our piss pretty soon."

"Speak for yourself," whispered the baker. "Someone will come — la Migra, o un ranchero —"

"Or the fucking Minutemen," said the baby-face man.

"Turn the phone off," I said. "You're wasting the battery."

He turned the screen toward me. "What are you saving it for?" he asked. "Do you know something we don't? And why are you talking all the time?"

"We're going to need it if the bars come back," I said. "Turn it off and give it to me."

"No bars on it now," said the baby-face man, holding the light on me. "You have his phone — and his water also." And then to everyone, "Isn't that right? How can he talk so much without water?"

"¡Dios mío!" said the baker. "How can *you* talk so much?"

He put the light on César and the only thing moving on him was his chest, up and down like a pump. The blood on his face was dry and pieces were breaking off like old paint. He turned the light back on me. "You took his water, didn't you?"

"He cares for him all this time," said the Maya. "Making the bandage, talking to him, giving him water. It is why he still lives."

"He gave you some?" asked the baby-face man, pointing the phone at the Maya.

"What have *you* done for anybody?" asked the praying woman whose son's head was still cradled in her lap. "Besides break that pendejo's fingers."

The baby-face man pointed the phone at me again. "My water's gone," he said.

"Because it's all in your feet," said the baker. "Now turn around, put them up on the wall, and for God's sake give us some peace."

Even whispering, you could hear in her voice that she was used to telling people what to do. I thought about what she said about his feet, and I understood that the women would last the longest. With their hips and chichis, they are full of water, like camels. The baby-face man was trying to turn around and having trouble so the baker made room for him. "You can put your head here for a little while," she said and patted her lap. "How old are you?"

"Twenty-six," said the baby-face man.

"The same as my son," she said. "He's in Texas now. You even look like him." She held her hands out to him and with no more words he laid his head in her lap and slowly moved his feet up the wall. For a moment the screen light went across the face of his friend. The man's lips were white with foam and his eyes were open, seeing nothing. He was breathing, but only enough for a much smaller person. I wondered if he was really a friend of the baby-face man, and if he would be the first to die.

12

I told César in his ear that I am holding his water, keeping it safe for him, but to myself I say, Only as long as I can.

My greatest fear, AnniMac — besides dying in here — is for my mother to learn of it on *Primer Impacto.* This is her favorite program with news, celebrities and always some catastrophe — a plane crash or narco violence or dead migrantes — Mexicanos with more wounds than Jesus Himself, and on *Primer Impacto* they show every corpse and cut and bullet hole. Since we moved to el centro my mother is addicted to it. The neighbor has a television and whenever she can she is over there watching. There are enough of us in here, I think, for *Primer Impacto* to notice, especially if we die. Because in Mexico death is our national drug, the god everyone worships but no one will name. And I can see mi madre with her neighbor, Lola, in their braids and skirts and aprons, sitting in their plastic chairs when that hot presentadora comes on with her white teeth and incredible lips and chichis bigger than your head, and she's telling the story and my mother is thinking, Qué lástima, more dead paisanos on the border — until she sees the pictures and hears the names and understands that no, these are migrantes from the south — Oaxaqueños — *Zapotecos* — her own son! Mi madre has suffered enough.

I will tell you about my mother because if you can see her, then you can see me. Her name is Ofelia. She is darker and shorter than my father and so am I, and our eyes are the same shape and color brown. When she smiles her face is a dark room with the sun coming in and to see it will make you smile also. Mi mamá is wide now and stands to my shoulder, and I am only one meter and sixty-five. There is a thing that happens to a woman after she has some children and spends a few thousand days in the field, and to a man after he carries a few thousand bricks and follows the plow for a thousand kilometers, and that is you stop walking forward with your legs like a horse or a dog and start moving from your hips — side to side like a lizard or the Hulk — stiff as an old burro. That loose way of the girl or the dancer goes away, the muscle turns to something else, and you start looking like the pots they made in our pueblo before plastic came. Everything in our old pueblo is low and sturdy like the people and you may wonder if we built the houses and the pots to fit us or if we have grown to fit them. If you are the way I imagine you, I think you will need to bend down to come in our door, but my mother will make you such a feast. Maybe she will teach you her recipe for mole — thirty-seven steps and two days to make it. She can feed a hundred people like nothing.

Mamá wears her hair in the same braids like those ladies on the Diego Rivera bags that the tourists used to buy, with ribbons woven in and tied together at the bottom. It is pretty, of course, but that is not why she does it. She does it so her hair won't catch fire when she's cooking. Mamá tried pants once, but Chinese bluejeans are not made for the Zapoteca body and Papá said they make her look like a pile of tires so now she is back to the skirt and apron and huipil. Most of the time there is no reason to wear shoes, but she has some little rubber ones. In the pueblos nothing is new but Pepsi bottles, plastic buckets and babies, and none of these stay new very long. When I was little, except for the Chevy Apache and some clothes, just about everything we owned or ate came out of the ground.

Where I live, it is the truck that makes the difference between a slave and the free man. This is what my father always told me. The Chevy Apache was his pride, un clásico with the V-8 and four speeds. The engine sounded like river stones in a dump truck. Papá bought it before I was born when he was working up in Chihuahua for Don Serafín. It had holes in the back gate and Papá said they were made by bullets. On the windshield is the polarizado, the special band for blocking the sun, and this one says GON MAN. There is one photo from that time when the Apache was all black, and with its desert tires and long bed it looked to me like the Batmobile.

You could always tell Papá's truck from the others because it was covered over in dents like some crazy person beat it with a hammer. This was from the only time Papá drove into Texas. I was still a baby and there was some kind of storm up there. Papá was alone on the highway when it happened and he said there were balls of ice coming down the size of guayabas — oranges even. They came so many and so fast he didn't know what was happening. The noise was incredible, he said, like thunder under your hat. He thought it was one of those warplanes Tío told us about and he was sure he was going to die. Together with all the dents, the windshield was cracked all over. When finally he was brave enough to come out, the sun was shining and near him in the grass was a dead coyote in a circle of smoking white ice balls. He drove straight home after that because in his mind it was an omen. Since then, he had bad dreams about it — sometimes it was the coyote lying there, sometimes it was him. He asked Mamá to see if the Bible mentioned such things with the frogs and locusts and hemorrhoids, but she said no, maybe it is a new punishment from God, special for Texas — for killing John F. Kennedy. My mother crosses herself whenever she hears his name because he was a Catholic also.

Only once did Papá take me with him to Chihuahua. It was just before we left for el Norte and Papá was making a delivery for Don Serafín — peanuts and other things too, I think, but Papá did not talk about it because I was so young and because what matters is only the work. In the night that highway from Ciudad Chihuahua to Durango is full of trucks, nose to tail like a string of burros and driving so fast, 120 kilometers, sometimes more. No federales and the only way off is into the ditch. Everything is dark beyond the road — just the wide plain stretching away on every side, black like space and between the towns not a single light. It is dangerous and only the santos and virgins keep us alive. But even with hundreds of them they are still too busy — so hard to watch over everyone at once.

And we are driving the peanuts — cacahuates. You must hear SpongeBob sing that song: *¡Soy un cacahuate! — Boom Bam Boom Bam — ¡Eres un cacahuate! — Boom Bam Boom Bam — ¡Todos somos CACAHUATES!* And he is right. Out here we are all peanuts and SpongeBob sings it like he will die if he doesn't — like a true

Mexicano, like Vicente Fernández. Of course you know this song. It was my first ringtone.

But this story here is from before the time of SpongeBob and celular —

It is late and we are driving and Papá is so still and quiet he is like a statue of someone driving. But this is normal, he is used to driving all night. I have eaten so many peanuts I never want to see another and I am trying to sleep against the door when all of a sudden the brake lights are on in front and we are going from 100 to 10 like that. Flashers everywhere and mi padre is cursing. He doesn't talk so much, but he curses con elocuencia. Many, many chingaos in all their different positions. So now everything is very slow in both directions and Papá pulls his head down into his neck, shoulders by his ears. He does this when he's not happy and it makes him look like a turtle sulking, but I would never tell him this. "¿Qué chingado es esto?" he says. "¿Una chingada calenda?"

There is a bend in the road and a rise in the land and on the other side a glowing. The sky is dark without the moon, but there is a light in the sky, big and orange like the sun is coming up early. Papá whistles and he pats the virgin on the dashboard — Juquila, por supuesto. "¿Qué es *esto*?" he says again. It is so slow now, like we are riding in an ox cart instead of the Apache, and when we finally get to the top of the rise we can see it. It is a fire — muy grande, como el infierno, and I wonder what can make such a fire like this. Most of the vehicles out here are panel trucks or vans with people, and these are not so big. But up there burning is something else, something enormous. Papá is holding the wheel tight with both hands and staring into the fire that is too bright to look at, and I am staring also because it is too bright not to look at. There are shapes in there — humans, black and thin, waving in the flames like puppets dancing. Monos in sombreros. After seeing this it is always how I imagine souls in Hell — in the dark by the side of a highway on an empty plain — el páramo despoblado — floating in fire. If it was Mexicanos writing the Old Testament, this is what it would look like.

We can see now that it is a truck, a Kenworth by the cab on it, and all of it is on fire — the cab, the trailer, the wheels even — like it was made of dry sticks. Papá whistles and crosses himself. I know I must cross myself too, but I do not, I don't know why because it is a habit with us — when you pass a cemetery, a church, a funeral, an accident, maybe a really pretty girl — for all these you will do it. It is a sign of respect and also for protection. But out here on this lonely road full of people, I have a feeling, a knowing, even though I am so young, that this will not protect me from such a disaster. It is too small an offering. I think about that moment sometimes — like now — and wonder if this is when God saw me turn away.

Slowly, slowly we drive past, and Papá is right — it is a calenda, only this one is silent — no music or roquetas, no shouting or dancing. There is only the low sound of engines and the fire — so big it makes its own wind, pulling the world into itself and eating it alive, so hot it makes everything around it bend and twist and shimmer. The truck is melting over itself like wax, the grass around it is burned down to the dirt. Even the dirt is burning, and I can see the dark floating men better now. They are standing in a circle around it, heads tilted so their sombreros block the heat from their eyes. I don't know how they stand it. When we pass, it is so hot I must close my window, so hot there is no smell, only the rushing wind racing up into the sky, sparks and stars together.

After this is a minivan, facing the other direction and looking like a broken accordion. Nothing is moving there. There is no police or ambulance or bomberos, only the traffic stretching away forever with nowhere to go. But what could they do anyway? What can God do but watch, tilting His sombrero to shield His eyes?

It happens every night, but how to mark a thing like this — este milagro oscuro that seems impossible and still it happens before your eyes? The families will come later and there will be crosses for sure. Maybe they will build a little capilla for candles and flowers, and it will be one more. If you rise up and look at Mexico from far away like an angel or a spaceman, you can see lines of crosses marching across the land — here and there capillas and then cemeteries and more crosses leading to more cemeteries and churches, basilicas, cathedrals and pyramids — in all directions across time. It is what binds the country together, this web of death and remembering. And who is the spider weaving this?

Fri Apr 6 — 10:59

With the days gone there is no time, and things I did not think of for years come back to me like yesterday. There is something outside now making sounds like the first time I carried a plastic bag. It was just after Papá and me got back from Chihuahua, and Mamá sent me to the tienda to buy some soap. There is a kind we use in the pueblo — Tepeyac — and it is the biggest soap you ever saw, like ten of your el Norte soaps, maybe because in Mexico there is so much dirt. It is a slow and lonely walk home when you're five years old and the older children are in school and all the adults are working in the forest or the milpa, and when you're alone there are so many things to be scared of. On that morning there was nothing to see but clouds hanging low over the metal rooftops and the leaves nodding and winking, shiny with the rain. Not even a stray dog did I have for company, only this giant golden soap in the plastic bag with its strange slippery weight, so different from a string bag or the basket. To give me courage I was swinging the soap around my head, hearing the bag rattle in the wind and I never heard such a noise before. Faster and faster I went until there were two tones together, a kind of growling, so I made a fierce face and imagined that sound was coming out of me and that my soap was a great stone and with it I can kill Goliath and knock down his house. But I was so young then, and what did I know about anything?

Oye, AnniMac, I never talked to anyone like this before. Where I live, not a lot of people talk about the life inside because, really, who wants to know? It's hard enough outside, right? Maybe there are some poets doing this, but who is listening? You try this in a mezcaleria and they will say, "¡Güey! What do you think this is, Neuróticos Anónimos? Have another chínguere and shut up."

It is a real place — yes, the mezcalería — but also Neuróticos Anónimos. One time in my first year of university, before I met Sofía, I went there myself, but when I was in the lobby, looking at their brochures, I felt like everyone walking by could see me in the window, and in my mind I heard them saying, "Will you look at that poor neurótico in there. He's probably still a virgin."

Yes, well, there is no Virgens Anónimos in Mexico, and when I tried it in my mind I could not make myself to say, "Hello, my name is Héctor and I'm neurotic." When I think such words I see only my father's angry face saying, "Why is my only son such a woman?" In one of the brochures there was a question, and it was "How do you want to feel?" No one ever asked me this before, but in that moment I believe how I want to feel is like I'm buried to my balls in the hot little neurótica I hope to meet in Group. Of course I know they will not accept this answer, and I put the brochure back and for some reason I say to the receptionist who looks familiar like an old teacher or something, "I'm sorry, I have a medical condition so I am unable to answer all the questions."

Then I hurry out the door, but in my mind I hear her calling, "Don't worry, Tito! Virginity is nothing to be ashamed of! There is now a cure!"

I am not handsome like César, but I am handsome enough — that is not the problem. The problem is that in Oaxaca virgins are the most precious and desired of all God's creatures so it is impossible to have only a girlfriend because with her comes all her posse — the mother, the sisters, the aunts and abuelas, the godmother and probably the brothers too — and all of them watching you like a family of hawks, thinking you're a thief and a dog trying to steal from their princesa preciosa her one thing that can never be returned. And maybe they are right, but what if you don't want to marry when you're sixteen? And you don't want to go with a puta? These are important questions, and for a young man they never stop being important.

The first time I got an answer was from Sofía on the park bench on the Llano. She is Mixteca, born in the campo but living in el centro and also the first in her family to go to university. I did not notice her until last spring when, one day outside Customer Service class, someone said how burros and Nokia 1200s cost the same and she said, "But with the burro you cannot change the ringtone." I looked at her in a different way after that. Behind her glasses she was prettier than I realized, and funnier. We had an ice cream on the Zócalo. She said she wanted to be a doctor, but her father is a waiter now and he said no, it is better to be a manager in a hotel. "It is better for me too," I said, "because I would never meet you in medical school."

Everyone in Oaxaca lives with their family so the only way to be alone with a girl is outside. For this, Sofía and me would look for a quiet corner in a park, but there are so many of us looking that it can be hard to find your own bench sometimes. That afternoon on the Llano it was May and warm. There was a breeze blowing and it carried mist from the big fountain and with it the smell of meatsmoke and trees. Together the wind and water made a kind of whispering sound so everything else — the children playing, the band practicing, the traffic — all seemed far away and it felt like only the two of us there kissing. After some time she put her leg over mine with her backpack across her lap. It was a surprise for me the difference — her cool thigh and then that sudden heat around my fingers, hotter than her mouth — and this together with my tongue and hers, all moving in time — so close and fast we could believe for a little while it was really me in there.

Both of us were walking funny when we left that place, and it was hard to look her in the eye. My lip was bleeding also and when she kissed me goodbye she noticed this and laughed and kissed me again. I could not be seen to walk her home from there because already she was late for vespers with her mother and sisters, but when she was gone I licked my fingers to remember and the taste of her together with my lip was something new and delicious and of course I wanted more.

13

Fri Apr 6 — 11:23

It is so hot, but when I touch my neck, my forehead, there is no sweat there. And when I do this, touch myself, it makes a cold shock through my body so my hair stands up and I am covered in turkey skin. The thirst is making us sick and not only with the headache. Our brains and bodies do not work properly anymore. I can hear it when the others try to talk, like their tongues are too big for their mouths. All my life, if I was near to a sick person I could feel their fever coming into me, even across the room. That is how it is now —

like a pressure growing, infecting me also and pushing me into the wall which is too hot to touch.

His water. If César wakes up, who will have it?

It is the devil's question and I must not think about the answer.

So many times I went with my abuelo to the Sunday market in Tlacolula. Always around noon Abuelo visited his friend at the juice stand there, in the arcade down the street from where they sell the wooden yokes for the oxen, next to the lady who sells the cheese and across from the escritora who writes letters for any campesino who needs one. Someone told me she charges extra for love letters and someone else told me they were free, but I never asked her because I can write my own. Every time I saw her she was sitting there in the same lady business suit that she bought up in Puebla a long time ago, with the same dusty typewriter she must have bought then also. Sometimes Abuelo tried to flirt with her, but she was, like they say, all business.

At the juice stand Abuelo would order a polla in a tall glass. Abuelo's friend, whose name is Pancho, would fill it to the top with red wine from a jug, then he'd take two eggs and crack them into the wine where they would float like a pair of chichis. Every time, Pancho would ask if he wants cinnamon on top and every time my abuelo would say, "You know I do, damn it," so Pancho would sprinkle some on there and smile a little smile. Once, when I was about fourteen, Abuelo nodded at the two eggs staring up at him and made a hard-on with his forearm. "*De chuppá chuppá*" he said. "For strength." Sometimes, if he was in a good mood, after selling all his corn or getting a deal on some turkey chicks, Abuelo would take up his glass and try to catch the eye of the escritora. If she looked his way, he would wink at her and suck down one of the eggs. She would stare at something far away then and press her skirt down close around her thighs.

Always since I met Sofía I believed that it — la conchita — was a necessity, like air and water. But now I know the truth, that it is only another luxury like happiness and love, and this makes me sad because what is a man, you know, without it — without this wanting? It is like being dead already. Now all I want is the water.

Juquilita, virgencita llena de gracia, lo siento, mi madre morena y generosa. I am afraid you are too small for this trouble we are in, too far away.

Pobre César. His water — the promise of it, it is hard to think of anything else.

How can he be so cool when it is so hot in here?

Fri Apr 6 — 11:57

AnniMac, you are a gringa, no? With a name like that? What is your sign? I am Sagitario and I came exactly on the eighteenth of December, la Fiesta de Nuestra Señora de la Soledad, Our Lady of Solitude. This is why my name is so enormous — Héctor María de la Soledad Lázaro González. Soledad came here a long time ago by accident and stayed, and now she is the official virgin of Oaxaca. Down there, she is even more important than la Virgen de Guadalupe. My mother will only approach her on her knees. I did not come easy to my mother and because of this, and because my birthday is her feast day, Mamá always took me with her to la Basílica de la Soledad en el centro. I never liked going in there, but whenever we got close and I tried to run away Mamá would hiss through her teeth, "¡Diablito! You are her special servant. You owe your life to her — and mine too." Then, if I did not stop pulling away and complaining, she would slap my face and squeeze my hand until I heard the bones inside my skin. But I would not cry.

I am sorry about that now. I never had her same devotion for Soledad because I was never sure whose special servant I really was, the Virgin's or my mother's. I am the oldest in the family, but there were two others before me, both dead before I was born. Maybe in her mind I am not one son but three.

La Basílica de la Soledad is the only church I know where they keep the holy water in a tank—AGUA PARA USO SANTA. But that doesn't mean you can drink it. The doors are big enough for a truck and always when we were inside Mamá would kneel down and walk like this all the way to the altar. La via dolorosa — the way of suffering — is long and my mother took her time. It was on this slow trip down the aisle, stopping to pray at each station of the cross, that I noticed the pulpit sagging lower and lower. The padre there is not such a fat man so maybe it's from the words he says. I must confess I liked it when Mamá was on her knees because this made us the same height and I could pretend I was her husband, which is better than being a servant. I walked beside her straight as a soldier and when she crossed herself I made a salute to Soledad until one time a nun saw me do this and gave me such a stabbing with her finger and another with her eye that I never did that again. But Mamá never looked at me — only straight ahead — her eyes on the Virgin like she was hypnotized. I tried to look at the Virgin as my mother did, but all I could see is what you see when you look at a ghost or a clown — a white white face and white white hands. There is nothing else to her, you know, this particular virgin is only hands and a face. The rest of her was not revealed in the vision so they filled the space with a great pyramid of black velvet and gold, life-size. To some it looks like a Spanish gown, to others a Zapotec temple with a head and hands. In the pueblo Mamá had a shrine for her with candles and a gown she made herself. When we moved to el centro, she bought Soledad a new gown from the saints' store on Independencia.

This is also when she started collecting los niños — Baby Jesus in the manger, Baby Jesus in his glorious robes, Baby Jesus in a doctor coat with the stethoscope and many other scenes and costumes. There is even a Baby Jesus magazine and special stores for all His accessories near la Basílica de la Soledad. Mamá knows them all. She spends a lot of time with her niños, especially when she has a black eye. I was the same with my action figures and Transformers. Once, I was arguing about this with her, saying unkind things like, "Why do you have all those niños when they just sit there? Look at my Transformers. Look at all the things they can do."

When she was tired of listening to me, she said, "Hectorcito? How long have there been these Transformers?"

And I said, "Always, Mamá. Since I was young."

And she said, "Yes, well, that is not so long. Our beloved Jesus has been a Transformer for two thousand years."

I wonder if she saw the black Mustang GT that is driving around Oaxaca now with Barricade's Transformer promise painted on it — *to punish and enslave . . .* Two weeks ago, I saw it in Colonia Reforma near the hospital. If my abuelo was with me that day, he would have jabbed me with his elbow and said, "Look, the bishop is visiting."

Even last year, with the eye of death upon him, Abuelo said the church was only a tienda selling Spanish goods. Es una blasfemia, but he had his reasons. Many times he told me how long ago the padres came to our pueblo and made the people tear down our temple and use the stones to build their church. The people did this because they would be beaten or killed if they refused. During this time, he said, there was an indio spying for the padres. When the people found out, they killed that traitor right there — Abuelo's ancestors did this, and for this the padres burned them alive on the plaza of our pueblo. But do you know what made Abuelo spit when he talked about it? That spy is a martyr now, a saint — with his own chapel. Verdad, you can see his bones in the cathedral in el centro with paintings of burning indios, and this is why Abuelo would never go in there. "What is the difference," he said to me, "between that chilito in the cathedral and the ones who killed your cousin in the strike? If you ask me, it is only the weapon that is different. Inside, they are all putos."

The Spanish gods never spoke to my abuelo. Maybe because he would never speak to them. There are other gods, he said — his gods — living right inside our church. Back when his ancestors were first building it with the temple stones, they made a secret place inside the altar for them — the Serpent and the Jaguar, Cocijo the god of lightning and rain, Pitao Cozobi the god of the corn, Xipe Totec the Flayed One who the Aztecs stole from us and dressed in a human skin. For more than two hundred years they stayed in there until the same earthquake that destroyed el centro knocked down our church and broke the altar. When this happened, Abuelo saw them with his own eyes, and when his uncles helped to build the church again, all those gods went back inside the altar.

Always it seems someone is coming down here with a new god to sell.

I was on the Zócalo one time when two tall hallelujahs came over to me in their costume of white shirts, black pants, black neckties and plastic nametags. These ones were Testigos de Jehová — what Papá calls Testículos de Jehová. He says you can always tell them by their size and whiteness. Well, these two were trying to talk to me in Spanish and one of them says, "Good day, friend, do you know Jesus?"

It is a common name here and I say to them en español, "Por supuesto, I know many. For which one are you looking?"

This confuses them and the other one says, "What is your name?"

They are so serious I cannot help myself so I say, "Jesús."

"¿Hey Zeus?" says the first one. "Moocho goosto. ¿Too air ace Catholeeko?"

"No," I say. "Zapoteco."

They look at each other and the second one says in English, "That's a software company, isn't it?"

I am trying to hold my face still when Number One says to me, "¿Too tennis computa?" which is funny in Spanish, and I say, "No con puta, solamente con Jesús."

They squint their eyes and nod. "Muy bono," they say together, and Number Two reaches into his bag and gives me that little newspaper.

"Muchas gracias, Señores Enganchadores," I say. "Es por un pescado, no?"

They are not sure what I am saying so I try to help them: "¿U-sted-es es-tán pes-ca-dor-es, no?" Their heads are turning like curious dogs and I can see them thinking and thinking. "Como San Pedro," I say. "The fishing man."

"¡Sí, sí, amigo!" they say. "Saint Peter! Yes, we are fishing for men!" They smile hard with their big American teeth and they shake my hand. "¡Vaya con Dios!" they say together and walk away.

So who is the better bargainer — me who got a good laugh and a free newspaper for wrapping fish, or them who think they got a free soul?

Fri Apr 6 — 12:46

I am wearing only my chones and sitting on my shoes with my feet on my backpack and my arms around my knees. The wall is too hot to lean against and this is the time of day when I have to lie down next to César. I rolled him onto his side so I will have a bit more room, then I put my shoes back on and made a bed of my clothes and backpack. My water bottle has only the piss in it now. I put a sock over it and use it for a pillow. I am lying across the tank, between César and the back wall. In one hand is his phone and in the other is my abuelo's jaguar head. César's water is in the backpack and I can feel it by my hip. This is all that matters now, and I must keep them safe. César's battery is going down faster than I thought — one half already. It is the heat, I think, so I will turn it off now.

Fri Apr 6 — 16:51

Hello. It is the afternoon. I tried to sleep.

There is still only one bar. If it was a problem with the tower there was time to fix it by now. Where the fuck are the other bars?

Fri Apr 6 — 17:11

My god, I'm cold. I don't know why. The tank is still warm, but my clothes aren't enough so I must stay close to César, as close as I can. My body isn't making sense anymore.

I have been sucking my ten-peso coin to keep the saliva coming. I did not know money was so bitter. As long as he keeps me warm, I say, I will not drink his water.

Fri Apr 6 — 17:23

Can you hear that? I am recording it. The small plane comes again, closer this time, but it does not turn. I am sure it is la Migra patrolling the border. Somehow, we are invisible.

14

Fri Apr 6 — 17:44

The sun is gone now. I can feel it in the wall. Many times I checked for the signal, for a message from you, but there is nothing. How can no one see us? Where did the coyotes leave us? I did not say this to anyone, but I wonder if we are in some parking lot with many other trucks so no one notices. Migrantes have died this way before. But this cannot be — the road was so rough. I don't think we are on any road.

Maybe this is how it is en el infierno — burning and freezing en la soledad con los extraños. And all you want you cannot have.

Fri Apr 6 — 17:52

I think the old man is dead. Someone said this. I never knew his name. I don't know what happened — if he gave up or suffocated or his kidneys failed him. Maybe others have died also — the baby-face man's friend, but I don't want to know. Only the water matters now. No one talks about the mechanic or la Migra anymore. There is only the breathing.

Once, when I was young, I saw a traveling circus setting up by the highway. There were camels in a corral and an elephant with no tusks and its ears had long cuts in them like banana leaves. In a cage was a bear lying so still he looked like he was dead. Maybe he was. It was hot that day — too hot for a bear. But it is the tigers that will not leave my mind now. They were all together in one cage and so many it was hard to tell them apart — just fur and stripes blending one into the other, piled like pigs in their own excrement, and so close I could touch them if I dared. The smell was — how can I tell you — ¡Guácala! — so loud and sour it made my eyes water, and in the sand under the cage were puddles of urine baking in the sun. The tigers made no sound but their breathing and it gave me a strange feeling — this knowing that the air going out of their lungs and into my lungs was the same air — like we were sending invisible messages to each other with no sound from anyone in all that heat but the breathing.

There was one especially big tiger. So big it was hard to believe — his feet were the size of my head. He was walking this way and that, panting and pacing, and I don't know how he kept from walking on the others. From end to end he went like this, stepping in the same places each time — with the same foot — a slow and terrible dance he did over and over, backward and forward through the others like a fish in a tank without stopping or seeing — like he was blind to them. Like they were not even there. I have seen crazy people do this in el centro, but I did not know that tigers can go crazy too. After this, I had no heart for the circus anymore.

Fri Apr 6 — 18:13

I wanted it so bad — more than anything because you don't know how the thirst invades your mind. I am holding it now — his water — and Dios ayúdame, the only thing I want more is the door out of here. The weight of it in my hand as heavy as a heart, and in my throat just one capful — éxtasis, you cannot imagine. I couldn't wait and I took more, filling my mouth with it. I knew I was stealing something from him — his chance to live — and I told myself that if I drank some I could help him, but it is a lie — even as I gave him some I felt this. Always the padre told us that the wine is the blood of Christ and it's Him you're drinking from the cup, His life on your lips. But the padre was wrong — blood is not life, water is.

And mine and César's are together in this bottle.

Fri Apr 6 — 18:27

All day I heard it and now I know what it means — that plant growing on the walls begins to taste like a good idea, like something delicious. It is on our clothes also, but no one cares about that now, only the thirst. No one imagined they would be sucking on their own pants or licking these walls for the water, feeling the rust crumble on their tongues — that sweet electric taste. These are things no sane person wants to imagine. At first I thought they were trying to get out. I could hear them scraping the walls with their fingernails and prayer cards, with the straps from their backpacks, but the water is bad and so is the plant and it makes them lose the liquid even faster. Everything is louder in here. More and more the tank is feeling and smelling like the intestine of some animal, slowly digesting us. When the old man died, it was a bad omen, una maldición.

People will believe anything, you know. The trouble is that in here all of it is true.

Fri Apr 6 — 18:38

I am sitting here like a farmer waiting for rain.

My ass is numb. My back also. There are only so many ways to move. My toes are buzzing and my fingers. It is harder to work the phone, not only because of the cold. But I found something in there, a file called SED-THIRST, with documents about the desert and first aid for dehydration. César was thinking ahead. It says you need salt and water and shade. All these things are in here and none of them are good. In there also is a document called Thirst Disease from an American magazine — a story about a Mexicano called Pablo Valencia. But I think it is about us too. This Pablo was a gold miner on the border with Sonora and Arizona and his compadre, Jesús, did to him the same as the coyotes did to us — abandoned him — no horse, no water, somewhere close to here. It is August so Pablo is in trouble and he goes searching for help — for water. For seven days he does this, walking and then crawling more than one hundred miles. Es un milagro macho. To stay alive, he drank his urine and ate cactus, spiders, scorpions — anything he can find with liquid in it. But he was dying anyway — day by day and drop by drop, just like us, and every time he stops to rest the vultures and coyotes come closer. In the end, he was found by some kind of scientist doing experiments out there — the one who wrote this. His words are too much for me, but I can copy this part and send it with the text. Maybe you can understand better what is happening to us in here. Because this is a true story also —

Pablo was stark naked; his legs and arms were shrunken and scrawny; his ribs ridged out like those of a starveling horse; his abdomen was drawn in almost against his vertebral column; his lips had disappeared as if amputated, leaving low edges of blackened tissue; his teeth and gums projected like those of a skinned animal, but the flesh was black and dry as a hank of jerky; his nose was withered and shrunken to half its length; the nostril-lining showing black; his eyes were set in a winkless stare, with surrounding skin so contracted as to expose the conjunctiva, itself black as the gums; his face was dark as a negro, and his skin generally turned a ghastly purplish yet ashen gray, with great livid blotches and streaks; his lower legs and feet, with forearms and hands, were torn and scratched by contact with thorns and sharp rocks, yet even the freshest cuts were as so many scratches in dry leather, without trace of blood or serum; his joints and bones stood out like those of a wasted sickling, though the skin clung to them in a way suggesting shrunken rawhide used in repairing a broken wheel. From inspection and handling I estimated his weight at 115 to 120 pounds. We soon found him deaf to all but loud sounds, and so blind as to distinguish nothing save light and dark. The mucous membrane lining mouth and throat was shriveled, cracked, and blackened, and his tongue shrunken to a mere bunch of black integument. His respiration was slow, spasmodic, and accompanied by a deep guttural moaning or roaring — the sound that had awakened us a quarter of a mile away. His extremities were cold as the surrounding air; no pulsation could be detected at wrists, and there was apparently little if any circulation beyond the knees and elbows; the heartbeat was slow, irregular, fluttering, and almost ceasing in the longer intervals between the stertorous breathings.

At the end, this man Pablo was living and dying all in the same moment, and still he kept going —

As the sun rose he sought the shade of a shrub and there knelt in final prayer for the dying; then he laid himself down with feet and face to the eastward, made the sign of the cross with a pang over the absence of consecrated water, and composed himself for the end. There — and this was his clearest concept, unreal though it be — with the rising of the sun he died, and his body lay lifeless under the burning rays, though his innermost self hovered about, loth to leave the material husk about which the buzzards waited patiently. The sun swung across the shimmering vault, and darkness fell; in the chill of evening some vague shadow external to his Ego stirred and then struggled aimlessly against chapparal and cactus along the most trying stretch of El Camino del Diablo. Sometimes he felt half alive and wrung by agony of severing spirit and flesh; oftener he felt that the naked body was pushed and dragged and belabored and tortured by something outside; he knew its voice, tried to cry out in protest or call for rescue, but did not feel the voice his own. So the night dragged on and on, until at early dawn the vague consciousness knew itself near the camp with the certainty of relief, and was dimly surprised at the bellowing break in a final call.

They found him this way, on the seventh day, by the roaring sound of his breath — this man Pablo whose body was dying all around him, who kept going without knowing if he was alive or dead or dreaming in between. But in here, we have no trail to follow and no one is finding us. So how do we keep going? In the morning my mother makes the fire from nothing, only by blowing on the gray ash. You can't see it from the outside, but the fire is in there waiting for someone to notice, waiting for some reason to burn again. Waiting — en español "to wait" is the same as "to hope" — esperar. Besides chingar, esperar is the other official verb of Mexico, and it is what I do for you all this time — all these hours and days and words. Te espero, AnniMac.

Fri Apr 6 — 19:07

But what if there is no hope? And what if your patience runs out the same as water? You know what kept this Pablo Valencia alive all that time, besides the dream of drinking? The dream of putting a knife in Jesús who abandoned him. And what if he is right — that hate is stronger than hope?

Maybe you did something once and when you looked at it after, you could not believe you were so stupid. Or that someone could do such a thing to you. I cannot believe Lupo can just throw us to the coyotes. I cannot believe I owe money to be in here and that my father may have to pay Don Serafín, the same man who sent his son to die. I cannot believe Don Serafín is partly Zapotec and has lived in Oaxaca his whole life and that my father looks up to him like he is on God's right hand. For this I condemn Don Serafín — for taking all our money and sending us, his own people, into such a disaster. I condemn Lupo and I condemn those coyotes whose names I don't even know. What if hate is stronger than death and I live to find them all, one by one like that killer in *The Godfather,* my father's favorite movie.

But even if I find them, even if I could kill them, it will not begin to pay for what they did to us in here — so many chingaderas in one small place. Now those maletóns made me their compadre, their accomplice — just by living so long in this situation you will not wish on your own enemy. For this I condemn them all. I condemn myself and I condemn César. This was César's idea to go in the truck — to stand up at the wrong time, to give me his phone and all that it holds.

15

Fri Apr 6 — 19:29

In Altar there was a lot of waiting — for me and César almost two days. Most of the time, César stayed in Lupo's choza and spoke to no one, only writing things into his phone. In the evening we sat outside Lupo's garage drinking beers and talking until it got too cold. At first we talked about nothing — cantinas we knew, old ones like El Farolito where they used to have the best pechuga before they renovated it for the tourists, and La Casa del Mezcal where they serve green oranges on the side with the gusano and pass the bottles through the air, and he told me about a knife fight he saw once. When I asked him about newer places like Nuevo Babel or La Biznaga he said he'd never been there. This was strange to me because that is where an educated person like him would go, especially if he had money. This is when I understood better that the accident with the taxi was simply one more story in César's house of misfortunes. I pressed him then. "You're hiding from someone," I said. "That's why you came back to Oaxaca."

César picked at the label on his beer bottle. "Let's get over the line," he said. "Then maybe I'll tell you."

But already I think I knew the reason — the problem for César was knowing which god to serve. Because in Mexico there are so many, even in a little town like Altar, and each one demands a different kind of sacrifice. Besides the church of Guadalupe, there are other shrines and chapels made by the people for all these pilgrims. I saw one for Jesús Malverde who is a real man — our own San Narco. Dead now, por supuesto. He tells the gospel from the New World and many people pray to him, especially los narcotraficantes. But San Narco is not as popular as la Santísima Muerte. I must tell you, AnniMac, in these days there are many saints who are giving up on God — and even life — and going into business. You know why Guadalupe and Juquila are so important to us indios? Because they are morenas too. Well, Santa Muerte is no color at all. She is only bones so she looks like everybody — everybody who is dead, and I can tell you she is the only virgin you're ever going to see smoking a cigar. She has Death's big scythe in one bone hand and in the other she is holding the world like an Aztec priest holding your heart, but someone painted this one big like an eye looking right back at *you*. There were many offerings at Santa Muerte's shrine — flowers and seeds and fruits and tequila and candy and incense like you see at shrines all around Mexico, but here also was a small knife, some bullets, a Cadillac medallion, a bloody T-shirt, a can of Red Bull — and lots of money. People give money to saints all over Mexico, but in Altar, Santa Muerte is the only one who does not accept pesos. Maybe the coyotes learned it from her.

Santa Muerte is new for these times, AnniMac — new for NAFTA. You can say she is our Santa NAFTA Muerte because many people turned to her in the nineties when the dying started in the pueblos — so many leaving and never coming back, and then the maquiladoras closing down because the jobs went to China, and the fence is being made and the laws are being passed, and the narcos killing more and more and more until it is like a war down here. It was the same for us when Cortés came — the distance between Hope and God and Death growing smaller and smaller until it is impossible to tell one from the others. This happens, I think, when new gods battle the old and too many prayers go without an answer.

I told you of some saints who have given up on God and gone into business, but in Mexico now there are also businessmen who are becoming saints. Right in our own cathedral is a shrine to San Charbel, the patron saint of Mexico's richest man, Carlos Slim. Many Oaxaqueños believe he is getting some special assistance from San Charbel, and if Charbel is making such billions for Carlos Slim maybe he can make a little something for the rest of us too. Charbel's statue is only small and must share a chapel with Guadalupe, but you should see the offerings there now. Some people say it is not San Charbel the people are praying to but the billionaire San Slim, and this is his great cleverness — not only is Slim the faithful servant of San Charbel, he is also the faithful servant of Telmex'telcel, the Aztec god of communication. We all worship him here. I was worshiping him myself until I ran out of minutes. These are the times we live in, where the Spanish god of Jesus and the ancient gods of Mexico and the modern gods of business are harder and harder to tell one from another. But I'm telling you, AnniMac, it has always been this way. And maybe this is the other half of our destiny together — not only to be the United States of América, but to be One Nation Under Gods.

You can add your own.

If we asked César what god he would add, I'm sure he would say Juquila, but he must also say SantaMaize and this is the problem for him. SantaMaize is a big and powerful seed company with shrines all over the world. Their specialty is the corn and they are sending their hallelujahs everywhere these days. But hasn't it always been like this, new gods coming in to challenge the old? Because that's where the real power is — in the old gods — water, lightning, fire and war. SantaMaize understands this very well and it is why they are so interested in the corn. It is not only the Spanish god performing miracles now, SantaMaize is doing it too. And one of these miracles — el Milagro de SantaMaize — is even in the Oaxaca Codex, a story for these times. Ever since the strike, pieces of it have been appearing around el centro on the walls and buildings. Our Governor Odiseo calls it graffiti, but it's not. It's the story of our people and of the gods they serve and the battles they must fight again and again for all time. Odiseo and his men try to clean it off and paint it over, but the story keeps bleeding through.

The first time I saw el Milagro de SantaMaize in the Oaxaca Codex was last fall on Calle Cinco de Mayo near the intersection with Chapultepec. How could those artists know, but they told the story of César's situation and just like all of us here, his story begins with the corn — one beautiful stalk painted on the wall with the ears fat and ready for picking. It is not only Chia Pets and bobblehead saints and megachurches and migrantes that come from Oaxaca. All that corn you have up there for your sugar and whiskey and cereal and gasoline? That came from us too, and César told me this himself — corn is the most valuable crop in the world, but not everyone values it the same way.

It is this knowledge and the proof of it that César carries with him. For César and for all of us this journey is more than going to another country. Many of us fail and some of us die. Even if you make it you may never see your home again, and that is another kind of dying. Not all of us understood this, but I think César did. On that last night before we got in the truck he bought two singles of tequila and six Tecates and he told me about el Milagro de Santa-Maize. It was the last time we talked and I wonder now if he saw this coming, that those things he said were for him some kind of confession.

Lupo's garage was set back from the highway in a sandlot with cement walls and broken glass on the top. On the side facing the road was a solid metal gate wrapped with concertina wire. Lupo told us we would be leaving around midnight so me and César waited outside by ourselves against the wall of the garage, sharing a piece of cardboard for a seat. César had his jacket zipped to his chin and I had my sweatshirt, but even with the hood it was not enough so I sat as close as I could to César without him knowing I was doing it for the heat. The moon was growing smaller and now it was just a crooked smile in the dark, hanging over the lights in the parking lot. On the edge of town where the desert began, tall cypress trees stood out against the sky and beyond them rose the mountains of America, la via dolorosa where migrantes found and lost their way. I had been looking at them for two days. In the afternoon those sharp ridges turned from brown to red and a blue haze gathered at their feet, but now all that color was gone and in its place stood a black sawblade with stars twinkling between the teeth.

As we sat there drinking and talking, we watched people like us coming and going in trucks and vans, many more than in the day because on the border, night is the time for travel. Here and there against the walls, groups of fifteen or twenty migrantes stood waiting, shuffling their feet, a couple of them smoking or looking at their phones. There were even some children, standing with their colored backpacks like they were waiting for the bus to go to school. Every few minutes a truck or van would pull in for gas and sometimes Lupo would come out and talk to the driver. You could tell by how the vehicles rolled from side to side in the potholes that most of them were filled with people or other heavy things. Sometimes an empty truck would pull in and one of the groups would get in and drive away, heading for the Sásabe crossing and the long walk into America. All around us was dusty and busy and everyone was for sale to somebody. Except for a sex club, never before was I in a place that felt so empty and so full of wanting at the same time.

César opened his single of tequila so I opened mine, and after raising our bottles to el Norte we drank them down. "What's the first thing you're going to do when we get across?" I asked.

"Fuck my brains out," said César. "Which reminds me — I've got more time on this." César reached into his back pocket and pulled out a phonecard. "You can have it."

I took the card from him and I wondered who he had called. "It worked OK?" I asked.

"Worked for me." He was smiling.

"You look happy," I said.

"I haven't seen my girlfriend in a long time and she's coming to meet me."

"Where?"

"What, you want to watch?" He laughed and slapped my knee. "Get your own."

I was missing Sofía very much, but things had been difficult for us since I left the university. She was still there studying for her degree and she already had a job in a hotel. The last time I called her she said, Maybe next week, but I knew what she was really saying.

"OK, OK," I said to César. "But where are you going after we get across?"

"It's better if you don't know." César let out a long breath and leaned his head back against the wall. "Just a few more hours."

I must say to you, AniMac, that I wonder if César's girlfriend is you. I searched in his phone, but there is no Anna or Anni or AniMac anywhere but the directory.

In all the time we were in Altar, César went outside in the daylight only once—that last morning to the church of Guadalupe, which was three blocks away. "With all the Oaxaqueños coming through here you'd think there would be a shrine for Juquila," he said. "This is where we need her most."

"You really believe in her?" I asked. "Or are you just lighting candles for your mother?"

"My father taught me that in every kernel of corn is the Creation. For me," said César, "Juquila is the face of that mystery. When I look at a kernel of corn, that's who I see."

"They always looked like teeth to me," I said.

"Maybe you didn't look close enough."

César finished his beer and opened another with his belt buckle. I was on my second and trying not to shiver. César took a sip and looked off to where the stars faded into the glow of Nogales and Tucson. "You know in the Sierra on a clear night when the stars seem so close? Did you ever imagine you could reach up there with your finger and move them around?" César snapped his bottle cap across the parking lot. "That's what they taught me to do at UNAM."

"With the corn?"

"They aren't just studying it up there," he said. "They're taking it apart, one gene from another, and putting it back together in a different way and saying it belongs to them, like they invented it. What would God say to that, I wonder. It is the reason I still pray to Juquila. I am the first Zapoteco to see these things, to understand what our ancestors understood without seeing. But we're like children playing with the master's tools."

"How do you do it?" I asked. "Move the genes around."

"For corn you use a gene gun."

"No mames," I said. I thought he was playing with me.

"¡Animal! Es verdad. This gene gun is a real thing, and it fires golden bullets —"

"No estés chingando." I turned away then because I was cold and had no patience for jokes.

But César said, "No, Tito, I'm not shitting you. This gun is powered by CO_2 and the bullets are tiny grains of gold. Each one is coated with DNA, with the transgene, and you fire it into the cell of the plant you wish to change. This is how it's done. In the lab we call it transformation, but into what? That's the question, right? Because you don't aim a gene gun, you point it in the general direction and shoot. The bullets come out like a shotgun blast and the genes go everywhere. They're like spies, you know? Or assassins — working from the inside. And once they're in there, they can do things you didn't plan on. They can mutate, they can sterilize themselves, they can make food with less nutrition or none at all, and the bugs they're supposed to kill can become resistant. And what happens when these transgénicos pollinate the native corn? Nobody knows yet.

"But what I know for sure is that the ritual of corn — the cycle of planting, harvesting, saving and planting again — this is the rosary of our existence, unbroken, every kernel a bead touched by someone's hand, and we are telling those beads, and they are telling us, who we are, over and over, season after season, year after year — not in a circle, Tito, but in a spiral, a double helix. Can you see this? One side is us and the other is the corn. In that DNA is the oldest manmade codex. I have read it myself and in every kernel is a message

from the past to the future — the story of *us,* and that's what I'm trying to understand." He looked at me to make sure I was listening. "It
is the story of how *teocintle,* the grandmother plant of all the corn,
was transformed by our ancestors, generation by generation, from a
wild grass into our closest companion, more loyal than any friend,
sweeter than any milk."

"My father doesn't give a shit about the corn," I said. "But you
would have liked my abuelo. When he saw a few kernels spilled
in the road, he'd pick them up and say, 'Would you step on your
mother too?'"

But César wasn't having a conversation. "For eight thousand years
this has been happening," he said, "since long before the Zapotecs
or even the Olmecs. Corn is where civilization comes from — from
here — not only from Babylon and China. Güey, the corn made
possible everything we do and are — pyramids, writing, astronomy,
art. It happened here first, and we're part of it — all that time we
spent as kids stripping the corn and sorting it and putting it in the
sack — some to eat, maybe some to sell, always saving some to plant
next year. Sometimes I'd get bored doing this and I'd sort the kernels by size or color or shape, like candy or precious stones, because
there are differences, you know, if you look close enough and long
enough. When I was about ten, I counted how many kernels were
on a single ear and the first one I counted had six hundred and
sixteen so that was my lucky number. After a while I noticed that
the rows were paired, always even numbers. I could see there was
an order to it, but I didn't know what it meant." César was smiling
as he talked, but he wasn't looking at me. It was more like he was
remembering for himself.

"One day, my father got some other corn from our cousins across
the valley, from Santa Magdalena. It was mixed up in a bag with
ours, but as soon as I held it I knew something was different. I was

twelve then and I said this to my father — that there was something funny about this corn. He asked me how I knew and I showed him the kernels, the shape of the ear. He went and told the padre and the padre said, 'Maybe he will be a scientist.' It is thanks to my father and that priest that I went to Guelatao for schooling, and I do this work for them — for my family because for us corn is family."

He took another sip of his beer and I could hear him swirling it around in his mouth before he swallowed it. "You know the young corn," he said, "when it's still sweet? I like to take a kernel of that and roll it around on my tongue until the shell dissolves and you get to the sugar inside. When I was younger I might be thinking about a girl and she would mix together somehow with that sweet taste in my mouth and I'm telling you . . ." He was laughing and I wondered if he was a little bit drunk. I never heard someone talk about the corn like this before so I just listened, and you know if you talk to César, mostly you're going to be listening because you never met someone so full of words as him. "Back in school when you borrowed my copy of *The Savage Detectives* — you read it for the blowjobs and those crazy sisters, right?"

I almost choked on my beer. "What?"

"I'm telling you, man, when you look close enough into the milpa, there's so much fucking and sucking going on it makes those chicas look like nuns. Corn especially — she doesn't care where the pollen comes from, just as long as she gets some, and that's why she's all those colors — because our corn has many fathers. When you hold it in your hand you're holding her eggs, and those strands of silk — there is one for every kernel — that's how the pollen travels down to fertilize them, but not all the pollen is the same. Maybe in your pueblo you have two or three varieties of corn, but in all of Mexico there are sixty, maybe more — for making tortillas or atole, for growing in the mountains or the valleys, in a lot of rain or a little — every color and climate, and it is us who made it that way, who modified it. But the corn modified us too. Corn is the mother of us all, hermano, it's what we're made of.

"But when I first got up to UNAM, all that mattered to me was the scholarship, the status and the chicas." He tapped his bottle against mine. "Imagine if it was you, some campesino from Oaxaca, an *indio* from the Sierra fucking *Juárez,* and suddenly you're in D.F. and they're paying for everything, even your computer. Y el coño — fue un milagro," he said, crossing himself. "So it took me a while to understand — you may be going to UNAM, but if you're working in that lab, you're working for SantaMaize. They opened it the year I got there and it's where I did all my graduate work. You should see it, the building was designed by this crazy Danish guy and it's state of the art, a cathedral for worshiping corn, all glass with one wall five stories high, shaped like a pyramid and covered in a mural that looks like it was painted by Rivera himself. One half is scenes from Aztec life — temples, markets, floating gardens, and in front is a milpa with men and women planting and harvesting corn, sorting the seeds and grinding cornmeal, dancing in feathers at a fiesta. On the other half is an enormous field of corn, stretching to the horizon with a combine harvester moving across it like a ship in the ocean and no people anywhere. Where did they go? I don't know, but some of them are in the lab and you can see them in the mural at the bottom, men and women with pipettes and microscopes and video monitors showing the corn and all its parts — pericarp, endosperm, plumule, all the way into the cell, the nucleus, and finally the DNA itself, all so beautiful and possible, in such vivid colors. And rising up over everything like the sun, joining these two worlds together, is the SantaMaize logo — a single ear of glowing golden corn with the husk parted like the Virgin's robes and bright green rays coming out just like the ones around Our Lady of Guadalupe. Every day going to work, this is what I saw."

César leaned his head back against the wall. "And now I'm in that mural too." It was the first time I ever heard something like despair in César's voice. "You know how sometimes you'll get an ear of corn that's all yellow with only one or two dark kernels? That's me in the lab," he said. "I'm the dark one with the mask on his face — the indio they taught to take the corn, this generous being that is ancient, that is ours, and break her down like a fucking car engine."

"César," I said, "I have seen these people myself." And I told him about the page from the Oaxaca Codex I saw down on Calle Cinco de Mayo, which is not only a picture of some corn — there are also men wearing suits and masks. One of them has a big needle and he is shooting something into the corn or sucking something out, maybe its *pitao* — its life force. The codex doesn't say.

"I know that one," said César. "Near the first-class bus station? That's who I work with, that's what I do. One of my first professors said that transgenic crops would be to food what the Internet was to communication. 'You don't know how lucky you are,' he told us, 'to be coming in now. Mexico is going to be a huge market and Syngenta, Monsanto, Pulsar, SantaMaize, all of them will want you.' I still remember the way he rubbed his thumb and fingers together.

"A few of us students were worried about these transgénicos coming into Mexico, not as food but as seed, because that corn is all the same — the diversity is gone so one disease can kill it. It's happened before and we didn't want some corn invented in a lab last year to be mixing with native maize that has taken thousands of years to develop. But NAFTA and the Mexican government allowed SantaMaize into Mexico — only in the north, they said, on an experimental basis, but that's like saying migrantes will only work in Texas. Corn is a migrante too. So we put together a petition calling for a moratorium on GMO corn. The problem for us is that NAFTA isn't interested in some indio with a little milpa of one hectare growing native corn and taking a bag to market a couple times a year. NAFTA wants big farms and all the same corn — lots and lots, all the time, and this is who our government is subsidizing now, not the campesino. They're telling us to leave the pueblos and work in the maquiladoras. Well, would you send *your* kids to Tijuana or Ciudad Juárez? But Mexicanos want their tortillas, right? They want them right now, and who do you think wants to sell the seed to grow the corn to make all those tortillas? This is the magical realism of NAFTA, Tito — Mexico, the birthplace of corn, is now importing surplus corn from el Norte — millions of tons driving the price down so campesinos can't afford to grow it. Exporting people and importing corn. It is backwards, no?"

I will admit I didn't know this, but I know my father and uncles. "If you don't leave the campo," I said, "how else are you going to get money to buy a truck or build a house?"

César spat. "You can't eat a truck, cabrón. This is our *land* we're talking about — nuestra soberanía. One of my professors was an old-school liberation theologist from Puebla, and he helped me get a little grant to go to Oaxaca and see if transgénicos were growing there. I suspected this because my father told me about some corn he saw at the market in el centro, corn like he'd never seen before — almost white, and cheap. Because this is the strategy, Tito, same as the narco — first they make it easy, but once you're using, they raise the price and make you buy more every year."

"How can they make you?"

"They come to your pueblo with a contract. But they're trying to get approval for suicide seeds and that will save them the trip."

I thought I heard him wrong and I looked at him.

"Corn with a terminator gene," he said, "what they call a V-GURT, so it sterilizes itself. That way, even if you save the seed, it's no good for planting. You must buy it new every time. Well, saving seed is what we *do,* no? It's how we *got* here. When I saw what these terminator genes could do I began to understand the implications for us, and that's when I wondered if I made a mistake. SantaMaize is working on one right now. It's not public yet, but they're calling it Kortez400 — with a K. There are different ways to do it, but the Kortez uses this protein called an RIP. You insert the RIP into the gene sequence, and if it's ever planted again the seed kills itself in embryo.

"When I went into that program, Tito, I really thought I was going to make things better, and not just for me. Corn is supposed to feed people, right? How can that be a bad thing? But at SantaMaize, corn isn't food. It's control. It's life with an off switch. And corn is tricky because the pollen travels through the air. With the right wind conditions it can jump over a mountain and once their seed is in your milpa, once their corn is mixing with yours, how are you going to separate it?"

Before I could ask if this was why he was hiding, he said, "Imagine some pendejo finds your sister alone in the milpa and rapes her and she has a kid —"

Maybe it's the beer, but before I know it I am thinking of my sister Vera and I start to choke up, which is strange because I hardly see her now, but something César said reminded me of when I was fourteen, just before I left for secondary school, and my father slapped her for something — right to the floor. I was so angry and frightened, but I could only watch because I didn't want him to do it to me. Now I am sitting here trying to keep my shoulders still, trying to hide this from César, but it is hitting me hard that I am really leaving and I wonder if I will ever see Vera again, or my parents, and all I want in that moment is to go back, to go home. I start to stand up then because I have to walk, but César pulls me down and looks into my eyes, and I realize now that he thinks the tears he sees in there are for the corn and he keeps talking.

"— so now that kid is part rapist, but he's still your sister's baby, right? He's your blood too. So what are you going to do? You can't cut the kid in half and throw away the part you don't like. It's all of it or none of it and that's a problem when it's your family. But if SantaMaize can prove with science — by looking at gene markers and sequencing — that you're using their product, that your corn is part their corn, well, what are you going to do about that? Call your lawyer? SantaMaize got a thousand lawyers. They eat you like pollo."

This is what César is saying while I'm wiping my eyes and trying not to choke on my beer because I want to be hard, but it's hard to be hard, especially when someone's telling you the world that made you is being killed in front of your eyes and what can you do but wait for some men you don't know and don't trust to take your life in their hands and drive you someplace you never been before where all you have is your uncle's phone number and with this you're supposed to make some new kind of life because the old one is broken and you don't know how to fix it except to do what everyone else is doing and go somewhere far away with bad food, cold weather and people who hate you.

You know what I'm saying?

What would you do?

16

Fri Apr 6 — 20:48

So cold. No one speaks now because they can't — only the terrible sound of breathing. I should share his water, but with who? It will be gone in a minute. In the pueblo, in the hard times, people join together, but in here there is no history and no connection, only the thirst which has no conscience. So I guard his water like César guarded his phone because the only way to live is to be still and quiet — to wait longer. To wait until you come.

If the Spanish Church taught us one thing, it is patience.

Fri Apr 6 — 20:57

In the afternoon so many memories came to me disguised as dreams and this one felt so real — in the café on the Zócalo with Sofía from my Customer Service class. I was there, but I was not myself, I was el Valiente. Maybe you know him from la lotería — those bingo cards were famous with the tourists. Of them all, el Valiente es mi favorito — un hombre serioso como Benicio del Toro only taller with a bloody machete in one hand and a sarape wrapped around the other. On the card they show him with a sombrero at his feet. Maybe it just rolled off a dead man's head, or maybe his enemy threw it down in surrender — you cannot be sure.

We were sitting under the arcade, Sofía and me, alone for the first time, and I was trying to order two cold beers, but I couldn't get the waiter's attention. How I missed seeing Odiseo I don't know. Of course the café was crowded and my eyes were on Sofía, but even in a dream our governor is hard to miss — that sagging-mustache face and bad skin. I should have known there was a problem because we were dying of thirst and no one was coming. All the waiters were serving Odiseo and his posse, and I couldn't believe it was really him, the Matador of Oaxaca.

Around his table is a barricade of men in suits and leather jackets and from the outside they look like vultures on a kill, heads down, dark shoulders pushing for position. On the table is a plan of the city, because right now Odiseo is tearing it out from under our feet and the traffic is hopeless. His brother is in the cement business and of course all those gutted streets must be filled with something. Mexico is a democracy and Odiseo has only a short time left in office so he must get busy — many pockets to fill, people to kill and BMWs to buy. Because of him there are crosses now around el centro.

In the dream it is December so all the flower beds are planted with nochebuena por la Navidad, but with Odiseo so near those bright red leaves only make the Zócalo look like it's bleeding again. Thirty meters from our table is the municipal palace that Odisco was forced to abandon because the people hate him so much, and out by the fountains under the laurel trees are the common people who cannot afford a beer in a nice café with tourists and matadors. Between us and them Odiseo's indio bodyguards orbit like dark moons, hands in their coats, eyes flashing here and there, searching for anything that can put the planet at risk. They are matadors too, and the city is their killing floor. Men like them have been captured on film in the heart of our city shooting people down like dogs.

One of those people was my cousin Paquito, the son of my Tío Martín. They killed him last October in the strike. He was my age, but we never saw that part of the family much after Papá and me were deported. I went to the funeral, but I never saw Tío Martín. On the same day Paquito was killed, I saw a photo taken by a cameraman at the very moment the cameraman himself was shot. That day, the flame tree blossoms were falling in the street so heavy you could hear them hitting the pavement and from a distance they looked like seashells on fire. I was with some other students at the barricade across the big intersection by the Panteón General, and there had been a warning by phone that the paras were coming — not police but assassins with no uniforms and their own guns. These were campesinos who looked just like us and this made everything harder. I didn't see it myself, but I could hear the shooting and it was chaos — all of us running. I can tell you, the sound of a gun in the street is different from in the forest. There is only one animal who is hunted in the street.

I saw the photo after. It was posted on the Internet. There were three of them — all Zapotecos. The one who shot the cameraman looked a lot like our water guy — the same fat face with small eyes far apart and a big panza, only there's a smoking barrel staring right in your face. The cameraman died for that picture — right there in the daylight, in front of everybody with the flame tree blossoms all around him. But here is the Mexican part — the man accused of killing this cameraman? He is one of the protesters the matadors were sent to kill. I think he's still in jail.

Here, in the café on the Zócalo, the man who ordered those killings is sitting right behind me like nothing happened, our elbows almost touching. I could turn around and offer him advice. I could whisper "Asesino" in his ear. Jesucristo, I could kill him myself. But I'm as chickenshit as the rest of them, sitting there pretending this is only normal — just like at home when the father beats the mother and everyone sits down to la comida like nothing happened, and the son hates himself for only eating, for doing nothing to defend the one who feeds him.

Odiseo doesn't notice. None of those chingados notice, and it's hard to be told like that — right to your face with no words at all — that you have no power, that all you have is the fork in your hand and what are you going to do with that? Poke him to death? Ask him, please pass the salsa? And you know everyone else is feeling the same except for the Spanish café owners, the same ones who were saying last fall when buses were burning and business was bad, "What we need now es una *masacre.*" Those ones are glad to see Odiseo and his compas at the table drinking micheladas because it means there is order again, that the army has gone home and that the people have one more time been broken — and now that this is done maybe the tourists will come back.

In the end, I was not el Valiente. I was el Cobarde, and there is no lotería card for him. No sombreros rolled on the Zócalo, we never got our beer, and Odiseo lived to kill another day.

Can it be possible for a whole city to have la esquizofrenia?

*

Without putting a hand on me, the matadors killed something in me that day—by not seeing me even though I was close enough to grab their balls. They were a wall of backs and attitude, their table a compound. But that's Oaxaca for you—a city of walls. Getting inside can take a lifetime or a ladder. Getting out takes a coyote or a miracle.

Fri Apr 6 — 21:15

The battery is under half and César's water is going too fast. It takes all my strength not to drink it. I think it's the only good water left in here. I tried to give some to César, but I don't want anyone to see when I do this with my finger — make it wet and touch his lips, hold them open so some drops go in. His breath now is only a quick, thin scraping sound and his heart is beating too fast. Without him I can't bear the cold. I can hear someone's teeth rattling.

Death is in here with us now, cold and heavy. The only reason I am still functioning—besides César and his water—is because I am in the back and this is where the pipes are for pumping the water out. They are down near the bottom of the tank and one is closed, the one that damaged César, but the other is open. A child can put his hand through it, but a man cannot. Just outside the tank, this pipe makes a turn so you cannot see out, but some light comes in there. It looks to the west, I think, because the pipe goes orange at the end of the day and then it is not so long until the cold. Here, the air is fresh and even at midday it blows a cool breeze when you compare it to the breathless heat inside the tank. With my face by this small opening as big around as my own mouth, I feel some-times as if I am bathing in the air and I can forget this hot wet stink all around me.

*

Last year, before the strike, I was taking classes at the university and I had some hope for my life in Oaxaca. Even then I had to borrow money and work for my father who was filling the holes made by Odiseo and saying over and over, "Remember Tío Martín and his truck? You can have that too, so what are you doing here pissing your life away?"

Even with that voice in my ear I wanted to stay. Back then, I could silence it if I got far enough away — in class, in the Sierra with Abuelo, at the Milenio Cross up the hill from our house in el centro. You can see this cross from everywhere and some believe it is a good place for a sacrifice because that hill is shaped like a pyramid and the view is incredible, like you are an eagle flying over everything. Down below is the great Valley of Oaxaca, and in the summer you can watch the storms coming in from the ancient places — Yagul, Dainzú, Mitla — moving across the land like dark curtains, sometimes two or three at once from different directions, and if you want, you can imagine it is you calling them in.

The last time I went up there was in August. I was with Sofía and a couple of friends from the university, and we had three liters of Negra and a bag of chicharrones. That day, we found a dead turkey and the head of a goat lying at the foot of the cross in a circle of candles all burned down. Sofía didn't like this and we sat away from them on a rock, but they weren't smelling yet so Carlo and Dani sat next to them on the cement which was better for the bottles and no ants biting. I don't know if the pope would be so happy to know that indios are sacrificing animals and drinking beer under the biggest cross outside of D.F., but maybe if he came here and sat for a while he would understand. The hill comes to a sharp point up there and the air was blowing around us in a circle. Far above was a hawk turning the same way as the wind like he was the one making it blow. The flowers up there were finished already, but for some reason this little turning wind was filled with butterflies flying around and around us. Sitting there with Sofía and the view with the beer still cold and all those butterflies I was thinking I never want to leave. Dani, with a liter of beer in him, took out his big graffiti marker and tagged a rock with "CHPT"— Chingón Para Todo. This motherfucker's ready for anything.

On that day I was feeling the same way.

Then the strike came and for months it was like a small war here. I went with the others to the barricades, but after Paquito and that cameraman were killed and all those others taken, tortured or disappeared, I lost my heart for the protests, not only from fear but because that anger — it is a kind of poison, you know, and it stays in the body. What did I learn from the strike? Nothing but how fast I can run and that Coke is good for washing tear gas from your eyes. This is why, just before el Día de los Muertos and all the soldiers coming with the armored cars, I left the city and went back to the pueblo to be with Abuelo. By then he was close to dying and it was a kind of silent bargain we made — I took care of his body and he did the same to my soul, telling me of all the changes he saw and how he made it through.

He also reminded me of something Mexicanos are being taught to forget, and that is how to live without money. One day, he said to me, "M'hijo, everyone knows life for the Zapoteco is hard, but we are lucky too and we are forgetting this. Who else can grow all their food — sweets and spices, herbs and medicines, corn and beans and squash, even oil for the hair — on one hectare on the side of a mountain? Everything you need is right here — the sun, the seed, the forest, the water. If you can read and grow your own food then your mind will be free, your stomach will be full, and you can survive no matter how the wind is blowing."

I could not help thinking of my father and how for him the milpa has become a kind of enemy, those rows of corn a wall between him and what he wants for himself and for us. For so many years I thought Papá's anger — with Abuelo, with his life — was from being deported. It wasn't until I went to stay with him that last time that Abuelo told me about Zeferina and the Jaguar Man.

17

Hoping and waiting, waiting and hoping. In here it is all the same. If not for the pipe and these things from César and my abuelo, I would be no different than the others — dying already from thirst and despair. They say hope dies last, but I think it is the story. This is why I must tell it now — to hear Abuelo's voice again. And so César can finally know me, and you also.

My Abuela Zeferina was not born in our pueblo but higher in the mountains, in Latuxí, a pueblo that had no road. A long time ago, in the 1930s, when he was a little older than I am now, my abuelo got a job up there as a laborer for an archaeologist from New York, from a big museum. I will tell you what happened just as my abuelo told it to me. It is easier to remember that way, and it helps me now to imagine sitting in his house with the candles and a bottle of pulque.

There is often a lot of wind around el Día de los Muertos, from all the spirits coming back, and the night Abuelo told me was like this and cold. Even with the door closed there was a breeze moving through so our shadows danced around us and it felt like there were more people in that small house than just me and my abuelo. "Up in Latuxí," he said, "there was a lot of old forest, wide oak and pine and some of the biggest avocado trees I've ever seen. You could feed a wedding party from one of them. Lots of orchids in the trees also, especially the little purple ones, and many, many birds. A campesino was up there clearing land for a new milpa, burning it off, and next to the clearing was a stand of trees growing on a hill. Ooni'ya, that campesino is pulling tree stumps with his oxen and he's finding things in the roots — pottery, a clay figure of a dog and many square stones perfect for building. Nobody remembered that hill was a temple. He tried to sell these things at the market, but the mayordomo of Latuxí learned of it and stopped him. It was the mayordomo who took the dog and the pottery up north to the city in Puebla because there was more money there and he thought he could get a better price.

"At that time, there were some archaeologists — gringos — working on a site in Puebla and one of them was called Professor Payne. When he heard about this dog and the square stones he came down to see that hill right away. He was a young man and I think he wanted his own excavation, he wanted to find a tomb filled with gold like Alfonso Caso did at Monte Albán. When I heard the rumor that a gringo was hiring obreros in Latuxí, I walked there, all day through the mountains, because I heard also that gringos paid in gold and silver. It was a hard time then and few of us in the pueblos had anything. If we couldn't grow it or make it, we had to trade for it.

"I met Professor Payne the next day under the stone arch in front of the village office. He was the first güero who ever spoke to me besides a padre. He even shook my hand. No don would ever do that with a campesino, especially an indio. If they said anything to you it was Come here! Go there! Do that! But the professor was different. When I took off my hat he told me it was hot and to keep it on. He had dark brown hair, a mustache like a brush and green eyes. His face and hands were dark from the sun. Except for a wide sombrero, he dressed norteño in a wool jacket and a necktie with a gold pin. 'I'm looking for shovel men,' he said. 'Hard workers.' When I told him I had walked fifty kilometers to be there, he hired me, along with eight others.

"We were only simple men, not one of us could read, but the professor tried to explain his work. He told us he was studying la estratigrafía. It was by this method—by knowing how deep one thing was next to another—that he guessed how old they were because in those days there was no other way to know. He told us the pyramid was made by our ancestors—by Zapotecos, and that the things buried there were like lost words in a great story which was our story also. With our help, he said, he wanted to learn this story so he could tell it to everyone in Mexico and all over the world. Well, m'hijo, I can tell you we were not interested in stories, we were interested in money and this gringo was not offering as much as we had hoped. But the professor was a clever man—he hired girls to cook for us, pretty ones, and this together with the money was enough to keep most of the men coming back. But I stayed for other reasons.

"The professor put us to work on the south side of the pyramid, digging out a careful square with strings and measuring sticks.

Each side of the square was five meters and we went down into the ground in steps, slowly, layer by layer, first with a pick, then with a shovel and then with a stick and a brush and a spoon. It took many weeks to do this and some of the men became impatient and quit. Others broke things, or stole them and were fired. I had never made a hole this way — with a straight wall where you could really see time passing layer by layer, and I was amazed that the professor could look at a broken piece of stone or clay and know by its color and texture which layer it had come from and how old it was.

"Over time, the excavation came to look like a pyramid, only upside down. After one layer was excavated, we went down into the next and I was the one to break up this new dirt. It was an important job and the professor offered bonuses — for finding things, for not breaking them — and I was good at this. Using the shovel every day, it becomes a part of your body the same as a machete and you can feel things with it. You can tell the difference between dead wood and living, between stone and metal, clay and bone.

"Ooni'ya, about three months into that first season, I hit something deep in the dirt there and it didn't feel like any of those things. It was softer than stone but harder than clay so I put the shovel down and dug it out with my fingers and a stick. I had never held jade before, never seen anything like it — smooth as a tooth and green as a tomatillo. It was a jaguar, sitting. Its face was half cat and half man and it was wearing a crown. The figure was about the size of my hand and its weight was strange, like it was too heavy for itself.

"Most of the things we found were broken because time is hard on everything, but the Jaguar Man was perfecto — como un milagro. Not a chip, not a crack. It was a treasure without price, but how could I know? And where would I sell such a thing anyway? Besides, I liked the professor — he was a kind man, kinder than most, with many jokes and good Spanish. He even had a few words of Zapotec. I didn't know what this thing was, but I knew it would make him happy so I took it to him in his tent where he was smoking a cigarette and working. The tent was open and he said 'Hola' when I came in but did not look up. When I put the Jaguar Man on his worktable next to his papers he didn't say anything at first — he just stared at it with his mouth open. When he looked at me his eyes were so big I thought he might faint. Finally, he picked up the Jaguar Man with both hands and said to it very quietly, 'My god.' He looked at me again and then down at the Jaguar Man. He closed his hands over it, took a big breath and opened them. I think he was afraid it would disappear. 'Oh my god,' he said.

"It was like that gringo was holding the bones of Jesus Himself."

Abuelo showed me the professor's face with his mouth hanging open like a door. He said it is the same face he would make if the pope showed up at his house with a cántaro of mezcal. But then my abuelo got a surprise too. The professor stood up and hugged him — like a brother. This is an unusual thing for a jefe to do and it was only then that Abuelo began to understand what he had found. He said the effect on the professor was not the same as gold, and he knew what he was talking about. Gold makes a man mean and greedy, like coca or bad mezcal. This was something more like the first time you touch the skin of someone you might someday love. That is how the professor was holding this little Jaguar Man, how he was looking at it and stroking it with his fingers — like recognizing someone you've never seen before.

"In the professor's mind," said Abuelo, "the Jaguar Man was a key to something, to a door he didn't know was there. When I asked him how old it was, he said, 'Older than Jesus. Maybe much older.'"

*

"At night by the excavation it was dark as a cave," Abuelo said. "The forest was deep and the clearing was narrow so looking up out of it made the sky look small and far away. When the night birds flew they moved across it only as a separate blackness against the stars and it was hard to tell how close or far they really were. This and the pyramid so near gave all of us an uncomfortable feeling and some of the men walked back to Latuxí every evening because they were afraid to sleep out there. The rest of us slept on grass petates, close together in one large tent, and next to us was a smaller tent with some of the professor's students. Professor Payne had his own tent and slept away from us along with the best pieces from the excavation.

"You know, Héctor, that I am at home in the night and sometimes it is impossible for me to stay still in the blanket. On such nights I would walk out of the camp and up into the forest growing over the pyramid, just to watch and listen. I saw things there glowing blue and green in the trees, maybe worms or fungus, maybe something else, and I heard sounds I never heard in the day — insects walking, roots pushing through the ground, bats calling loud as birds. Even the smells came differently — more like voices than smells. Most campesinos don't like to be in the forest at night because there are spirits and maybe that's what I was hearing. The night is a different country with a different language, but I feel I understand it.

"It was on the pyramid one night that I learned we were in the territory of a jaguar. I didn't see him, but I smelled him, and I understood who it was. He was marking the trees up there — all around the camp. I followed his scent and I made my own marks to let him know he was not the only one around. Not long after that I saw his track by the stream below the clearing — a single print. I looked around to see if anyone was watching and then I stepped into it, covered that track with my own, and my foot fit right inside there — the ball and the toes. I had a feeling then I can't explain — coming out of the ground, coming right up through me. All over my skin was prickling, my hair standing off my head. I never told the professor, never told anyone what I saw there. Someone would have shot him.

"That jaguar showed himself to me only one time, at the end of our second season. It was by the stream in the late afternoon when I was washing. There was a wide place below a small waterfall where the water was deep enough to swim, and I was in there floating on my back, looking up through the trees which blocked out the sky so all was in green shadow. To the side of me, in the shallows, were hundreds of bololos — tadpoles — the size of rosary beads with eyes the color of blood. I had tried to catch some, but they were fast and I was hot and tired from working. Ooni'ya, I was floating in the water with my feet against two rocks, to hold myself in the current, when I heard a sound separate from the waterfall. I thought it was one of the men coming to bathe and I looked over, but where I expected to see a man, there was a jaguar. It was the first time — the only time in my life I have seen one, and it was a shock for me, the size of him. He was five meters away, but even so close it was hard to know where the forest ended and the jaguar began. He was not so much a separate thing as he was — how can I say it — una perturbación, like ripples in water. His spots could be leaves and the spaces between them at the same time, the line of his back a branch or its shadow. All but his eyes — they could be only one thing.

"And there I am, naked in the water. My throat, my stomach, my privates — everything was exposed to him, but what could I do? One jump and he would have me like a calf. So I stayed where I was and watched him from the corner of my eye, trying not to move, not even to blink or breathe. But I could not stop my heart and you should have heard it then, beating under the water. I had thrown my clothes across a bush and the jaguar was sniffing at them, especially my pants. For some reason these were interesting to him. He was so close I could hear his breath, hear him smelling, even through the water. I wondered what was in my pants that could be so interesting, and then I understood. He was recognizing me — here was the one who had been marking in his territory. I wondered if he would be angry and what he would do. Ooni'ya, I found out.

"As soon as he finished examining my pants he turned around and sprayed them. It was almost funny until he looked at me. At that moment the water turned ice cold and my body was covered in turkey skin. It was his eyes that did it, they closed that distance between us to nothing. They were green like jade — like the Jaguar Man, and his pupils were round and black as bololos. He sat down at the water's edge and studied me floating there and his tail was twitching. It was thick and strong and when it hit the ground it made the sound of a heavy step. I wanted to look away — to get up and run, but how could I?

"Then something in the water caught his attention. I could see his round ears come forward and his head turning quickly from side to side, following it. He lifted a paw over the water and it was moving too, together with his eyes, tracking this thing until he brought it down with a splash. Then again with both paws and he was jumping in the shallows there, this way and that. He was chasing the bololos. After that I wasn't afraid anymore, only amazed that we were there together, noticing the same things."

In the evenings, my abuelo worked in the professor's tent, cleaning the things they found in the day. Many men were careless and some were stealing so they were not allowed in there, but Abuelo was careful and curious so he was. Sometime after that big find, Abuelo said to Professor Payne, "That face — the one on the Jaguar Man — he looks like someone I know."

The professor did not ignore him or laugh. He wanted to know who that man was — who his people were and where they came from. "It is not the man I know," said Abuelo, "but the jaguar."

The professor held up the Jaguar Man and compared it to the face of Abuelo. "I think he looks like you," he said. Both men were laughing, but at different jokes. Then the professor asked my abuelo a funny question—"For such a thing to exist, must the man eat the jaguar or must the jaguar eat the man?"

Now, AnniMac, we are Zapotecs and we share the jaguar with many others around here—Mixtec, Mazatec, Aztec, Maya. Jaguar is our ancestor and my abuelo had to explain something that is obvious to most people. "Professor," he said, "the Jaguar Man is not made from eating. He is made from copulating. Like all of us."

Then Abuelo told the professor how he came to know this, and he told it to him the same way he used to tell it to me.

"Our people are descended from two brothers," he said. "Long ago, they came into the Sierra from the Valley of Oaxaca, searching for water and a safe place to live. They left their home because there was drought in the valley and a third brother, a powerful cacique, drove them away. 'There is not enough here for all of us,' the third brother said. 'Go now or I will kill you like the rest.' Because they were his blood he would not enslave them. The two brothers went north into the mountains, sick in their hearts and believing they were alone in the world. That night, as they sat by a small stream wondering what to do, a jaguar appeared to them. His eyes were glowing and when the brothers saw this they were afraid and raised their weapons.

"But the jaguar did not attack, and he did not run away. He spoke to them. 'Is that any way to greet your grandfather?' he asked. 'Do you not remember who I am?'

"The two brothers lowered their weapons. 'We are sorry,' they said. 'We believed our grandfathers to be dead. For years there has been fighting among our people. Many have died and it has damaged our memory.'

"The brothers had nowhere to go and the jaguar understood this. 'I accept your apology,' he said. 'If you like, I will take you to my home in the mountains.'

"At this the two brothers bowed their heads in gratitude. The jaguar turned to the older one and said, 'You, climb on my back and face where you came from.'

"Then he turned to the other and said, 'You, climb on after and face where you are going.'

"The brothers did as they were told. They sat on the jaguar's back facing each other with their knees touching.

"'Now look down,' said the jaguar, 'and tell me what you see.'

"Between them the brothers saw the diamond shape made by their legs, and they told this to the jaguar.

"'What do you see inside it?' asked the jaguar.

"'Fur,' said the older brother.

"'Spots,' said the other.

"'Draw a line across my back,' said the jaguar, 'from where your knees touch on one side to where they touch on the other. When you have done this, draw another line down my spine. Where the two lines cross, tell me what you see.'

"'Fur,' said the older brother.

"'Spots,' said the other.

"The jaguar snapped his jaws together. 'Look again.'

"The brothers looked again. In the center where the two lines met was a dark outline in the jaguar's fur with two black dots inside it.

"'I see a cloud and two birds,' said the older brother.

"'I see a lake and two fish,' said the other.

"'My skin is a map of the world,' said the jaguar. 'What you are seeing is a valley surrounded by mountains.'

"'What are the two dots inside it?' asked the older brother.

"'Those are the pueblos you will build there.'

"All night the jaguar carried the brothers through the forest, higher and deeper into the mountains. The next day when the sun was at its height, the jaguar stopped at the top of a ridge. Far below them lay a green valley ringed by mountains. The brothers had no idea where they were.

"'You are the first humans to see this place,' said the jaguar. 'This is my home. I invite you to share it with me.'

"'Thank you, Grandfather,' they said. 'But how can we repay you for this kindness?'

"'All I ask in return,' said the jaguar, 'is that you remember who brought you here.'"

18

How we remember Grandfather Jaguar in our pueblo is with the dance, but my abuelo was the last man to do it. He told me it was the oldest dance he knew, and that it came with the two brothers who settled our valley. Before the Spanish came, he said, the people honored Grandfather Jaguar because he alone kept order in the forest and the milpa both. The people tended their crops and the jaguar tended the animals who ate the crops — rats, badgers, javelina, deer. Even the puma stayed away. The Spanish feared the jaguar, but not as much as they feared our faith in him. They called the jaguar a false god and a creature of darkness, but only the second part was true. Then they ordered us to kill our own grandfather. With guns and poison they did this, with threats and promises of more, later, in a world beyond this one. We gave up many things when the padres came, but we would not abandon the jaguar.

"The Spanish god can share the day with Grandfather Jaguar," said my abuelo, "but the night in the Sierra is enormous and complete, and all of it belongs to him."

The padres tried to stop the dances and for years the people danced in secret, until the time my grandfather was born. A new padre came to our village then and he was a clever man. He allowed us to bring the jaguar back into the light, but only for Carnival week just before Lent when all the powers that govern the Spanish world are turned upside down. That padre died a long time ago, but the jaguar dance stayed with us and every year it was a contest to see who could spot him first. Once, he crawled out of a bread oven. Once, he drove up in a car. Once, he rode in on a burro, a sack on its eyes to calm it, and another time he ran out of the church. But no matter where he came from, the new padre was unhappy to see him because the jaguar is his own god and will never be converted.

When I was very small I didn't understand that the dancer saw where he was going by looking out the jaguar's mouth, and the first time I saw the dark eyes of a man shining back at me from behind those teeth, I believed the jaguar had eaten him — a Jonah in a bone cage looking from the inside out. All my life it was my abuelo who danced the jaguar to the music of the flute and drum through the smoke of copal burning, but when I was young I didn't know it was him, only that you never found the two of them together. No one saw him put it on — not the mask he carved himself or the suit of spots Abuela made. Some said he got the paint from the men who made the highway — black and yellow for the skin, red and white for the tongue and teeth, his own hair for the whiskers. I still don't know where he found the eyes and he would never tell. When I was older I understood that they were made of mirror glass and when he came close — close enough to bite — it wasn't only his eyes staring at you but your eyes also. For a moment you were the jaguar too.

To the end, Abuela Zeferina cheered the loudest because he danced it for her. They spent their lives together, but they never shared a god. Hers lived in the church and his lived in the mountains where the trees meet the stars. She did not condemn my abuelo for refusing the Spanish god because, in the Sierra, God is everywhere — in Jesus and the jaguar both. Once, when she thought they were alone, I heard her call him mi felino — my big cat. The way Abuelo danced it, the tail was a separate thing, trailing its master like a second thought, like it had other plans. Sometimes it was just a tail, other times a whip, a snake, a cock with a mind of its own. Tender or cruel, no creature was safe from it. Sometimes he would wind it around Abuela's waist and pull her into the dance with him. She would protest, of course, but in a way that only pushed her closer. The band could not resist then — horns and drums came thundering in to swallow whole the little flute while the padre only bowed his head and prayed harder. For him, the jaguar was chaos — big as a man and almost as hungry.

Behind their masks the others danced their animals — burro, goat, sheep and ox — while Grandfather Jaguar ran like the devil through the pueblo. Only the mayordomo was his human self behind his human mask with his great mustache, his carbine and machete. Him and his masked dog, they entered at last to hunt the jaguar, drive him back to the mountains and make the pueblo safe again for Christians and their helpless beasts. But they did not kill him, because he protects the corn. This is the compromise we made with that old padre, and the ones who came after respected it.

That mask and suit, I don't know where Abuelo kept them the rest of the year. There was no place in his small house to hide them. When I asked him once, he just smiled and pointed toward the mountains which were everywhere around us. What I know now to be true — when the jaguar was there my grandfather was not, and now they both are gone.

I asked him once, Who will dance the jaguar after you? "Whoever carves the mask," he said. "You know where my tools are."

I promise now — to him and to you — if I get out of here, I will go and find them.

Fri Apr 6 — 22:32

I don't know why, AnniMac, but the old gods have been showing up lately in some strange places, not only on this truck and in the Oaxaca Codex but at la Basílica de la Soledad. I saw them myself when I went there with my mother two weeks ago on the Sunday of the Passion. It was my first time in three years because I refused to go. I told her I am not a boy anymore — I am barely even a Christian because of all the things Abuelo told me. But Abuelo would have smiled to see what I saw that day at the basilica — jaguars have appeared on that great church. No, I am not imagining it. They are real, carved from the stone, new but in the baroque style — two of them right at the top on each side of Soledad herself. Es misterioso, no? Más jaguares de uso humano. I asked my mother how they came there, but she could not see them, or would not. "Those are renovations," she said. "They were supposed to be for the milenio, but they were late."

"They renovated the basilica with jaguars?"

"Of course not," she said. "Who would put jaguars on a basilica?"

"You mean you can't see them — the claws, the eyes?"

"Those are flowers in the Spanish style," she said without looking. Lower down, over the doors, is a carving of María Magdalena kneeling at Golgotha with the skull carved so deep it looks ready to fall on you. Mamá looked only at this, crossed herself and walked inside.

Why do I tell you these things? Because I cannot tell her, and I am afraid that I am dying. I wish I could see my mother — not only for comfort, but to ask her forgiveness. I understand now I should have gone with her to the church more often, but I confess that I was influenced by Abuelo who did not respect her because she is a servant to the pope. Also because once she called him un pagano. But I can see now that for Mamá the church is more than that. For her, it is security and comfort and love in a life that doesn't have enough of those things — from anyone. Not from her husband and — I am ashamed to admit this — not from her son. But two weeks ago I was in a different darkness and I couldn't see this. The only reason I went with her that day was out of pity because she was crying so much and because I am her only son. Somehow she knew I was leaving even before I did.

On that last Sunday before I met César in the taxi, Mamá and me walked over the hill from our house to the basilica. It was a hot day and as we walked you could hear seeds from the jacarandas falling hard and loud in the street. In a maguey bag my mother carried flowers and other things wrapped in a newspaper. She walked with no shoes on, and this should have been a sign to me that this day was important, but I was thinking only of my own problems and where can I find a pair of Puma Ferraris for cheap. How is it two people can walk side by side across the same stones with the same blood in their veins and their minds so far apart?

When we arrived at the basilica it was between the services and quiet. Just inside the doors is the rock where the mysterious holy burro died and the box holding the vision of la Virgen de la Soledad was discovered. This is where Mamá went down on her knees just like when I was young, and just like then I walked beside her carrying her bag. I could smell the things inside it now, plants from the pueblo, and suddenly my throat was thick and my nose was prickling and I didn't know why. She stared straight ahead, polishing the tiles with her knees, and angels held the lights to guide her way. I was towering over her, but I was not the only grown son there with his praying mother. There was another sitting at the front, clean like his mother just washed him but with spike hair, a knife-cut pentagram on his T-shirt and chains on his pants — a good boy from the pueblos trying to look like el diablo is his compa. I never liked that kind of music myself, and Mamá would never let me wear such clothes to church. She ironed my jeans the night before and the polo shirt I wore was a false Lacoste with an armadillo she bought for me in Abastos market. I am wearing it right now.

On her long journey to the altar Mamá went through the stations, hands to her lips, eyes on the Virgin, thoughts who knows where. Next to her I was far away, thinking of Sofía on the park bench and do I have the cojones to go back to el Norte, or even to D.F., but you know twenty million people is a lot for one city and the news is bad coming from there. They have this T-shirt now, *I Heart D.F.,* only the heart is exploding from a bullet. Anyone can be a martyr these days, but who could wear this? My mother would kill me. In Oaxaca we have our own T-shirt from the strike — la Virgen de las Barricadas wearing a gas mask, with a cloak covered in burning tires. But Oaxaca is only a small village compared to D.F., and what would I do up there anyway?

All around us the sweet stink of incense hangs off everything like moss in the forest. It is almost noon and the sun is coming down into the church in dusty rays, sharp fingers pointing out all our defects — cracks in the tiles, peeling paint on the wall, missing only by centimeters the hole in my heart and landing on San Francisco's cracked plaster toes. ¿La devoción es peligrosa, no? Even now the saints suffer. But right between Francisco's broken feet is a single egg lit by the sun because you must offer what you can, even if it is only an egg or an orchid. I try to avoid those searching rays, but of course it is impossible. My hands are empty and I cannot hide this.

When finally we arrive at the altar, Mamá makes the sign of the cross with the seventeen touches, finishing with a kiss on her thumb. Then she does something she has not done since I was small. She turns me toward Soledad who is floating there above the altar in her big glass box. Somehow the rays are in there too, falling on her perfect white hands so they seem to glow and almost move even though it is dark all around her. Hanging in the shadows above her is Jesus bleeding and over Him is God Himself in a red cape flying. Like Superman, I used to think, only older and with a beard.

I can hear Mamá behind me whispering the blessing—"mi cariñito, mi angelito, mi vida, niño doradito"—such tender things, over and over, trying not to cry, but it is no use because Soledad is her virgin and the Virgin is alone because she has lost her only son and soon my mother will lose hers and how can she not feel the Virgin's same sadness, especially with Easter so close? And how can I not cry also in the face of all this? It is too much so now it is both of us there with the tears coming down and in my mother's hand are roses and herbs like we use in the pueblo for the temazcal ceremony, for making the body and spirit clean—yerba santa, chamizo, albahaca, ajenjo—too many to name, and with these she is stroking my body, caressing me like she did when I was born—the top of my head and then my cheeks, across my shoulders, down my spine, and her crying and praying all at the same time so that I am glad she is behind me because I cannot bear to see her face, but when I look at Soledad it is as if this sadness is everywhere around us, and I remember how I felt as a boy in Señora Ellen's arms in el Norte—those bony white hands, and how much she is not like my mother and never can be and how empty and hopeless such a feeling is—even as that sad church air comes suddenly alive with the smell of flowers and herbs all the way from the pueblo — the very breath of that place filling my nose and lungs — as Mamá brushes the leaves and petals down my bare arms and hands, across my backside and then the front and down my legs, making circles there around my feet to protect me from some harm in the future that she fears but cannot know.

19

Fri Apr 6 — 23:02

I can hear someone gagging and I know it's from drinking urine. I have heard this sound many times today. And someone else saying, "Porfiz, porfiz," like a child begging. But they are strangers to me now. If I knew them I would go mad. Many times I watched my mother pray and it was like she was leaving her body. I thought she was giving herself away, and I couldn't understand why she would want to. But now I think I do — it is only in the effort of telling, of calling up the story, that I can escape, and it is such a shock to come back. I am so tired. So cold.

I am rubbing César's hands to warm them but also mine. Then, carefully, quietly, I put my finger into César's water bottle and drip some in between his lips. Still he lives and there must be a reason for it. When I take a sip and hold it in my mouth, I swear I can feel my cells swelling with it, and there is in this a kind of grace.

When I speak of my abuelo it is almost like he is here with me. And if he lives — even if it is only in these words — I can also.

Professor Payne always took a special interest in my abuelo, and not only because he found the Jaguar Man. He could see that Abuelo was strong and intelligent so he taught him to read in Spanish. It was hard for him, but Abuelo saw the professor and his life and listened when he told him that books were a door into other worlds that you can visit from anywhere — D.F. or New York or even Latuxí. He told Abuelo that it was because of books he came to Mexico, and so because of books they met and the Jaguar Man was found. For Abuelo this was a powerful idea and he told the professor he would like to read also, to see what was on the other side of all those doors.

The first book the professor gave to Abuelo once he could make the words himself was *Los de abajo* — *The Underdogs* — by Mariano Azuela. In a year or two he was reading whatever he could find. The first time Abuelo told me *The Underdogs* was a good book, I asked him why and he said, "Because it is short — much shorter than the Bible — and more true." Abuelo knew many men who fought in la Revolución. He was too young for it by just a few years and that was hard for him. When he was younger he believed if he had been there he could have helped his father and maybe then he would have lived. But that book let him see for himself that if he was there or not, it was ending all the same. What could anyone do against those German guns, cutting men down like cane in the field?

*

For many nights after he found the jade Jaguar Man, Abuelo saw the shadow of the professor in his tent, bent over in the lamplight like he was studying something. Abuelo had an idea what it was and one night he crept up to the tent where there was a hole for looking through. The professor was there in his folding canvas chair and in his hand was the Jaguar Man. But the professor wasn't studying it. No, his eyes were closed and tears were streaming down his face. Abuelo said when he saw that, he turned away quickly and was ashamed as if he had surprised his parents in their nakedness. He went back to the tree where he'd been sitting, pulled his serape around him and wondered to himself what was in that piece of jade to make such an important man from so far away so sad. The Jaguar Man was a very old and powerful thing — so old and powerful that the professor took it with him back to New York.

In the end, Abuelo got to hold the Jaguar Man for only a few moments because the professor cleaned it himself and kept it in a special place. But he could never get it out of his mind. It was the first time he ever came close to that kind of power in a man-made thing. When my abuelo found it, he could barely write his name, but pulling the Jaguar Man from the earth like that — with his own hands, and being the first man to touch it in who knows how many lifetimes — there was something wonderful to him in this, in holding a thing so ancient and fine that carried so much inside it. He said that for a moment he was raised up out of himself like in the stories and was able to see across the mountains. I don't think he knew what he was seeing exactly, but he hoped I would and this is why he told me of it. Last November, when Abuelo was near to dying, he said to me, "M'hijo, if you ever go back to el Norte, go to the museum in Nueva York. Find that thing. Hold it if you can."

*

The professor was a gringo and a scholar, but most of the people he talked about were Mexicanos and artists, people like Rufino Tamayo, Diego Rivera and Frida Kahlo. He told Abuelo that Rivera was one of the bravest men he knew because he was not afraid to shout when other men would only whisper. With his great murals he looked Henry Ford and Nelson Rockefeller in the eyes and told them the truth about themselves. And they paid him to do it. Abuelo never saw those murals and he didn't agree. He said Diego Rivera was too rich to be a man of the people and too fat to be a real Communist. He called him un rábano — a radish — red on the outside but white on the inside. Abuelo told me that the professor and Rivera would smoke together sometimes, and not only cigars. It is something, no? The great Diego Rivera got that güero high.

This is a world Abuelo never saw himself because no campesino did, but it was interesting for him and in the evenings he would sometimes bring the professor some yerba rolled in a corn husk, or mezcal in a gourd. The professor would talk then, and he told my abuelo many stories from his life. I think he must have been lonely out there so far from home, and why not? What kind of man would do such a thing — leave his home and family to dig in the hard dirt of a foreign land?

It is a trick question. The answer is Mexicanos. All the time. By the millions, but not back then.

At the start of their third season in Latuxí, the professor was still talking about the Jaguar Man. "It was an obsession for him," said Abuelo. "There was something about it that troubled him, and one night the professor said to me, 'I've asked everyone at all the museums, and no one has seen anything like it — not from here or anywhere else in Mexico. Tamayo wants to buy it from me.'

"That time," said Abuelo, "we were leaning against a big avocado tree on the edge of the clearing, smoking and watching the stars. 'It's so small,' I said to him. 'It could have been carried from far away, from anywhere.'

"'You think it was a gift?' said the professor. 'I had a dream about it, you know.'

"I rolled some more yerba on an old metate and passed it to the professor who lit it with his silver lighter. 'I didn't see it exactly,' said the professor. 'I felt it — the texture, as if my fingers were dreaming.'

"'Sometimes ten eyes are better than two,' I said.

"The professor laughed at this. 'You think I was carving it in my dream?'

"'No one knows it as well as him who made it.'

"'I am sure there are other memories at work besides the memory of man,' he said. 'I am sure there is memory in the earth, the stones, the clay. This is what I am trying to recover. And those trees with their roots deep inside the temple — what do they know? What are they seeing? If a jaguar could talk, what would it say?'

"'There are plants,' I said to him, 'mushrooms and herbs that can help you to see these things, to understand this language. They can even speak to you themselves. I have been told the mushroom can find lost things and answer questions that have no answers otherwise.'

"Of course the professor wanted to know more, because he wanted to know everything. He was a man greedy for knowledge. 'What are they called?' he asked.

"'*Teonanacatl*,' I said. 'Flesh of the gods.'"

Abuelo laughed. "You should have seen that gringo going for his notebook.

"'There are many names for them,' I told the professor. 'In the rainy season they grow all over the place, especially in cowshit.'

"'How can I get some?' he asked.

"'I do not eat them myself,' I said. 'It's not in our tradition. But I know you can't use them just anytime, like yerba or aguardiente. They are a sacrament, for seeing and healing and cleansing. There is a ceremony for it.'

"'Who leads the ceremony?'

"'A curandera,' I said. 'One who is called to it. But you will not find such a one in Latuxí or in my pueblo. For this you must go into la Mazateca — three days walking to the northeast.'

"'I don't have time for that,' he said. 'Can you bring me some?'

"'Professor,' I said, 'it's not safe to take them alone, not without a guide.'

"'Sit with me then, will you, Hilario? You can keep me safe.'

"'Maybe from what's outside, but not from what's inside. It is another country there and I can't follow. Besides, it's too dry for mushrooms now.'

"But the professor was a stubborn man and early in the next September, after the rainy season, he sent me across the mountains into la Mazateca where they spoke no Zapotec and little Spanish. It took me a week, but I found a curandera who knew the right ones and she tried to give me some instructions in her language. On the night I returned, after all the obreros had gone to sleep, I set up a small three-legged quemador on the dirt floor of the professor's tent and I lit some copal. The professor sat down with me in front of the quemador and he opened the curandera's medicine bundle. It was made of bark paper tied with a vine and inside, wrapped in herbs and grass, were twelve fresh mushrooms with long thin stems and brown caps. This much I understood from the curandera and I told it to the professor — 'Before you eat these, you must know why you are doing it. It is dangerous to go to that place without a guide, but even more dangerous to go without a reason.'

"'I am going,' he said, 'to see who made the Jaguar Man.'

"I was afraid for him, and I took his hand then. 'Bueno,' I said. 'But you must promise to come back.'

"The professor laughed at me and I did not like that, but he promised to come back. 'You eat six at one time,' I said. 'The curandera was very clear about this, but maybe since you are new to it you should have only three.'

"The professor smiled at me like I was some worrying old woman. 'They are small,' he said, 'and look at me.'

"The curandera had tried to tell me the right words to say, but I could not understand any of it except two words of Spanish, 'holy children,' so I said this and some words of my own in a prayer—

> These Holy Children are yours,
> given us by the Launching Woman who sends
>   her people on the journey,
> by the Sky Woman who flies in every form,
>   by the Water Woman who swims in light and darkness both,
> by the Reading Woman who knows all pages of the great book,
> and by the Landmark Woman who guides us home again.
> To you and to them we say, We are humble men
>   who live by the law as we are able.
> Please receive this prayer and find us worthy
>   of your sight and protection.

"Then I sprinkled some yerba and tobacco on the burning copal until it flared and crackled, and I poured some mezcal so it sizzled and spat. 'There,' I said, 'I hope it is enough.'

"The professor ate the mushrooms then—first one, then two, and the last three together. He was a strong man who did not shrink from chiles or mezcal and the only way to tell how badly these mushrooms tasted behind his mustache was by the motion of his nose. He drank some water from a gourd and lit a cigarette, and we waited. After some time, he leaned back against the leg of his work-table and closed his eyes. 'You are sure about these?' he said. 'The curandera was trustworthy?'

"'I asked in three pueblos and she was known and much re-spected in all of them.'

"'Nothing's happening,' said the professor.

"'I asked her how long it takes, but she would only make a circle from west to east.'

"'All night?' The professor wasn't happy about this.

"'I think that was for the journey,' I said.

"After three more cigarettes the professor was impatient. 'Six isn't enough. You people are so small and look at me.'

"'No,' I said. 'Please do as she says.'

"The professor got up, went outside, came back and sat down again. 'I don't feel a damned thing,' he said. 'I'm not even light-headed.'

"And before I could stop him, he ate the other six. All at once he did this. Then, after another drink of water, he sat down cross-legged on the ground. He was reaching into his coat for his cigarettes when he stopped, doubled over and vomited between his shoes. When he came up again his eyes were big like a mono, and he looked about him as if he could see through the walls of the tent. He no longer recognized me or, I think, even himself. I went outside quickly and got a shovelful of dirt to cover his mess and then, through the copal smoke, I watched the professor seeing things I could not see. After some time, he began to lean so I helped him to lie down on his side and I put a folded blanket under his head. His eyes were still open, only staring now, and his mouth moved, but there were no words. The moon was setting when he closed his eyes, but I did not sleep.

"It was still dark when he opened his eyes again. 'Water,' he said.

"I helped him to sit up and gave him some water from the gourd. 'I saw it,' he said. 'I saw it in the stone. I saw it being carved, and with every cut of the tool there was blood running.'"

20

Whenever he came from D.F., the professor brought new books for my abuelo to read — *Don Quixote* and *Great Expectations,* also *The True History of the Conquest of New Spain* by Bernal Díaz. They were in Spanish and Abuelo kept them always on a shelf in his house under the altarcito Abuela made for Juquila. It was from these books that Abuelo taught me to read after we were deported and my father left us in the pueblo. He tried to teach my father when he was young, but Papá could never do it, could never make the letters stay together in his mind. I have seen him try and his eyes are devils playing tricks, every word a shell game. To be like this and to live with a man like Abuelo who was reading all the time, and then to have a son like me who learns so easy and is so little like him — maybe you can imagine how it is for a proud man. In el centro, or far away in el Norte, he could stand it because no one at home would see anything but the money, but in the pueblo, in front of his own people, it was too much for him. One time Abuelo said to me, "These days, the Mexican man is a baby." I didn't understand what he meant until later.

In that summer before the American war with Japan, the professor wrote to Abuelo telling of his plans and asking him to come a week early to help organize the obreros and set up the camp. He said also that there was a new cook coming from Latuxí and he would bring her to the camp himself. The cooking was always done at a stone fireplace under a palapa made of sticks and petates, but in his letter the professor asked Abuelo to build a new cocina from adobe and bamboo with a pine needle roof. "Make it nice for her," he said.

Abuelo built the cocina and when the professor arrived at the camp with the new cook, he understood why. Her name was Zeferina and she was pretty — Zapoteca, por supuesto. But she wasn't just another campesina. There was something about this girl, the way she looked and held herself — como una princesa. "She looked like a painting I saw in one of the professor's magazines," Abuelo told me. "Those big eyes turned almost like a cat's, the mouth a bit crooked, but full in a way that only makes you want to open it. Understand? To taste the juice inside." Abuelo was ninety-six years old telling me these things, but still he liked to smoke and drink a little and he offered these to me also. I'm telling you, with your mind buzzing from all that, it was something for a young man to hear.

Professor Payne was married with some little children up in el Norte, but Abuelo knew it only from a picture on the professor's worktable. The professor never spoke of them and he always came to Latuxí alone. Often he made drawings of the artifacts they found and he taught Abuelo to do this also, but in that last season the professor was making more drawings of Zeferina than of artifacts. They would do this in the afternoon during the siesta, and sometimes they didn't come out of his tent for a long time. "One evening," said Abuelo, "when I was in the tent helping the professor to clean some things we found that day, I saw one of those drawings behind the worktable. The professor was a good artist and many times at night, and even in the day when I was working, I would think about that picture."

Of course Zeferina did not spend the night with the professor, ever. Always she walked back to her parents in the pueblo before sunset, coming back early in the morning to start the fire and cook for the men. It was a long walk from Latuxí, and one morning Abuelo surprised Zeferina by making the fire himself and the coffee too. "I will do this every morning," he said to her, "and then you can sleep longer."

She refused this and said the professor was paying her to do the cooking, but Abuelo didn't listen and kept getting up early to make the fire and the coffee, and when he did this he thought about the things he was touching that she would touch later and at least it was something. One morning, after maybe ten days, Zeferina came late, but everything was ready so all she needed to do was pat out the cornmeal for the tortillas and fry the eggs. Even the beans were warming in the shoe pot, buried in the ground by the fire. "So, you accept my offer?" said Abuelo, and that was the first time she looked him in the eye — and smiled — both at the same time. Always after that she came a bit later.

"Ooni'ya, I was her prisoner then!" Abuelo told me. "I decided I must marry that girl. You know, m'hijo, I was married one time already, but there were problems and it was hard to have the child. We saw the curandera and finally she was with the child, but when it came time for the baby I lost them both. I was there in the house with the curandera and my tía helping when this happened and it was terrible — there was blood enough for three. After that, I had no heart to be with a woman again.

"Zeferina was the first one who reminded me what that feeling is, that wanting. But it caused problems for me — it was harder to look the professor in the eye. Something about him was changing also, no longer would he talk with me in the evenings as he had before. And it wasn't just me and the professor noticing Zeferina, it was every man in camp, even the professor's students. The obreros were not allowed near the cocina or the professor's tent, but even from the excavation you could see her walking, bending over, and I must tell you it was something how she moved. Even when she wasn't there that girl was vibrating in the air como una chicharra. It was the first time in five years of knowing the professor that I counted the days until he was gone. But how could I know then what was going to happen?

"I don't know if it was because of Zeferina or other troubles in his mind, but the professor spent more and more time in his tent and left me in charge of the digging. Of all the men, I had been there the longest and I was the only one who could read, or draw the artifacts as they truly looked. In November, after we all came back from celebrating el Día de los Muertos, the professor made me a kind of jefe and now it was me telling the other men where and how to dig, making sure they were doing it correctly and not stealing anything. I was proud the professor trusted me this way, and of course I was glad for the extra money. He paid me in gold that year — forty American dollars. I will never forget the beautiful weight of those coins.

"Never again," said Abuelo, "did we find anything as fine as the Jaguar Man. But the professor could not forget that one — he even wrote about it for a magazine. He showed this to me, and seeing those photographs was like seeing an old friend. I studied them carefully and I also studied the words, but the name of him who found it was not there. It was in that last season that the professor told me he was going to write a book about the Jaguar Man because now, after years of studying, he believed he knew who had made it, and it wasn't a Zapotec. He believed it was Olmec. The Olmec came before us, from the Gulf coast of Veracruz, but no one in the Sierra remembers those people. They were great artists like us and it was them who made the clay statues with babies' faces and those giant stone heads in the jungle, but it wasn't until we found the Jaguar Man and the professor studied him that anyone understood that all of these things were made by the same people, or even who those people were. Back then the Olmec didn't even have a name. It was Professor Payne who made the connection, and he made it through the Jaguar Man.

"I asked the professor if I could keep the magazine and he said I could. He also told me it was the mushrooms that showed him, that allowed him to see beyond the faces and past the lines that made them, all the way to the tools and the hands that pushed them through the stone. 'Once I saw this,' he said, 'I understood it wasn't a question of design. It is the method that unites them.'

"It was then," said Abuelo, "the professor told me some important news — to prove this idea for his book he needed to leave Latuxí and find a new site on the border with Veracruz. He asked me to go with him, and do you know the first thing I thought? That it will take me away from Zeferina. Everyone knew she was the professor's mistress so it was not a good situation for me, but for some reason I was hopeful. She was in me somehow, and I hoped I was in her. The professor said this new excavation was a special chance for me — maybe I could come to Nueva York and work in the museum there. It was a big door opening, and that strange feeling I told you about from holding the Jaguar Man? I remembered this and wondered if it was a premonition—maybe I would travel across the mountains and meet the Jaguar Man again. So I said to the professor, 'Yes, I want to go with you.'

"But secretly in my mind I was thinking, 'Only if Zeferina refuses me.'"

"This is how it was when the professor left in the beginning of December to return to his family and the museum. When we were packing up the camp, Zeferina would look only at the ground because seeing faces made her cry. I don't know what the professor told her, but I can only guess it was goodbye—forever—because of course her parents would not let her leave Latuxí alone. On her last day I was too busy packing artifacts in the professor's tent and I never saw her leave. My heart was sick that day and I wondered would I ever see her again. My pueblo was a day's walking from Latuxí and I didn't even know her family name. I'm telling you, Héctor, in those days it could be hard to meet the chicas. I told myself maybe, if I'm lucky, I will see her in Tlacolula at a fiesta.

"The next day, we were loading everything onto the burros and walking out to the road where the professor had hired a truck for the long drive to D.F. I was in charge of the burros and I was praying—sí, mi joven, it takes la conchita to make this viejo pray!—I was praying I would see Zeferina somewhere in the village. But I did not. When I said goodbye to Professor Payne there were shadows around his eyes and he looked like his mind had left already, but he shook my hand and said again that he wanted me to work with him next year, and he would write to me in the spring."

"In the new year of 1942, America was fighting in the war with Japan. For a campesino like me there were not many changes to the life. We were far from everything and we had no radio, but there was a bus driver I knew in Tlacolula who brought newspapers from el centro. I was thinking about Zeferina all these months — so much that my mother thought I was sick and my brothers who were all married a long time were making rude jokes to me in the milpa. Also, there was no letter coming from the professor, and this made things harder. Finally, I could not stand it anymore. After the first corn harvest in June, I waited for the moon to grow to half so I could see my way through the mountains, and then I walked again to Latuxí. All night I did this so I would have the greatest chance of seeing Zeferina in the day. Maybe she was married already, but I had to see her. I had to know. Ooni'ya, there were two big surprises waiting for me there.

"I arrived after sunrise and the first person I see to speak to is the padre who is on his way to the village office. He knew the professor and he had visited the excavation, but he was surprised to see me at this time in the year. When he understood that it was me, he said, 'M'hijo, I have sad news.'

"Well, the first thing I think of is that something has happened to Zeferina. It shows you how out of my mind I was because there is no way the padre could know my feelings about this. Then he looked in my eyes and said, 'I am so sorry to tell you — el profesor está muerto. May God rest his soul.'

"I could not breathe for a moment. I had been thinking only of Zeferina and I was so shocked I didn't know what to do or say. The padre put his hand on my shoulder. 'Forgive me for surprising you like this,' he said. 'It is a terrible loss. We learned only last week in a letter from the museum to the mayordomo. They wrote to say the funding for Latuxí is finished.'

"'How did it happen?'

"'They say only that it was a tragic accident. There are no details.'

"I was staring around like a blind man. I didn't know what to do with myself. 'Padre,' I said, 'is the church open?'

"'Of course,' he said. 'Always.'

"So, I go into the church. It is dark and cool in there and I sit down on my heels against the back wall. I did not know until then how much hope for my life I had attached to Professor Payne, how in a moment it could be finished—just like that. So many doors closing at once. For some time I sit there feeling sick in my soul before I understand I am not the only person in that church. Up in the front, kneeling at the rail, is another, a woman. I was in a bad condition, but I would know that calabazo anywhere and I cannot believe it. I am so tired from walking all night and so sideways from the padre's news that I wonder if I am seeing things. To be sure, I go up to the altar very quietly—I have no shoes—but she doesn't move and she doesn't disappear. I kneel down at the rail some distance from her and I see two things then—one, that she is crying into her hands, and two, that she is with the child.

"So, I ask you, m'hijo, how much can one man stand? First I was kicked by a horse and now I am run over by the wagon. I didn't know what to say to her, but I couldn't bear to leave her. I looked up at Jesus and He was hanging there like always, looking bad like He just lost a knife fight. He is no help so I lean on the rail, wrap my hand around my fist and rest my cheek there. I cannot believe how tired I am. 'Zeferina,' I say.

"Her shoulders start to shake and she is making little sounds. I want to go to her, but I do not. 'Zeferina, it is me, Hilario Lázaro, from the excavation.'

"'I know who it is,' she says without looking. She doesn't sound happy to see me.

"'I've been thinking about you all this time,' I say. 'I miss you.'

"'You will be over that when you see me.'

"'I can see you,' I said. 'And still I miss you.'

"'I want to die.'

"Now she is really crying. 'No,' I said. 'You can't do that. There is too much of that already.' It is all I can do not to start crying myself. And then, before I know what I am saying, I said, 'I will help you.'

"She looked at me for the first time then and she did not look like herself. Her eyes were red, her cheek was purple and her lip was split open. I understood then she was not married and that this must be the professor's child she carried. I was angry to see her hurt like this and I slapped the altar rail. 'Who did this?' I said. She covered her face again and was just crying. I was thinking to myself who could do such a terrible thing to such a beautiful face. 'Your father,' I said.

"'He says I can go to Hell and he will hold the door.'

"'Your mother?'

"'She is only crying and crying.'

"'Well, there's no Hell where I live.'

"'Of course there's a Hell,' she said. 'I'm in it right now.'

"'Not where I live, and it's only a day's walk from here. Maybe you'd like to visit? Right now we have a baby burro. He is a very sweet burrito and everyone knows there are no burritos in Hell.'

"'You're teasing me.'

"'No. This burrito is the sweetest one you ever saw. Wait until you see his little nose. Maybe your baby would like to play with him.'

"'My life is ruined and you're making jokes. What's wrong with you? Go away!'

"'Nothing's wrong with me, but your man on the cross here is having a very hard time. There's nothing I can do for Him, but I can help you, Zeferina. I want to be near you for the rest of my life.'

"'I am a sinner.'

"'Who cares?'

"'Who cares? Jesus does!'"

Abuelo stopped then and said, "I have to tell you, Héctor, I couldn't believe I was having this conversation, but at least she was talking to me. So I point to el Señor who is bleeding from every hole and I say, 'Look at Him, will you? Look at the problems He's having — and so many. Do you really think He's worrying about you?'

"'He is bleeding for my sins.'

"'No, chica, you are. And one crucifixion is enough.'

"'Es una blasfemia.'

"'Hermana, la blasfemia is thinking you are the center of His attention. Look at this world we're in — los Nazis, el Comunismo. Fighting and bombs. What are we in all of this? Nada. Insectos. He has no time for us. That poor cabrón can't even help Himself.'"

"She was looking at me like I had horns but I would not be stopped. 'And look at her.' I pointed to María who was off to one side in her glass box. 'Is she married to the father of *her* child?' Zeferina jumped like she was being burned but stayed where she was, forehead pressed into her knuckles. 'Does it matter?' Now I am almost shouting. 'No! She loves her baby, doesn't she? The baby is fat and beautiful, yes? And white! Now that is the real miracle.'

"Zeferina began to cry again. 'You are beautiful too,' I said to her. 'Como un milagro.'

"Ooni'ya, I never said such words to anyone before. But many things were coming clear to me — most of all that I'm in love with Zeferina and not just the idea of her. 'Come home with me,' I say. 'Right now, today. I have a place for you and I will take care of you and be a father to your baby. I promise. If you want we can be married also.'

"She did not say yes to this, but she did not say no either so I left the church to find her father. It was hard to leave her because I was afraid she would disappear and I was not strong enough to lose another that day. When I asked some people outside for the home of Zeferina, they would not answer because Latuxí was far from the main road and the people there were suspicious of anyone they didn't know. Finally, I found a boy who would tell me and I went alone to Zeferina's house to speak with her father. The house was small and by itself, and in front was grass cut down close to the ground by a burro which was tied with a long rope to a dead guayaba tree. On the edge of the yard were calla lilies growing for the market, covered over with weeds. There were chickens running, but besides the burro, no other animals. The house had only one window and this was covered by a goatskin with the hair scraped off and nailed in with wooden pegs. The door was made of cane stems with adobe to fill the cracks, and the hinges were of leather. It was a poor man's house, even for that time.

"I stood outside in the grass and announced myself, and a man who must be Zeferina's father came to the door. He was drunk with no shirt and his eyes were red and hot. I told this man who I was, that I understood he had difficulties with his daughter and that I could make a home for her in my village. 'Take her,' he said, waving his hand down the road. 'Take her to Hell if you like. She has no home here.'

"At that moment, a woman ran out of the house and threw herself down in front of me. If she was drunk I could not tell because the man had beaten her too, and her face was covered in dirt and tears and something that looked like cornmeal. She was on her knees in the short grass, pulling at my pants leg and crying, begging me not to take her daughter from her. But the man had no patience for this and he pulled her to her feet by the hair, hit her again and drove her back inside, shouting, 'I swear to God, if I see that coño in my yard I will kill her with these hands!'

"Then he looked at me, holding his two fists. He was breathing hard and I could see in his eyes that, drunk or not, he was a dangerous man. I did not want to fight him so I took my hat off and held it in front of me. I don't think he was expecting this and he reached out his hands to me with the palms showing and said, 'To her family, to this village, to the Virgin — that girl has brought only shame and misfortune. After two harvests we still have no corn to sell and barely enough for seed. Why? A month ago our calf died. Why? Now the gringo is dead and there is no more money for our family. Why are these things happening to us?'

"The man looked at me as if I might know the answer. 'With your permission,' I said, 'I will take your daughter, and maybe things will be better.'

"And so I did this — took Zeferina home with me through the mountains. For a month she cried, but her belly grew, and at night while she slept I could feel the baby in there kicking. I tried to imagine what it would look like, but all I could see was the professor's big mustache. I'm telling you this was no simple thing for me and I wondered, with her sadness and a child that was not mine, if I had made a bad mistake. I tried to make her comfortable and my mother tried to feed her, but her heart was broken and everything she wanted was far away and impossible to have. To make things worse, she would not let me touch her except her back because it was hurting from the baby. Ooni'ya, I have always been good with animals so that is what I did — with my hands I calmed the muscles there, and in this way she came to know me. In time, I came to know her — very well, but it was the baby who first lifted her from sadness."

There is more, but now you know a little bit about how my abuelo came to be with my abuela, and about her baby who is my father. Sí, AnniMac, this Professor Payne is blood to me, and whatever was in him — good and bad — is somewhere in me also.

One day, after Abuelo told me all this, I was alone with my father and I asked him about the professor and why didn't he try to find his family.

"Look at me," he said. "You think they would accept me?"

"You could explain —"

"What, that I'm their bastard half brother from Mexico?"

"If you told them about Abuela —"

"And what was she? A gringo's milk cow. Nothing more."

"You don't know that," I said.

"And you know less."

"Abuelo showed me his picture," I said. "You look like him."

"And see the good it does me." He hawked up and spat. "I cannot speak his language, I cannot read it, and I am not welcome in his country. *Biche*," he said, like it was a curse, "green eyes is all I got from him."

After this I looked at my father in a different way. To have a gringo father with so much — money, respect, education — and to be cut off from all of it, for Papá this was almost worse than having no father at all. His mother loved him of course, and Abuelo was a good man most of the time, but in our pueblo to be half gringo and a bastard also es una maldición. Our deportation, the ice storm with the dead coyote, not being able to make his letters — all these things and more were connected in my father's mind. Each one, another punishment for being born.

21

Sat Apr 7 — 07:31

In here, we are not dying, we are evaporating. The weakness — from
no water and bad air — it creeps in like a fog, pulling the life out of
us with every breath. I know this because when I move away from
the pipe, I can feel it — a drifting out of myself. I am used to the heat
because up in the Sierra, the sun is closer than God, but in here it
reminds me of a game we played after school when I lived in the
pueblo. Chuy, the witch's son, taught it to us. He called it Ojo de
Dios, God's Eye, and you play it with the sun and a piece of glass. It
is like a test — how much pain, and the smell is terrible. I still have

the marks. I haven't thought of it in a long time but I am thinking of it now. This and the water.

Dying of thirst, there is a madness that takes over a person. I heard it, but I tried not to see it. You will take off your clothes no matter who is there and you will suck on anything to make the saliva come — coins, scapulars, your wedding ring, maybe some stone. It is like being a baby again — you turn into one big mouth. The rest of you is only there to carry it around, and the more thirsty you are the bigger your mouth grows, the rest of you getting smaller and smaller and farther away until you disappear and only the thirst is left.

Any of those who still have the voice to speak simply beg for water — Please, God. Señor, por favor, just one drink. And every time is like the stabbing from that nun in the basilica because I am the devil in the corner who will not give it. In here, our prayers go nowhere. God cannot hear us. Or will not. But I am still praying — for someone to find us, for the bars to come back, because you are César's friend with the American code. And because I have nothing else. Is this why my mother does it? Is this what brings her to her knees? Tell me, AnniMac, do you understand the connection between believing and desperation? Would you ever do such a thing like this? Who do you believe in? What do you believe?

My Abuela Zeferina was such a strong believer she would set herself on fire to show her devotion to the Virgin, and she is not the only one. Five years ago was the last time we made the pilgrimage to the pueblo of Juquila, high in the southern mountains where the Virgin appeared to a campesina washing the clothes. Abuela made a new gown for her and she wanted to offer it in person, but the waiting list to dress Juquila is long. In her church there is a room stacked to the ceiling with tiny gowns. Not hundreds, AnniMac — thousands. Juquila has clothes to wear until Judgment Day.

In the plaza by Juquila's church are tables with mounds of clay and from this the pilgrims make their own milagros—a leg that must be healed, an airplane for a safe journey, a sick relative in bed. For these blessings they bring offerings of money and food and dresses, and some, like my abuela, dance in the dark street with rockets shooting out of their heads. They say the Chinese invented fireworks, but it is Oaxaqueños who dance with them and become that fire. For the saints we build castles of fireworks as tall as a church, and for Juquila some women will carry smaller ones on their heads. The coheteros build them from wet cane that you can bend into any form—a church, a bull, a ghost, a virgin. To this you attach the spinning wheels made also from the cane, and then the rockets. Some shoot high into the air and explode in all the colors, and others are flaming jets. It is the jets that turn the wheels and set the castillo in motion.

Abuela knew it was the last time she would make this pilgrimage and she was determined to dance on the plaza in front of Juquila's church. It was December the eighth, the night of her fiesta, and there was a crowd of pilgrims—many hundreds—with a band of twenty horns. Abuela wore a green skirt, wide at the bottom so it made a bell when she turned, and over that was a huipil she wove herself on the loom and sewed with flowers. Even as a vieja she was beautiful in the way she moved and held herself. Abuelo was with her and he gave her a shot of mezcal before she went out—to light the fire inside. Then she checked the wrap of her rebozo on her head one more time. The coheteros had the basket ready with the castillo—a statue of Juquila—with all the fireworks in place and the fuses connected to set them off in the proper sequence as she danced. It was Abuelo who helped her set the basket and castillo on her head and walked with her into the plaza. A cohetero followed, and when he asked if she was ready she smiled Yes and closed her eyes. Then he lit the fuse.

This is the signal for the calenda band to play, drums and tuba keeping time while the clarinets scream like rockets and the trumpets sound the blasts. All eyes are on Abuela who is now a tower, a dancing castillo four meters high. She moves carefully in the empty street, dancing simple steps because there is a bomb up there. It is a kind of duel that way between her and the fire, and no one will come near because it is hers alone to do. She will make her own light now. When the rockets go off, they fly from her head in all directions, exploding over the street, the church, the band — everywhere sparks and fire and bits of burning this and that coming down like falling stars, reflecting in the church glass, in the shining bell of the tuba, maybe burning a hole in your jacket or in Abuela's huipil. And when she feels it coming through, burning her skin, and all that fire and heat is sucking the air out of her lungs, she shows no pain but only prays harder and keeps dancing because she is not your grandmother anymore, she is a Zapotec volcano sending a message direct to the Virgin and you are her witness en el centro de la creación.

It is now the jets begin to fire and the wheels on her head begin to turn, faster and faster until they disappear into halos of burning light spinning in the dark all around Juquila, until there is so much smoke and fire and color it's hard to see the person anymore, or to know how she can breathe, or even to believe that inside all of this is your own abuela dancing, proving her devotion in body and fire and prayer. We are all clapping now, cheering for her courage and beauty and faith because she has stopped time and with her dancing freed us from the past, the future, all the burdens we must bear. But only for a moment — the spinning wheels will slow, the last rockets will fly, and the bamboo frame will collapse upon itself in little fires burning here and there. Maybe the music grows softer and stops or maybe it doesn't, but you go into the street then and help your abuela take that smoking basket down.

This doesn't happen only once. Many women go out to do this dance and prove their faith, to send this glorious message to the Virgin they love and who they are certain loves them more. And if you are still there and awake at three in the morning, you will see a strange and wonderful sight. Most people have gone home now, but there may be a cohetero with some rockets left, reminding Juquila and God in heaven that we are still HERE. And of course Juquila is there in her shrine, on her little altar with flowers everywhere, even on the roof, and her robes fresh and shimmering with loops of orchids around her neck, a crown upon her head, hair flowing to her feet in a dark river.

Juquila is never left alone, and in the coldest, quietest part of the night, just before sunrise, is the time for "Las Mañanitas," the morning song, our birthday song. And for this the band comes dressed in black from head to boots, with wide sombreros and wool ponchos over their small jackets, and black pants with silver conchos down the side, made to catch the light and throw it back. Not two, not four, but eight of them appear in the solitude of the night. They are mariachis, but here, at this hour in the dark street with their black suits and cases, they look like some strange vaquero priests come with their tools to make a sacrifice. One by one, they enter the church taking off their great sombreros that can together fill a room. They set these on the chairs and their cases on the floor, and they take out their guitars and guitarróns, a big bass, a violin and one small silver trumpet. Then they arrange themselves around our Juquilita to sing and play for her. There is no audience but her small holiness and our great loneliness, unless you are there watching from the door, listening to the deep sweet voices and that falsetto weaving in, all of them rising and falling together and around, weaving a braid of sound — eight voices making love in the air and offering it to Juquila —

On the morning you were born
All the flowers bloomed at once
And the nightingales sang at the baptismal font
To honor you, our finest one.

And more like this:

With flowers and herbs, today I come to greet you.
Today for your saint's day we come to you and sing.
From the stars in the sky I need to lower two,
One with which to greet you and the other for goodbye.

For an hour and more they sing, filling that mountain church which is made for song so everything and everyone is multiplied in there, building on each other until their bodies and skulls are vibrating like the instruments and the church is transformed into one big box of sound, singing from itself through the open doors and windows, out into the valley to mix with all the others gone before. And when they are finished, these dark men cross themselves, pack their instruments and go away into the night, eight sombreros floating over laughter and a bottle passing. It is their secret gift to her, and us too.

I ask you, AnniMac, how can Juquila not hear this? What god could bear to turn away?

Sat Apr 7 — 08:01

What does it mean when the only proof of living is the pain you feel? I can see my abuela, eighty years old with the fire all around her, dancing as her lungs burn and her skin also. The heat did not weaken her, it made her stronger, because what is faith unless it is tested?

22

Sat Apr 7 — 08:17

My abuelo is dead now since November, but two days before he closed his eyes for the last time, he asked me for his bag. It was made from the ball sack of a burro and he kept it always on his *payu* — a belt of red cotton that only fiesta dancers wear now. He was in the bed so much at the end that his bag was hanging from a nail on the wall. I got it down for him and with his eyes he told me to untie it. Then he took it from me, reached inside and pulled out this little clay head, the one I carry with me now. It's old — a thousand years or more, broken off with an ear gone, but you can see it is a jaguar by the teeth and the eyes.

"The professor let me keep this one," said Abuelo, "because it is Zapotec and so am I. Now, I am going in the ground soon, but this was down there long enough already." He held it out to me. "I think if he had the chance to know you, your gringo abuelo would want for you to have this. There are some ways you remind me of him — the way you hold your head when you are listening. And your curiosity. Be careful where it leads you."

Taking that little clay head from my abuelo's hand made the tears come to my eyes because I knew he would never carry it again. In that moment I saw only dead men holding this, passing it on from one to the next since long before my grandfathers, and who knows when I will be one more?

In my abuelo's last days we would sit together outside his house, sometimes for hours saying nothing, looking out across the valley at the green ridges all around. Just being with him was enough. It was on one of these days in the beginning of November that the army ants came. This time they took the tree of golden flowers that stood behind the granero where Abuelo stored his corn. From there, the ants came marching right across the steps of Abuelo's house in a perfect line, one behind the other by the hundreds and the thousands, each with its own golden flag. Day after day they came, waving their golden flags until there was nothing left of that tree but the bare branches. After three days, Abuelo looked at the dead tree and at the line of ants disappearing into the forest and he said, "It is the same like us, no?"

Sat Apr 7 — 08:53

To Lupo and the coyotes I say, Chingate, no estoy muerto. With every word I say this. But what can I offer you, AnniMac, when I am asking for so much? Salvation is no small thing. How could I know that water and light were so important? Who is keeping me alive right now is my abuelo. So he is my offering to you — his strength and this story he told me only one time.

In those last weeks, Abuelo was pissing the bed like the Apache was leaking oil. It was me who took out his petate every day and washed it down so I was glad the wind moves through that old house so easy. Every morning it wasn't cold, he sat on a little bench outside, leaning against the wall of his house, facing south, warming himself in the sun and many times lizards would be there with him doing this also. The adobe in those walls is old and made from the dirt around the pueblo so you can see all the things going into it. Along with the rocks and mud and grass is the sole of an old huarache, pieces of clay pots, the jawbone of a goat, a cotton rag, some wire — it is the story of our pueblo in there. By Abuelo's head where he sat, there was the funnel hole of a spider, but it never bothered him. So many creatures fell on my abuelo or crawled across him in his life, like he was only another piece of the Sierra. Even scorpions he would not kill, but only cursed and swept aside. So many times in my life I sat like this with him and saw these things framing the picture of his face with all those lines in it. For me those lines were a map, helping me to find my way through.

In front of his bench there was always a stump of wood with a couple of nails sticking out, and this was his workbench where he carved little animals, mostly burros and bulls. Sometimes he would paint them, but paint is expensive and at the end his hands were not that steady. For him the knife was easier. When I came to visit I'd bring some small nails with me and this is how he attached the legs — so close it was hard to see the joint. The horns and tail went in with no glue, only sap from the tree. Most of this work he would do with a machete and a goat knife, but he had also an old saw blade and a file with handles made from corncobs. It was something, what he could do with only these, and it helped him pass the time. One morning, when the sun was warm and he was out of nails, he told me the story —

"It was not long after el jaguar Pancho Villa was assassinated," he said. "They shot him in a Dodge, you know. I don't know the model, but after that we called it el Dodge Emboscado."

Abuelo looked at me and winked. It was a joke he had not thought of in almost a hundred years, but I told you his Spanish name is Hilario.

"I had maybe eighteen years then, so that will make it 1925 or 1928, but who can count it now. Ever since la Revolución many men — not just soldiers and assassins — were carrying guns because there were so many of them around. People were used to this from all the fighting, and many men felt something was missing without some iron on them. I didn't have a gun then because it is too expensive, but I can also see how the man who has one is often getting shot himself. You know what we called a bullet in those days?" He was smiling to himself. "A nice little warm one. It makes it sound not so bad, almost like a woman."

He closed his eyes then and hummed to himself, tapping his finger on his knee. Then he began to sing in a breaking voice, "I'm off to battle with my .30-30 / I entered the rebel ranks / If it's blood they ask for, blood I'll give them / For the people of our nation."

He was humming and frowning, searching for the words. After a moment I said his name. He opened his eyes then and was surprised to see me. "Abuelito," I said, "what are you singing there?"

"'Carabina Treinta-Treinta.' This talking reminds me of it. Many men had the Winchester rifle in those days and that song was very popular. I always liked the tune. It's about us, you know." He closed his eyes again, nodding to the invisible music and reaching back in his mind. His eyebrows lifted and he smiled, waving his arm to the rhythm. *"We're headed for Chihuahua! Your black saint is leaving town. And if I catch some bullet. Go and mourn me on hallowed* ground. ¡Viva Mexico! ¡Viva! I'm off to battle with my .30-30. I entered the rebel ranks. Yes, that's it. Más o menos."

"I think I know that song," I said. "I heard it on the radio."

"On the radio? Me lleva la chingada. Ooni'ya, if you like that, I must sing for you 'The Gravedigger.'"

"Abuelo," I said, "you were telling me a story — from when you were a young man."

"Yes, that's right," he said, and I could see him thinking again — an old man with so many things who has put one of them down and can't remember where.

"Ooni'ya. In this time I have no wife or child and I am short, but not as short as now. It is the market in Tlacolula — Sunday, and it must be April or May because it is hotter than hell and I am going there to sell some turkeys — you will see why I remember this, and also the terrible music. Well, I had a late start that morning." He smiled and took a drink from his thumb. "Already I was walking many hours in the heat from the village with a headache and my burro and the turkeys in the baskets, one on each side, and I heard the music even before I came into the Zócalo. This music — if you must call it that — is caused by an accordion and when I get to the Zócalo I look for it because I am wondering to myself, Who can be making such sounds? It is like an animal doing this. Ooni'ya, you know the cantina opposite the church? Sitting by the wall there is an indio I don't recognize. He is the one with the accordion and he is playing 'La Adelita' over and over, so out of tune it is like he is torturing her. Maybe the accordion is broken or probably he is drunk. And now that I am close I can hear also that this cabrón is trying to sing! It is a kind of moaning that is so wrong I think he must be an imbecile and I don't understand why he is tolerated. Well, there are some light-skin gachupines there also — younger sons of hacendados — drinking aguardiente at the cantina. They are sitting under the arcade and I can still see their cántaro on the table there and the clay copas all around. But it is before noon so normally no one is too drunk yet.

"Ooni'ya, I walk past the cantina with my burro and the turkeys and I hear one of these young machos shout, '¡Paisano!' At first I don't think he speaks to me because why would I think such a thing? I have nothing of his and nothing to say to such a man. Also, this donkey music is a distraction. Again I hear, '¡Paisano!' and still I do not look. Then, 'You! Sawed-off! Mud-in-your-ears — with the turkeys!'

"I hear them all laughing now and I look over there and then at one man in particular. 'Yeah, that's right,' he says to me. And then to his friends, 'I'm telling you, those little fuckers know much more Spanish than they let on. ¡Joven!' he says to me. 'I want to buy a turkey!' He laughs at this and his friends smile into their cups and shake their heads. 'What else you hiding in there, amigo? Your sister maybe?'

"The man saying these things is a little bit older than me and Spanish by his look — at least the father. Anyway, he is the kind who has done nothing and thinks already he is some kind of pesado. I can see this by the way he dresses, like a charro who lost his horse! He has goatskin pants with the conchos down the side and a fine gamuza jacket that shows his waist and the silver on his belt. On his high boots he has the kind of spurs no workingman will wear, they are like wagon wheels back there and very shiny. On top he has a Tejas sombrero so big with so much gold stitching it looks to be from a woman. He also has a sword on his belt which is not so common at that time. Maybe he is a relative of someone visiting from some other place, I don't know, but I am looking at him and wondering where is the fiesta.

"Luego, it is so hot already and I don't want a problem with these men, so I turn straight ahead and walk. Now there is a wagon by the cantina with a load of ollas in it and hanging on the side is a broken yoke strap for the oxen. The strap is made of oxhide — very heavy and wider than a belt. This pendejo sees he has an audience now so he gets up, takes the broken strap from the wagon and he walks toward me, wrapping one end of the strap around his hand. I walk faster, trying to get into the market before he can reach me, but he sees this and moves more quickly and cuts me off. 'Where you going, little friend? That's no way to treat a good customer.' Then he looks over toward the cantina and the men there, smiling and nodding at them like he said something very clever. 'Now, let's see those turkeys!'

"He grabs the lid off one of my baskets and this surprises the burro who turns suddenly and steps on his foot. Now his friends are really laughing because this one is wearing very nice boots that go up past his knee. It is embarrassing for him and also painful so he draws back and whips the burro across the hind legs with the strap. The burro leaps forward and it's all I can do to control him. This is also upsetting the turkeys and I tell that chingado he can't hit my burro. 'The hell I can't!' he says, and he does it again. I am trying to get between him and the burro who is bucking now and also trying to keep the turkeys in the baskets. I am shouting at him to stop and trying to push him away with my free hand and then he tries to hit me! Ooni'ya, it is too much to bear and when he swings the second time I catch the end of the strap.

"'*Bíttu!*' I say, and there we are — him at one end and me at the other with just an arm length between us. He is pulling hard on the strap, but I was strong then and will not let go. He is much taller than me, especially with his boots and hat, but our eyes meet and lock like dogs will do. That moment I think is worse for him than for me because he has so much to lose. For such a man it is intolerable to be challenged by an indio. You understand la Revolución is finished, but in those days campesinos are still stepping aside for the Spanish — any güero — taking off their sombreros and looking only at the ground. Ooni'ya, he calls me a very rude name, drops his end of the strap and reaches for his sword. He is shouting something like, 'You little pagan prick! I'm going to beat your black ass back to the campo!'

"He didn't intend to kill me I don't think, but a beating from a sword is very serious and can do some bad damage. I let go of the burro then and *Ya* it away. Now we are alone in the street and I am trying to make some distance between me and this loco from who knows where. Some people are backing up under the trees. A couple of his friends are telling him to come back and sit down, but others are laughing and cheering and clapping their hands. To make things worse, that cabrón with the accordion won't shut up, and it is so hot the sun is its own burden. I have never been in such a situation like this, but you know my father fought in la Revolución and it is a waste of a man. He died fighting chilitos like this, and now, after all that, here is one more trying to slap me down like a woman — como una *béccu'nà* — and many people are seeing it. Ooni'ya, you cannot let such a thing go by without an answer, not if you want to live a normal life in that place. If you do nothing, every man will treat you that way. That is how it is. So now the people are watching to see what I will do — to see how I am made.

"My burro is gone, and now it is only me and this gachupín alone in the street. The sun is so high we make barely a shadow, only a dark hole around our feet. I remember the charro's sombrero is just a circle moving and changing shape across the ground — and the sword arm coming out. It is strange what you notice in the dying situation, the things you think of. The charro is slapping the flat of his sword on his palm and coming toward me — not straight on but in a circle, the way the hawk is climbing the sky. I am moving too because he is pushing me, leading this dance, but I can see that his boots with all that jewelry make him a bit clumsy. It can also be the aguardiente causing this. Maybe he is hoping I will run, I don't know. There is space in the road for me to do this, but it is not a real possibility — not with all those people watching. It is like that strap is still between us, holding us together. I can feel my heart inside me and my mouth is dry, but finally I find something to give back to this pendejo who has shamed me in public and hurt my burro. 'Why does your mother dress you that way?' I say to him. 'Is she blind?'

"I did not say it loud, but I think others besides him heard it and now he must defend his mother or whatever she is. 'You will die for that,' he says, and he means it. I know this because he is not shouting anymore. These words are just for me. That is how such men are and now there is no going back. Someone must finish it. Ooni'ya, you know I carry the machete always and on that day I had it on the strap over my shoulder. Let me tell you, that machete was an old one, the kind they call el Collins — made in America. Those ones held their edge and lasted a long time. You know I had that Collins for many years already, in my hand for many hours almost every day so it is like a part of my own body — my right hand, and that's where it is before I think of it. The charro sees this and he stops slapping his palm and prepares his blade. Some people are afraid, shouting at us to stop, but there are others there who are wanting to see some blood that day. It is cheaper than la corrida, no? And a dead indio will be something interesting to discuss at la comida.

"Ooni'ya, with two blades showing no one is coming near us. It is a strange picture, you know — one that no one in that town saw before. There is me, even shorter than you in dirty white campo clothes with no shoes and a straw sombrero, and this charro, tall and pale as a güero, looking like he is going to a parade — together in a duel! It is not an equal situation. If he kills me, maybe he pays a small fine, but if I kill him, I will be executed for sure, maybe shot on the spot. Also, the charro's sword is longer and so is his arm and this gives him an advantage, but also some false confidence.

"It is very quiet now, except for that fucking accordion, until someone yells, 'Shut up, will you!' Then the accordion makes a surprising sheep noise like it is being hit or thrown and it is finished. This is some kind of signal for the charro and everything happens quickly then — the circle growing tighter, the charro attacking, stabbing first to drive me back and then sweeping his sword around and across with such force like he will open me up or cut me in half. Ooni'ya, I have quick feet — you need them for dancing and to keep the animals from stepping on you — and I jump back, turning away like this, to my left. I can hear his sword behind me in the air, and I am lucky this time, but now my back is to him. He comes after me again, roaring now, swinging his sword up and over his head like an ax, and it is in this moment that one of his fine boots slips just a little on some stones. He must catch himself then, so down I go, as low as I can, like I am cutting cornstalks, and I come back like *this*."

Abuelo is so old, but his mind is eighty years away, on that hot street in Tlacolula. It is hard for him to stand now, or to bend so low, but his machete is there by him like always and he wants me to see how it was. I also think he wants to see it again himself. He makes me stand like the charro and then, with the machete in his hand he shows me his move, sweeping the blade around, away from his body and back, aiming for my right knee.

"I know very well how the animal comes apart," he says, "and I want to get this one on the ground as fast as possible so I go for the tendons. I catch him only with the tip of the blade, but it is enough. The Collins is heavy and sharp, of such good American steel, and it does not stop. One moment that charro is charging and I am a dead man, and the next his leg folds up like it has no bones — so quick he can't understand what happened. I tell you, that macho was on the ground como *Ya!* And his sword came down hard in the sand. I jumped away, not sure if he can come for me again, but he is finished — his leg is loose below the knee and the blood is running hard. It is a surprise for everyone, including me, to see this big charro stirring the dust in his fine clothes and making sounds like a girl.

"Of course with so much fighting in the past years, people are used to blood and already some men are there trying to calm him, offering him water and aguardiente, and one is with a goat knife cutting pieces from his pants to tie off the bleeding. Myself, I have no damages, but my heart is beating like the walls are not strong enough to hold it. Never again — not even with a woman — have I such a hammering in there. Now that the charro is on the ground without his big sombrero, I can see better how young he is, how soft his mustache, and I wonder what will happen to me. Right then, one of his friends from the cantina comes running into the street. I am afraid he may attack me and I raise my Collins again, but he is interested only in the sombrero. It is lying there, upside down and dusty, and he picks it up, brushing it off like it is injured too — like it is the flag of the republic. Maybe it is his father's, I don't know. I put my machete away, I didn't even think to clean it, and that is when I notice a strange wind blowing on my back. When I touch there with my hand I understand that my shirt is cut open.

"Ooni'ya, because it is market day there is a truck there from the army — the first one in Tlacolula — and they use it to take that poor cabrón to Oaxaca City. He is alive in the hospital there for seven days. In that time, they cut off his leg, but the infection goes to his heart all the same. I tell you, the authorities were fair with me — so many witnesses, and it is clear I am not trying to kill, but I think what saved me was going to confession. The priest knew the young man's family and after I confessed to him he defended me. He would not say it to me himself, but I heard later that this young man's father was ashamed of him, that he was drinking so much and making problems for many people, not only for me. But one thing the priest said to me alone and I never forgot it — 'Hilario, if you are prudent, you will not speak of this again.'

"You know I never want for this to happen, but I can tell you from experience, God's own shoes are better than Spanish leather. That day, it was my feet that kept me from dying like my father. I hope you are never in such a situation, but there is a saying from that time that I find to be true — *No es el tigre, como lo pintan.* It isn't a tiger, no matter how it's painted. With a nail I cut these words into the blade of my Collins and it was good luck for me. Even after I broke that machete in the forest many years later, I never had such problems again. It is a pity about the Collins, I could never find another, and these new ones coming out of Nicaragua are crap."

I asked my abuelo why he never told me this story before and he said, "Because I listened to that priest. Maybe it is the only time I do, but he protected me, and it is because of him I walked away from that. Those hacendados have power and influence and they can do anything they like to a campesino. The padre was right — if they hear I am telling that story, it will sound like I am bragging and it will cause a problem for sure. It is a long way to the market, you know, especially when you're walking, and there are many places for an ambush. *Xútsilatsi!* You're dead before you hear the shot."

At the end of November, Abuelo died in his sleep. A neighbor made his coffin and I dug his grave. The family came and Papá offered to help me dig. I knew he didn't want to so I did it alone. It was better this way because I cried like it was my father I was burying. In my mind when I was digging I saw him at the excavation in Latuxí — Abuelo with his shovel, making his way down into the ground until I couldn't see him anymore, until he found something deep under there that was softer than stone but harder than clay. I understood

then the bargain he was making with the Sierra, with the earth—
one Jaguar Man for another.

I know how my abuelo died because I was there, but my Grandfather Payne died far away with no one to explain it. Always there was a piece missing and that piece is in el Norte together with the Jaguar Man. This troubled my abuelo also, but the closest he came to an answer was the newspaper. "Two weeks after I brought Zeferina home," he told me, "I went to Tlacolula for the Sunday market and I asked my friend the bus driver if he had any newspapers. He did, and in one of them there was a story in the obituaries telling of the professor's life and his work at Aztec sites in Puebla and at our site in Latuxí. In there also I read that his death was not an accident like the priest said. The newspaper said he did it himself with a pistol. Always I wondered what could cause such a strong and healthy man to die in the middle of his life. It is a hard question. Because he was a gringo and a jefe there are things about him I could never know, but if it is so, if the professor took his own life, it would make him the only man I know to do such a thing, and it puts a shadow over everything. I didn't tell Zeferina about this for a long time. Or your father. Not until he was thirteen and he heard some people in the pueblo talking. Then he asked me why his eyes were green like a gringo's and not brown like mine. That was another hard question, and after I answered it nothing was the same between us.

"And the reason I am telling you," he said to me, "is because wherever you are going, you must know what you are made of, and who."

These green eyes like my father and the professor I do not have. I look only like my mother's son. If there is gringo in me, it's hiding on the inside. And now I'm wondering where.

Abuelo told me a strange story about him once, and always I

wondered if it was true. The professor was talking to Abuelo about Diego Rivera and his murals telling the story of Mexico. In one of them is the great pyramid at Tenochtitlán, and my grandfather told my abuelo how Rivera imagined it in the time of Moctezuma before the coming of Cortés — so many being sacrificed and their blood running down the steps like a waterfall.

"One night," said Abuelo, "the professor told me how Señor Rivera, he wonders if the Aztecs are only sacrificing these people or if they are eating them also. Well, Rivera is a man who will try anything. Just look at him — that mouth and that panza — nothing is safe. Señora Kahlo was brave or crazy to sleep in the same bed with a man like that. Who can say if it is true, but the professor and Señor Rivera were explorers, young and curious men trying to understand what it means to be Mexicano, and one of them says, 'I must try it.' And the other says, 'Yes, we must.'

"This is what the professor tells me," said Abuelo, "that Señor Rivera wants to know how it is to be a priest up there on the pyramid — to take a man, break his chest open and pull the living heart from his body with only your bare hands and a stone blade. He wants to know that moment with the manfruit beating in your hand, wants to feel that muscle still alive with all its colors bright and shining, beating and beating because it doesn't know anything else, beating because to not beat is to not be." And Abuelo is saying, "No, Profesor. No es verdad."

But it *is* true, AnniMac. Oaxaqueños know all about it because we are doing this same operation at home — pulled alive from our family, our pueblo, and put in a stranger's hands to beat and beat until we can't. Since forever.

And the professor says to my abuelo, "Sí, mi amigo, es verdad. Mira." He takes out his wallet then, and pressed in there, flat like a phonecard, is an ear. From a man. It is old and dry, but it is for sure an ear. Abuelo doesn't believe him completely because many men took such prizes in la Revolución and maybe this ear was from that time.

"You're not having a joke with me?" he says. "You and Señor Rivera really ate this?"

"Not this," says the professor. "The meat."

Maybe you can forgive my abuelo, but he asks him, "What does it taste like?"

"La ternera," says the professor. "Veal, but with a little something extra."

"Spicy?" says Abuelo. "¿Como la conchita?"

"No," he says. "Not exactly. In my experience it is unique."

"Would I like it?" asks Abuelo.

"I think you would need to be very hungry," says the professor. "Or a jaguar."

23

Sat Apr 7 — 10:59

The metal is hot now and I have folded my sweatshirt under my shoulder, my bag under my hip, and I have my sneakers on again. Because of the shape of the tank, my feet must go up the other side and I can't feel my toes so well anymore. I think this is pushing the blood into my brain and I can feel it in there — the pressure and the pounding — like my heart has moved into my skull. My stomach is clenched like a fist. I am lying on my side with my bottle for a pillow, and this keeps my face by the pipe where there is now a small breeze blowing. It is so hot, but I have discovered the secret to cooling my-self — it is in the eyes. That air — such soft feathers on my eyelids.

I keep them closed so there is less evaporation and because it hurts them now to be open. It is also why I speak so soft, trying to keep the water inside. I hope you can hear me. I understand now that this pipe is the only way back to the living world — to air and light and sound, and soon I will pass through it.

Sat Apr 7 — 11:33

Too hot for anything. One bar. César's battery one-third. His water three-quarters gone.

And breathing starts to feel like the sand on fire.

This and the waiting.

Sat Apr 7 — 14:22

Hello anybody. This is Héctor María de la Soledad Lázaro González. And I am still alive.

Sat Apr 7 — 17:31

I heard someone — a man, I think — begging to die. I could not recognize his voice because it was a raven talking, but I recognized the word — morir, and I put my fingers in my ears. I had water and air and I did not give it, and I put my fingers in my ears until the voice went away.

Sat Apr 7 — 17:42

In your country is it a sin to be a migrant? If it is a crime it must be a sin, no? Is this our punishment from your American god?

When I was small I asked my mother if I was a sinner. "You were born a sinner," she said. "But you are not old enough to confess.

Yet." But yet has come and gone, and you are my confessor now. Y este aquí es el confesionario más grande del mundo. I confess to you I would rather have some cool water right now than some long forever by the side of Jesus. To drown would be a blessing.

Sat Apr 7 — 17:54

It is a coffin in here. O una crisálida.

All of us had the same wish, but no one could see past themselves. We were together alone, no better than animals who in their panic only hurt themselves more. I saw a burro once, a young one, with his head caught in a barbed-wire fence. Every time he tried to pull his head out he cut himself, and every time he cut himself he panicked and cut himself more. The other burros in the field came over and stood with him, but what could they do, so that is how we found him in the morning — dead in the fence with the vultures on him and the burros standing all around. The only difference between us and that burro is we paid thirty thousand pesos. Too much for a coffin.

You change, you know, in such a situation. Who would want to be deaf and blind? But that is what I wished for today. Some of them went quietly — in the dark you don't even notice. But others threw away their beads and medallions, and I'm telling you, for a Mexicano that is the true sign of despair. They became angry, crazy, they hurt themselves and tore their clothes. I could not recognize their voices anymore. It sounded like animals in here attacking them, but they were attacking themselves. Because they saw things that weren't there. Because their skin stopped feeling like something that belonged to them. Because the pain you make upon yourself is easier to bear than the pain from the world outside. Some hit their heads on the tank again and again until there was only silence. Others clawed at the walls until the skin of their fingers came away —

until I came to understand the sound I was hearing was not the sound of fingernails but the sound of their own bones against the metal.

The human soul was not made to know such things and live.

Most of the people in this truck believed in God when they got to Altar. Even after the coyotes abandoned us they believed in Him and His mysterious plan. I know it because I heard their prayers. But now? If they could speak, I think they would raise their hands and say to you — to the pope himself, "*¿Qué plan?* God has no fucking plan!"

Unless it is to suffer.

24

Sat Apr 7 — 18:02

César — still he breathes, even with so little water. He is the strongest of us all. He is the only sound in here now. Listen . . .

Sat Apr 7 — 18:07

Are you still listening, AnniMac? Can you hear what I must tell you? When we were in Altar, César asked me for something and I would not give it. All this time I've had his phone I tried to make it up to him, tried to carry it and keep it safe. But I can't anymore. César's water is almost gone and I am out of time. This is César's confession, but it is my confession also. I will speak for him because he cannot. It's all I can do for him now.

This is how we came to the third part on that page of the Oaxaca Codex. If you walk along the wall there, past the beautiful corn growing and the men in masks with their needles and special plans, you will come to another figure. This one is a campesina — una Zapoteca como mi mamá, and César's also — no shoes, long braids, heavy skirt and huipil, a rebozo around her shoulders and another on her head. But this campesina's got a carabina, a .30-30, and she's pointing it at those men in the masks like she's going to blow those chingados away.

Midnight came and went past Lupo's garage and still we waited for the truck to be ready. All this time César talked to me, talking without stopping. "It's getting so late," I said. "Maybe we should rest for a while."

"No, hermano. You are from the Sierra and these are your people. You need to know what is happening."

Well, what am I going to say? It's hard to say no to César.

"Last summer," he said, "I went down to Oaxaca to ask people about their seed, what they were using and where they got it, and I discovered that yes, there is SantaMaize corn growing in the Sierra Juárez, right in my own pueblo. You could spot it from far away because the ears were so much bigger and, inside, the kernels were almost white. We were told this wasn't going to happen. We were told they were importing this corn for food only, not for planting, and that the government had promised to control it. So how did a truckload of this seed find its way into the Sierra? No one could explain this to me.

"And there was something else I learned from my father who had bought some of this corn himself. He grows two crops in the summer and after he harvested the first one he tried to replant some of the seed, but not a single one came up. He showed me and there was nothing in that milpa but weeds and beans with nowhere to climb. When I saw this I got scared because my father knows what he's doing and unless there's no rain his crops don't fail. So I took some of his new seed back to UNAM and when I studied the gene sequence I found the RIP, the cell toxin for Kortez400. I was in shock. What more do they want from us, Tito? Already we accepted their language, their government, their god. Must we beg them for food also?"

I didn't know what to say, and César didn't wait.

"So I have this data," he said, "but it's like finding a bomb and it's ticking and I don't know where to put it. The Ministry of Food, Agriculture and Rural Development doesn't want to hear about it because it will make them look bad, and SantaMaize doesn't want people knowing they have an unregulated product loose in the campo."

The beer was gone and I was feeling it along with the cold. "Cheche," I said, "I can see this is bad, but isn't it always like this? Already we buy water — at home even. If you don't make it yourself, you have to buy it, right?"

"¡Cabrón!" he said. "The corn is ours already! And the water is too. Can't you see the problem here?" César was quiet then. I thought he was waiting for me to say something, but he wasn't. "About a month ago," he said, "I had a dream. I was back in the pueblo, stripping and sorting a basket of corn just like when I was a kid. Everything was normal until I got to this one ear that was bigger than the others. In the dream I'm thinking, What's this? And when I pull the husk down, instead of kernels there are rows and rows of tiny white skulls."

A shiver came through me, and I knew the cold I felt was from César. In the Sierra, in almost every pueblo, there are certain people who can see things before they happen, who can feel things others cannot, and I understood then that César was such a one. In that moment, César — who I looked up to since I was fourteen — was asking me for something, something more than a favor. Always I wanted to have something he wanted — not so I could keep it from him, but so I could give it. Now he wanted me to see what he saw — to help him carry it. But the truck was going in an hour and I was so afraid, not only of the future in el Norte but also of the future César saw in Oaxaca. "OK," I said, "but what am I supposed to do? Why are you telling me?"

Well, AnniMac, his answer was a surprise. He said, "Because something might happen."

"Like what?" I asked.

César rubbed his face with both hands and looked up at the sky. He took a big breath and I could hear his chest shaking. "Last night," he said, "I had it again, that same dream. Listen to me now. Please. When I got back to D.F., I wanted so much to tell my colleagues what I had found, but my position there — the whole department — is funded by SantaMaize. I'm the only researcher from south of Puebla. Except for the janitors, I'm the only indio in that entire building. If I do anything or say anything that could discredit them, they'll send my ass right back to Oaxaca. For months I sat on this information wondering who I can trust. Maybe I am weak, but this was hard for me and finally, in January, I told my girlfriend who is here from the States. She's been in D.F. only six months and she says I must go to the press right away. I said to her, 'Do you know how much money is involved here? Do you know what happens to informants in Mexico? How many journalists are killed?' Then she tells me I should go to the foreign press, they will protect my identity. But how can I be sure of that? So I called my father. There is nothing but the radiophone in our pueblo so I reach the village office and they call his name over the loudspeakers. About five minutes later, my father comes to the phone. 'I am eating,' he says. 'Why aren't you?'"

"He's just like my abuelo," I say, but César wasn't listening —

"I don't want to give my father a lot of detail because he is standing there in the office, so I describe the situation in simple words. He reminds me that it is the Mexican government who gave me the scholarships and it is because of them I have knowledge to study these things. Then he says to me in Zapotec, 'César, you are a Mexicano and you are a scientist, but before this you are a Zapoteco from the Sierra Juárez. We fought the Aztecs. We gave this country Benito Juárez, and we still have our language. These are not accidents. You are the first one of us to study these things about the corn, and this is not an accident either. There is a reason you are speaking for us and for the corn. So don't forget — that is what you are doing. Now, la comida is getting cold already. Cuídate.'

"My father does not explain exactly what this 'reason' is, but I think he is saying I have a duty. I decide then that this is my country and if I have no faith in my power to protect it, then what am I doing here anyway? I made a plan to go to the Ministry of Food and Agriculture where I know people and I meet with the guy I trust the most. He's interested and asks to see my data, and I'm not sure what to do then. I have never been in such a situation. I decide to give him a copy because we came through university together and without the cooperation of the Ministry it will be impossible to fix this problem. What else could I do?

"I don't hear anything for a week and I am about to call when the Ministry calls me first. But it is not my friend on the phone — it is a man who says he is working with BioSeguridad, a new sister agency to the Ministry. He mentions my friend's name, tells me he is very impressed with my work and that he wants to speak with me. Well, I am suspicious about this, but I can see his phone number on the display and it has the same prefix as the Ministry so I am thinking it is probably OK. He asks me to meet him that afternoon in front of the Ministry building. This sounds safe enough, and — it seems ridiculous now, but it is a beautiful day that day, so I agree. I am still a bit suspicious so I call my friend to be sure, but he's not in his office. I call his cell, but there is only a message. What do I do? I decide to go anyway. What can happen in front of the Ministry? When I get there I realize I don't know this man's name or what he looks like, but a man there recognizes me immediately. 'Dr. Ramírez!' he says. 'Mucho gusto. I am Raúl López with BioSeguridad.' He shakes my hand and offers his card.

"I'm thinking his voice is not the same as the man on the phone, but I'm not sure. This guy is in his fifties and his chest and neck are thick like a bull's. He isn't tall but his hand swallows mine. He nods toward the street and a cab pulls up right away. 'We'll take this one,' he says. His arm is around me now and we are moving — or he is moving me, talking and talking. 'Do you know Café Verde in Coyoacán? Just opened. Fantastic coffee.' He is so close his head is touching mine. 'There's a waitress there. Incredible tits. Maybe you get lucky, get some extra sugar with your coffee today.'

"He is laughing and I am getting a bad feeling, but also a feeling like this is some kind of destiny, like this is a choice I made the moment I showed my data. For some reason I am afraid to resist him, afraid to make a scene in this public place, and all the time he is talking and moving toward the taxi. 'You know, my mother's family is from Oaxaca — from the Mixteca Alta, not so far from you — now those are some farmers! If you can grow corn up there with all that cactus, you can grow it anywhere. Don't you agree? Get in.'

"And then we are in the taxi. It was so quick, and I notice the doors locking as we pull into the traffic. Raúl opens his phone and sends what looks like a message of one letter, then he puts the phone away again. 'My boss is looking forward to meeting you.'

"I ask him if his boss is at Café Verde. It is so pathetic when I think about it now. 'We will go there after,' he says. Raúl never speaks to the taxista because the taxista already knows where we're going. And you know the traffic in D.F., well, this guy is a fucking magician, he is moving us through the city like there is no such thing as traffic, turning and turning so that I am not even sure where I am. Now Raúl isn't talking anymore. He only looks out the window like I don't exist, like his job is finished. I'm thinking about what can happen and what I can do. The door handle is there, easy to put my hand on, so I do it. Raúl is still looking out the window. I push on the lock, but it is on the children's setting and will not move. Whoever invented these did not think about all the situations. After maybe thirty minutes we arrive at a new office park. There is a gate there with an intercom and the taxista types in a code and says, 'Chaco.' The gate opens and we drive into a parking lot that has only one other car in it. The building is maybe ten floors, but it looks empty. I ask Raúl if this is the office of BioSeguridad and he says, 'Temporarily.'

"Now I am terrified. But I am more terrified to object, to try to run, because then the illusion of Raúl and Café Verde and the mother from the Mixteca will be completely broken and something much worse — some kind of truth — will replace it. The taxista parks away from the other car and Raúl is back now with his friendly voice. 'He's waiting for us,' he says. 'De acuerdo.'

"We all get out and this is the first time I get a good look at the taxista. He is not Danny Trejo, but he is a hard-looking guy with a lump under his coat and this is when I admit to myself what I was afraid of admitting before — 'Pendejo, you let yourself be kidnapped.' You hear about it all the time in D.F., but usually it's some businessman or his kid, you never think it's going to happen to you. But now it is, and I'm telling you, it's not like I imagined. It's like being caught in a powerful river, it has its own momentum and we are all in it together, floating along toward the door of the building which the taxista opens with a fob and then we're through it and into a stairwell, climbing up and up — the taxista in front, Raúl behind and me in the middle. I'm thinking now I'm going to be thrown off the roof and my legs are shaking under me so bad I must hold the railing, and when I do this I can feel both men noticing, bracing themselves for whatever I might do. All this time, I'm holding on to this tiny hope — as long as no one speaks there is still a chance it can go some other way — because this is a door I cannot bear to see closed.

"Somewhere around the eighth floor, the taxista opens a fire door and we go into an empty hall with no lights only a window at one end. The window is broken and there is a wind blowing so I have to cover my eyes because of the dust. There are doorways along the hall but no doors in them and, as we pass, I can see they all lead into empty concrete rooms with wires hanging from the ceiling. It is the same with the room we enter, only there is a man in there and he is sitting on a folding chair — the kind you take to the beach. It is the only chair in the room. Behind him is a big window, but it looks like the kind that can't open. The man is sitting next to a large spool of electric wire and he is using it for a table. On it is a cell phone, a bottle of Coke and my data — ten pages held together with a clip. I can see it's mine by the cover letter.

"I can tell you, when you think you are about to die, you notice the details and these are burned into my mind now. This man in the chair is maybe forty-five years old. He is dark — mestizo, but not from the south — with a forehead round like a pot. His hair is going and what is left is combed straight across. He is wearing a pink shirt with French cuffs but no jacket. His mouth is full and wide and crooked and when we get close I see his eyes are different shades of brown. Somehow this makes it seem like there are — not exactly two people there, but more than one. Raúl and the taxista are behind me now, I can feel them there between me and the door. The man in the chair picks up my data by the clip and, with his elbow resting on the arm of the chair, he swings it in a careless way. 'This is your work, Dr. Ramírez?'

"I am so relieved not to be on the roof that it makes me bolder. 'I think I have a right to know who I'm speaking to,' I say.

"'Do you know this building is state of the art?' The man looks at the ceiling. 'They're even installing a green roof—a milpa. And in this milpa they will grow corn and beans, and the people in the building will eat the corn and beans because that is all a Mexican needs.'

"'Who are you?' I ask again.

"'If it mattered, do you think we would be meeting here?' He stops swinging my data and holds it in the air. 'This is yours.'

"My strength is gone again and I nod my head.

"He drops it back on the spool table. 'Are you a terrorist?' he asks. He's looking at me very calm, and he picks up his Coke, slowly breaking the seal which sounds like whip cracks in that empty room. 'Is this your manifesto?' He nods toward my data. 'Your argument for sabotaging the future of agriculture in this country?'

"'What?'

"'You went to UNAM on government scholarships—master's, PhD—all paid for by us. That is an honor, and very expensive. So why do you hate Mexico so much? Why bite her tit like this?' He looks up at me like he really wants to know. 'Your father is a campesino, yes? Maybe he's in the milpa right now. Well, we have something in common, you and me. My father was a campesino too. I grew up in Morelos and there we use horses for the plowing, but it is all the same in the milpa and that is where I found my father. I was nine years old and he was younger than I am now, and I found him there one afternoon, dead in the dirt from a heart attack. The horses were just standing there like they would wait forever for him to get up. After that day, I went behind the plow with my brothers and sisters. We had to do everything because my mother wasn't herself anymore.'

"The man's arms are on the armrests of the beach chair and he opens his hands to me. 'And how long have we been doing this? Five hundred years? A thousand? The animals will do it for another thousand — forever — but we are men, no? Maybe you hate Mexico, but do you hate your father too? How can a young man given so much be so selfish?'

"He stands up then, walks to the big window and waves me over. I don't want to go near that window. 'Come,' he says. I turn to look at Raúl and the taxista, but they are both looking at their phones. I walk over to the man and stand sideways to the window so I can keep an eye on everyone. The man is looking out at the city, which looks from there like a rolling carpet of gray boxes. 'Twenty years ago,' he says, 'this was all forest and milpas, but don't those people still need to eat?' He turns back to me. 'What UNAM has done for you is the same thing we are doing for the corn — maximizing its potential. When we signed NAFTA you were still a boy, but this was my generation's gift to you. Not since Porfirio Díaz built the railroads and industrialized the sugar cane has a Mexican leader made such a strong commitment to progress. Thanks to Carlos Salinas, Mexico is becoming a modern country — and we are becoming a modern people. Tell me, how old were you when you got your first pair of shoes?'

"'I don't remember,' I said, which was a lie.

"He leaned toward me like he was sharing a secret. 'I was seven and I was not the first to wear them. Now I wear Magnanni. And look at you, a doctor of science, working at UNAM in a biogenetics lab with students of your own. It's incredible, no? In one generation your family has progressed from the Middle Ages to *this*. I can only imagine how proud your father must be. You can help us improve the native corn just as quickly. Transgénicos are the *future*,' he says, stepping toward me and pointing out the window, 'and Mexico is going to be a *leader*. You know as well as me that Mexico is the mother of the corn — for the whole world. And science is the father. Together we are making a better corn that will grow more, grow anywhere with no more lost crops, no more dead fathers and broken mothers. You know how hard it is so why do you, of all people, want to threaten the future of Mexico? This is a revolution, not only for the corn but for the people. Don't you understand what this means for us? For our families?'

"His eyes are wet and it makes the two colors in them even more different. He is asking like it's a question, but I can tell that for him it's answered already. I know this subject like my own hand, but I am scared and angry and there is something about his eyes. I'm having so much trouble collecting my thoughts. Finally, I get control of myself and I say to him, 'Señor, do you understand the risk you're taking? Nobody knows what transgénicos will do to the native crop over time, the science is too young. But what I do know'— and I'm pointing at my data now, stabbing at it —'is that I found Kortez400 in the Sierra Juárez, in four separate locations. Everyone in our lab knows there's a global ban on terminators, and everyone working on Kortez knows it's volatile. So what in the name of God is it doing in *Oaxaca*?'

"The man is standing two meters from me now and he sighs, looks at his watch and then over my shoulder at Raúl. 'It doesn't make sense,' he says, shaking his head. 'You call yourself a scientist and yet you have no faith in science to perform the miracle it is already performing in crops all over the world. It is a contradiction. It is bad for Mexico and, if you're not willing to hear me, it will be bad for you.' He walks back over to the spool, picks up his Coke, takes a sip and puts it back down. 'Listen to me now and I will tell you what this is.' He picks up my data and holds it in front of me. 'This is a dirty bomb. If you activate it as you are trying to do, you could do serious damage to millions of people and to a young industry that will bring Mexico wealth and respect in the twenty-first century. If you cause this to happen you will no longer be a scientist in our eyes, you will be a terrorist — an enemy, not just of Mexico but of our ally and partner the United States, and these are dangerous enemies to have.' He drops my data back onto the spool, but he keeps talking.

"'I can see you have a passion for this work, a gift even, and I'm willing to believe that you think you're doing the right thing. Now, Dr. Ramírez, with respect, I want to invite you to do exactly that — to be part of this green revolution that will transform Mexico. Already it is happening. Not only do we have the science, we have the support of NAFTA, the Ministry of Food and Agriculture, your Governor Odiseo and several multinational companies, including SantaMaize. But it will help the cause to have an indigenous scientist working with us, someone who can represent that population and give them confidence in the mission, to let them know we aren't taking anything away, we're simply harmonizing science with tradition. It will be a victory for you, for your people, for all Mexicanos. I can also say that if you join us you will be paid very, very well. I know for a fact that UNAM has secured funding for a new position on their faculty of sciences, a chair for a plant geneticist of native blood. Dr. Ramírez, you could be the first — the Benito Juárez of biotech.'

"The man is smiling now, like a patrón. 'It's the opportunity of a lifetime, but in order for it to happen'— he rests his hand on my data —'this must go away. As you know, we're in touch with your friend at the Ministry and we have his computer. We will need your computer now and we will replace it with the model of your choice. Maybe you need a new phone also. If there are other copies, in any form, you will need to find them. If this data or any part of it enters the environment — if it is reproduced anywhere at all — you will be held responsible and I cannot control what happens then. It's safe to say, at the very least, that your career at UNAM will be finished. But you're an ambitious and intelligent young man and I see another path for you.'

"He nods to Raúl who steps forward holding out a lighter. Again I am surprised by the size of his hand. The man takes the lighter and he looks at me, his face is open, almost beaming. 'It will be like planting time in the milpa,' he says. 'From the ashes, a new beginning.'

"Then he places the lighter on top of my data.

"I understand then what I am in this man's story. Already he knows what's coming next, and I am acting it out like some kind of puppet. More than anything I want to be gone from this place, but the lighter is one more thing I'm not expecting. I'm thinking this chingado can suck my dick if he thinks I'll burn my own work. This is the kind of thing they do to political dissidents and spies — not to scientists. Not to me. But I was still learning then.

"'You want me to burn this,' I say.

"'It's up to you,' he says. He is smiling like a cat and his different-colored eyes grow wider. I can't move. I am still trying to get this new idea into my head and it is just too big, too wrong. He sees me like this and says, 'Of course, if you need more time we can go up to the roof and see the milpa.'

"I know there is no milpa. I know the only thing up there is a long way down. And now I know that when you're afraid for your life you will do anything to save it. So I move myself and it is a robot doing this. I go to the spool and pick up my data and the lighter. The man stands back with his head down and his hands in front of him as if he is honoring a moment of silence. Raúl and the taxista put away their phones.

"I'm holding my data in one hand and the lighter in the other. The only way I can bring them together is to divide myself in two. There is the physical body with the data and the lighter, and there is everything else I am and believe floating overhead by the dangling wires. From there I witness my hand lighting the lighter and putting the flame to the pages. Like this I see the fire catch on the bottom corner and climb along the edges first, then race up the back, as if to burn is what those pages have always wanted to do. My hand drops them to the cement floor where the fire grows and the paper curls in on itself and then breaks apart, black and smoking. After a minute, the fire dies down, but there is some paper left, still showing some text.

"'All of it,' says the man softly, tapping his fingertips together.

"The body kneels and picks up the last part by the clip. The body lights it again and turns it in its fingers, feeding the paper to the flame until there is a smell of more than just paper. When it is all gone but the smoke and a few dark lines of text in the ash, the man nods to Raúl. Then he picks up his phone and the bottle of Coke. Raúl comes over and steps on the ashes, kicking them here and there. He picks up the clip and the lighter and puts them in his pocket. After that, he folds the beach chair and puts it under his arm. The man in the pink shirt looks down at what he thinks is me, still on my knees. 'Bueno,' he says. 'Ándale.'

"He draws his hand across his thin hair and moves toward the door with the taxista leading the way. With a wave of his hand, Raúl tells my body to come and it rises and walks out with him close behind. I am following overhead like a balloon on a string. Down the stairs we go with no one hurrying. Somewhere around the fourth floor, in the rhythm and echo of all those shoes and steps, in the shame and relief of being alive, I find my way back into my body. We come to the entrance hall and through the door to the parking lot. Before going to his car, the man turns to look at me. 'What we discussed,' he says, 'you'll take care of that today. Either way, I'll see you soon.'

"Raúl opens the door of the taxi for me and, once I'm in, he closes it, puts the beach chair in the trunk and gets in on the other side. The taxista starts the motor and as we pass through the gate the doors lock themselves again. The taxi is driving and there is nothing I can do. I am numb except for the blisters growing on my finger and thumb. I have never felt so weak. Never before have I had the life taken from me like that.

"'Café Verde,' says Raúl to the taxista like he is reminding him.

"'I don't want to go there,' I say.

"'It just opened,' says Raúl. 'The coffee's fantastic. And this waitress — my god.'

"He turns and looks out the window. I am looking too, and for a moment El Popo is visible between some buildings, snow running down from the cone in long blades, the ancient, endless smoke trailing away in the opposite direction from where we are going. Moctezuma saw that volcano, and so did Cortés, and I know for certain now they were seeing different things."

25

Lupo's head appears around the corner of the garage and says, "One hour," and I realize I've forgotten where we are. César doesn't even look up. His eyes are way out in the desert past the floodlights shining on this parking lot that looks now like a prison yard. A sick sad feeling comes into my stomach when I think of what's coming. But I never knew anyone in such a situation before and I can't help myself—I ask César what happened next and this is what he told me, más o menos.

"We were in the taxi for a long time," he said, "and no one says anything. I'm not sure where we are going and I wonder if I will have the strength to walk when we get there. When finally we pull over and stop, it is in front of Café Verde. It is a real place. The doors unlock and the taxista gets out and walks around to open my door. I look at Raúl to see if he's going to do anything, but he doesn't except for raising one of his giant fingers. 'That man we visited today,' he says. 'You saw his eyes? They are very good at finding lost things.' Then he nods toward the café and winks. 'Suerte.'

"I get out and walk away from the taxi in such a stupor it takes me a minute to realize that I am in Coyoacán, an expensive neighborhood by the university with shade trees and brightly painted houses. I feel dizzy like I have just given blood and I wonder if I'm being followed. I want to go home, but maybe someone's in my apartment already. Maybe I will get there and it will be torn apart, or I will be taken again. I go to a pay phone and call my girlfriend at her office and I can't tell you my relief when she answers. I ask her to meet me for coffee near the university. I don't usually do this and she asks me if everything's OK. 'Something came up,' I say.

"We meet at a student cafeteria on Churubusco where the kind of person who works for BioSeguridad will stand out. She is worried and asking me, but I make her wait until I've studied everyone and it looks OK. We get our coffee, sit down, me facing the door, and I tell her like I told you. Then I say I'm leaving the city and that she must fly home immediately. She is a stubborn güera and says she can't leave, that she's committed to her program and that giving in to fear is like justifying evil. I tell her that she is being arrogant and naïve, that Mexico isn't America, that this BioSeguridad guy is a very scary man who knows all about me and it won't help anyone if she is kidnapped and used for blackmail. I ask her where her passport is and she says it's in her backpack because she needed it for the bank that day. I ask her where her computer is and she says it's at her office. I tell her to go there, pick it up and go directly to the airport—to get out of Mexico and not come back until she hears from me.

"She's crying and I am saying how sorry I am, but I beg her to do this and promise I will contact her when I know more. Then this funny look comes over her face and she asks me if I've met someone else. I can't believe she's saying this, that she thinks I would make up such a story, so I take her hands in mine and lean in very close and I say, 'You're fucking right I met someone else. He wears pink shirts and has two different eyes and he scares the living shit out of me.' It was the only funny part of that entire afternoon. 'Mi corazón,' I said to her, 'you must believe me—and believe this.' I kissed her then and wondered when I would again.

"I never went back to my apartment and I never went back to the lab. I will not describe for you our goodbye, but letting go of her hand at the metro—that is when I became an exile in my own country. It was Orpheus who went down those stairs. I could feel her eyes on me, but I was afraid to turn around. At the bottom was a subway map covered in glass, and in spite of myself I looked at the reflection. All I could see behind me was a dark shadow against the sky.

"I took the metro to Centro Médico, withdrew my maximum from a bank machine, got a cash advance on my credit card and rode all the way out to La Paz. From there I took local buses to Puebla and then a Red Star overnight to Oaxaca. I knew a place I could hide safely, but every time the bus stopped I thought I was going to have a nervous breakdown—that Raúl would be there waiting, with his enormous hands. I was praying, but it had been a long time—I'd been so caught up in the work, and Juquila was far away. I was hoping she would be closer in Oaxaca, and I needed time to make a plan."

*

"The sun was coming up when the bus arrived at the second-class station and I took a taxi straight to my friend who lives alone near Abastos market and owns a taxi himself. He was home, thank God, and when he opened the door I started to cry. He hugged me, slapped my face like a brother and offered me a shot of mezcal. It was good to be back in Oaxaca. He made eggs and tlayudas and I tried to tell him. He was the right person, he had been active in the strike and it wasn't his first time hiding people. I didn't go outside for two weeks. I prayed a lot, especially to Juquila, and I apologized for neglecting her.

"In this time I grew a mustache and a small beard and made a plan to leave the country. I never wanted to leave, you know. I didn't know what else to do unless I wanted to work for those madres at BioSeguridad, but they wouldn't trust me now and UNAM would never take me back. My passport was in D.F. and I was sure they had it so I knew I must cross with a coyote. It was a big step—I wasn't sure I had enough money and that is how I came to drive the taxi. It is something I did in university and after two weeks in hiding I knew they would have searched my pueblo and found nothing. I hadn't been in el centro for five years and I believed I could be safe there if I was careful. My friend offered me the night and sixty percent minus gas. 'Just don't speed,' he said. 'And don't crash.'

"I thought I would make enough money in a month, but it took longer and all that time I didn't use my phone or my bankcard. I didn't go out in the daytime and I didn't try to contact my family or my girlfriend. It was a hard rule for me to live with, but I couldn't take the chance. I spent a lot of time working on an article to go with my data and researching the border on my friend's computer, but I would clear it every time. I left nothing with my friend and I put nothing in the cloud. I wanted no trace that might lead back to him or to Oaxaca. Always I kept my data and my money on me because I needed to be ready to run at any time. I had a thumb drive on my keychain, but the federales got that. Now the phone is all I have left. And my friend — I'm afraid I destroyed everything for him. My only hope is he can convince the federales that his taxi was stolen. Fuck. I can't think about that now."

César leaned his head back against the wall of the garage and groaned. "Since that day in D.F., my data and the dream of seeing my girlfriend again kept me going." César looked at me then and it was not a friendly look. "I was so fucking careful. For two months nobody recognized me. Then I have you in the taxi for two *minutes*." He took a sip of his beer that was more like a bite. "I never saw that truck coming."

"Cheche," I said, "if I had known —"

But he waved my words away. How can you argue with Fate?

26

I was so sure we would be found by now, that César would go to the hospital, that the bars would come back — something better or different than this. But to carry this for César — that is the bargain I made when I took his water. All his data is in here with his article in English — "Evidence of transgenic DNA and V-GURTs in native maize fields in Oaxaca, Mexico." Maybe it is the only copy that exists now. I tried to send it already, but it is waiting with everything else.

*

There is something else, AnniMac, and I only found it now — a pdf called VueloJetBlue. It is an itinerary for a flight from New York to Phoenix and the date has passed two days ago. But it was not this that sent the lightning through my body, it was the name. It is you — Anne Macaulay.

All this time.

You are in Phoenix now? Waiting? Looking for César? Pobre César. I believe it was you who kept him careful for so long. He did this for you and for the corn, and still he lives. I will tell him that you're close.

If you ever get these messages, please know I made it last as long as I could — his battery, his water, everything, but I'm afraid it's not enough and I cannot help him anymore. He was right — I should not have followed him. I should have left him in Abastos and gone back to my pueblo. If I had done that, he would not have gone to Lupo. But both of us wanted it to be true — that Don Serafín would help us, that things would be better if only we could get over the line. And there is something about César — he is a magnet, and such people can be dangerous.

Sat Apr 7 — 20:52

Here, but not here. There are night sounds all around me now — scratching and scuffling. The sound of soft feet. And birds — I think they're birds. Owls, maybe, calling. But no one answers. Once in a while something will crash against the tank, so loud and surprising it feels like a hammer on my mind. There is an echo when this happens, but it is too loud to be real. Maybe these are birds too — souls coming and going. There has been a lot of that lately.

Sat Apr 7 — 21:09

I should have shared my pipe — I know this, but I did not. I knew how precious it was, how if the others felt this cool air they would want it for themselves and I am not strong enough to defend it from so many. So I kept the pipe a secret and I saved this sweet air for myself. Before, when people were still moving in here, I sat against it, protecting it, feeling its breath on my back making my hairs stand up. And then when all was quiet I would put my face down to breathe and breathe and breathe.

There is no need to protect it anymore.

Sat Apr 7 — 21:13

I am killing time and time is killing me.

Sat Apr 7 — 21:22

It is when so many prayers go without an answer that the sacrifice becomes necessary. In Oaxaca we are always ready for this possibility, always practicing. With my own eyes at Día de los Muertos I have seen a man dressed like the pope standing in front of that church on Calle de la Noche Triste cutting women's breasts made of Jell-O into pieces on a plate and feeding them to the congregation while the devil in his horns and blood-red skin dances with a bottle of mezcal, pouring it down our throats like an injection. And across the street, hanging in the tree of the virgins, is a body made from old clothes and the bones of animals, a cow's pelvis for a face and blood or something like it everywhere around.

This is what we do in the good times.

And why is that? Before our troubles, many tourists liked to visit Oaxaca for Muertos. One time in the cemetery of San Miguel I was with a friend and his children at the grave of his young wife and their young mother where they had been working all day to build a scene around her stone, with mountains and trees and the ocean because she loved all these things in her life. Luego, into this scene about one in the morning comes a German tourist with his big cannon camera and two-meter girlfriend and he asks my compadre, "So, what is it with you Mexicans and death anyway?"

It is a funny question for a German to be asking, but my friend is a gracious man and he says to this giant cabrón, very calm and right in his eye, "Death is close by, amigo. Always." Then he taps this German on the back with his finger. "It is always just here, waiting. We know this, we recognize it and welcome it. It is not something to be afraid of because it is coming for all of us and who knows when."

Every year in the cemetery is a party — everyone you ever knew coming together again with candles burning on the graves, a band and food and many families, children playing in the dark with their dead brothers and sisters, and over there, under the laurel tree, an old man in a jaguar suit dancing with a lover only he can see.

Next year, I will be there also — one way or another, with this body or without it.

Sat Apr 7 — 21:34

Hello, am I talking to anyone?

I think someone is alive in here with me, but it's hard to know the difference now between us.

Sat Apr 7 — 21:38

Me llamo Héctor María de la Soledad Lázaro González y yo todavía estoy vivo.

Sat Apr 7 — 21:41

The wind blows sometimes and it makes a music in the pipe. I can hear the plantain man out there pushing his three-wheel Mercurio with the fire inside, blowing his steam whistle. That fire in the barrel is what I see at sunset when I look into my pipe. Next to the fire is a tank of water and it is the steam from this that cooks the plantains and makes the whistle blow. You can hear it all over the neighborhood — sad and hopeful at the same time. So many sounds, so many codes to understand. Many times I wake up to roosters and rockets and the man shouting ¡AAGUA*AAA!* ¡AAGUA*AAA!* coming to take your empty bottles and give you full ones.

But where is that pendejo when you really need him?

And that little flute which is the man coming to sharpen your knives, and every morning the mailman on his bicycle with the whistle that makes the dogs go crazy, and him with the metal can ringing his little triangle, but who knows what he has inside there. Remember that girl with the empanadas who looks like she's eight but can shout as loud as a man? And Señor Claxon with the ice cream, and that crazy banging in the morning telling you to get your trash down to the corner pronto, and the gas man with his ringing rings playing the Beatles so loud it will throw you out of bed? And all day the knacking of the looms, and all night the neighbor with the dog who won't shut up, and sometimes a calenda with its horns and monos who look over your wall and in your window and scare you half to death like they did last night.

This time I was sleeping maybe, dreaming. There was the moan and whistle in the pipe and then a scraping on the tank and then a banging and a scraping as if we are now some kind of instrument. You would not believe the tones, so many all together and in them I hear so many things — the mechanic coming back, the sexton's bell from the pueblo, mi madre asking ¿Quién es?, la llorona crying for her lost children, other voices I almost recognize, some creature trying to get in, others trying to get out. Señora Ellen singing in the hotel, and so much humming, the whole tank vibrating with it, moving through me like I am not even there.

But when finally I understand what is making these new sounds, I feel stupid — tricked again, and I remember where I am, in a universe where the governor is not God or Odiseo but Coyote. Because it is not only the wind doing this. It is the trees. This is why no one sees us. Jesus would forgive them, but I will not because to forgive is the gift of the weak, what you give when you have nothing else, when those chingaderas done to you cannot be undone or paid back. It is wrong to feel this way, I know — one more blasfemia. My poor mother.

Trying to think how a coyote thinks. We are not on any road. They took us up an arroyo and we are in some kind of forest, maybe a little canyon. In the desert this is the only place you find more than one tree together. Trees are like people that way, gathering by the river. There is a place in Oaxaca where the riverbank is made from cedar roots, solid wood like a canal. And the waterfalls. My god, it is a paradise. Who could leave such a place? But they do. For el Norte. Because they don't understand that water is the most precious thing of all. If I get out of here, I will tell them. I will be a hallelujah for the water.

Tell me, AnniMac, is it good fortune to be hiding in the shade? Or a cruel trick? The battery is getting low now, and the life of the phone is not the only one it measures.

27

Sat Apr 7 — 21:57

It is the first night I have been warm since I left Oaxaca and for this I must thank the others. There are so many clothes and bags in here and I have made a bed for César and covered him. At first I was afraid of them, so many and so quiet. I can feel them close around me now like a family of ghosts.

Sat Apr 7 — 22:31

It is hard to say this, AnniMac, because it means I must stop speaking to you, but the water is gone — all of it. Besides César breathing, the only sounds I hear are coming from outside the tank. I am cold now with the turkey skin, even with the extra jacket. It hurts down in my back, my kidneys, and I know it is from thirst, but I have only urine in the bottle now. That will be difficult, but there's no hurry about it because in here we have time, no? Una eternidad.

Sat Apr 7 — 23:18

I woke up dreaming of water and meat. I was lying with César. I had the phone on his shoulder, talking into it, and I went to sleep. When I woke up I was licking his face and I did not stop — could not. All the blood and sweat on him — his forehead, his eyes, his ear where it collected. I cleaned him like a cat.

It is another world in here, where your mind watches from far away, and need and pain are the only gods you recognize.

Sun Apr 8 — 00:07

It's César. It isn't César. AnniMac, there's no more breathing and his hand is cold. There has been a mistake. Why am I still here? It is his touch, you know — his breath — that keeps me sane.

El silencio es terrible.

Sun Apr 8 — 01:11

Dreaming of watermelons — many all together cut in half-moons. I am eating them one after another without stopping and somehow in these watermelons, in the eating of them, is something important, some kind of forgiveness.

But I am awake now and in my hands there are not watermelons but César's phone and my abuelo's jaguar head — the only things left that are not empty or dead, the only things in here that can make me brave. Who is brave? Not many, not me, but César is one. Even now. And my abuelo who keeps coming to me because he lived through so many things, I ask him, "Abuelo, why are you always sharpening and sharpening your machete?"

"Why?" he asks, like I should know the answer. "Because you never know what you might need it for."

His voice sounds so close by, but I don't see him until the accident with the taxi. It is a big surprise for everyone — the three of us walking home from the mountain with a load of wood, and the taxi comes around the turn sounding its claxon, only the claxon is a police siren. Isabel is tired and half asleep and it is not a sound she knows so she jumps the wrong way and up and over she goes — with the firewood and everything through the windshield.

The taxi stops in the ditch on the other side of the road and Abuelo is running like a young man. Isabel is in the front seat with glass and firewood everywhere. There are two ladies from San Jerónimo in the back and they are screaming and wiping Isabel's urine and shit from their faces and aprons. Isabel's head is in the taxista's lap. His nose is broken from Isabel or some wood and he is wearing a beard of blood. His hair is sparkling with the glass and all over his forehead are little wounds like Jesus has. Over and over he touches his eyes, saying, "Where are my Ray-Bans? Who took my Ray-Bans?"

But Abuelo is too angry to care about him, he just wants to save Isabel, and he opens the passenger door to untie her packsaddle. Isabel's eyes are open and he's talking to her in Zapotec, patting her face to let her know he's close by. It looks like she is maybe OK so Abuelo takes her by the back legs and tries to pull her out the door. I am just standing there, forgetting I even have a body, until I hear him shouting, "Héctor! Take it! Take it!"

So I take her tail in both hands and together we pull her out of the taxi. It is only then we see that one of her front legs is gone by the knee and Abuelo is clicking his tongue and saying, "Where's your leg, girl? That's no good. What has he done to your leg?" Isabel doesn't know her leg is gone and she's trying to stand up and walk, but she keeps falling down so Abuelo takes her by the halter with his face close to hers saying things I can't hear, and like this he leads her away from the car, stroking her nose and helping her to walk. Then, before I can see what's happening he twists her head so suddenly and — *Ya!* — she's lying on the ground with him on top of her holding her head down and covering her eyes to calm her, all the time talking in her ear until she stops kicking and trying to get up. She is breathing hard and her nostrils are big and round, their wind blowing up little clouds of dust on the roadside, moving small pebbles. I can feel this on my face and I can hear Abuelo breathing together in the same time as her and me.

Abuelo's machete is still over his shoulder in the fajilla and now he pulls it out with his free hand. He takes it short by the blade and puts it to Isabel's neck, feeling with his fingers for the heartbeat. When he finds it I can feel it too — like it is my own heart beating. Abuelo makes a strong hold with his other arm and slides the blade in so easy like he is only wiping it, all the time talking softly in her ear. I can hear every word he says and I know everything is going to be OK. Isabel barely moves. There is only her breathing and the bright blood coming, making small rivers in the dust and over my abuelo's hand, which is my hand also. Slower now comes Isabel's breath and more easy, her nostrils not so round, and it is the same with me and Abuelo until everything is quiet with only the sound of the wind on the road.

Sometimes life gives you such things to do, but not everyone can do them.

If I get out, I promise to them and to you I will make a pilgrimage over the mountains to the church of Juquila. I will light candles there for all of them and I will deliver the little gown César bought for her, the same one I tied to his head. I will tell the priest of César's sacrifice, and that Juquila must wear it now — just like it is.

Because it's coming, closer all the time.

Sun Apr 8 — 02:36

I heard someone crawling in the tank. I heard him breathing — a deep growling sound like an animal. I didn't know who it was and I had nowhere to go. I was sleeping, but I sit up then with my back against the wall and listen. I can hear his knees on the bottom of the tank, his hands on people's clothes, but no one makes a sound, only him. When he's on top of the Maya I turn on the phone and point the screen at him. I cannot recognize the face, the skin is pulled so close over his bones and his tongue is out of his mouth like Death himself. He roars at the light and then comes faster. I keep the light on him and when he's on top of César I kick at his face, beating him back with my heels. He tries to grab my feet, but it's hard for him because his hands are wet with something and my shoes come off. I am so strong with fear and every kick is for my life until I hear something break and his head drops down, but I'm afraid he will get up so I keep kicking. He's lying across César and with my feet I push him off until his head is on the floor of the tank, then with my heel I hit him again and again, but the growling will not stop, it only gets louder, horrible sounds no animal can make, and only when I bite my sleeve to calm myself is it quiet again.

Sun Apr 8 — 03:02

God is giving me one more day.

How do I know this?

When I am disappearing over and over again.

Everything is gone but the waiting. So I wait for my courage to come back because, in here, life and courage are the same. César — all of them — as close to me now as Odiseo in the café where all the laws are broken and no one seems to care, talking all at once but only about water. And you are water also — a cool and beautiful pool. I am swimming in the idea of you and it is keeping me alive. You and César and Abuelo are telling me to think the impossible thoughts, that all these bodies are only that. The throat is an empty hole, you say. The heart is a dry well. Alone in such a darkness I think you can lose your mind.

Sun Apr 8 — 03:51

Yes, it is me again. Because I am doing a difficult thing — searching for water. There is a lot of liquid in here and all of it is bad. I am only looking for the bottles. Looking — no, I cannot bear to look at them, I'm feeling around like a blind thing. My fingers are worms among the dead. The tongues are the worst — so big and hard it makes me gag. Most of the bottles are empty. Some have urine in them and I keep these because this is what a desperado must do. But God is smiling on me today. Or maybe it is you, because there is water. Sí, es un milagro. In a plastic bag tied under a lady's huipil — some people carry it this way. I can tell by the heavy sewing that she is the Maya from Chiapas. I remember her face because the last time I saw it she looked so frightened and it is hard to frighten those people.

It is wrong, I know, to put my hands where I put them to find that water. I remember from before, her chichis were big, but when I touch them now they are small, no bigger than the bag of water. This is what the thirst will do and I grow smaller also. Whispering to myself, to her, "Lo siento, hermana, pobrecita. Discúlpame, por favor." There is only a little bit, but now it is my life, not hers, floating in that bag and I will make it last. Because something is choosing me to live and I have made this bargain. By keeping my pipe a secret I have done this. By taking César's water.

Sun Apr 8 — 04:10

The tank is filled with light — bright as a sun and everything burning. I see their blackened shapes with orange rings around them, mouths open wide and it's impossible to breathe. I am afraid to look at anyone because what if they look back. What if they know?

Sun Apr 8 — 04:32

I did not pour the Maya's water into a bottle but sucked it slowly from the bag, each time only enough to make my mouth wet. It lasted longer this way, and with that bag in my mouth and soft against my hands I did not feel so alone as before.

I live another day, or maybe just another hour. And I try to reach you one more time because this — these words are my machete, and these keys are my rosary, and as long as I am telling them I know I am not dead.

28

My abuelo is here with his special stone, the one he found when he was plowing. Too old to have a name but heavy with a hole it. You hold it to the sun so the rays come through. Can you see this? Burning a hole into my head so you and God can see inside.

Tengo otra confesión.

I had a dream last night he reached into my mouth. I thought it was my own hand. I knew it was César only after — not by the sound he made because it was not the sound of a man but the sound of an animal — an animal choking on sand. His fingers were hard and his hand was clumsy, searching I think for something wet. I know because all of them were searching for this and I must have pity, but in that moment, in the dark, I was scared out of my mind. My mind is not working properly and I bit him. Without thinking, in my dream, I did this. It is wrong, I know, but it was like being a baby again — how they take without thinking. How they take like the world owes it to them. That is the kind of thirst I have. I could not stop myself, and I could not be stopped.

My tío tells me a drowning man will do like this — will climb over his own mother to only breathe. "I have seen it myself," he says. "Once, in the Río Bravo."

So hard to know now what is me and what is him. But it was there, in that moment of the taking that we crossed over.

These are messages coming down to you from the cross on the mountain. But you are safe there on the other side — and merciful, I hope, because I am needing some of this right now —

Dominus noster Jesus Christus te absolvat —

Sí. Por favor. Amén. But how can one absolve — or punish — this? The body wanting to live? Only if life is breathing and nothing else am I alive. My mother would not know me now. *Chamaco* she called me — *Diablito*. Then she was just angry. Now it is a prophecy.

. . .

Dark and water everywhere. Water spirits coming in the night when it gets cold, coming into me with every breath. I can feel them all around me now, rolling down the walls, onto my hands, my tongue. They have been trying to tell me all this time — we are being made into something new. So we can travel through the pipe, and join the others.

It hurts so much to do this, to leave the body — cramps and cold and cracking open, bones too big for the skin.

. . .

Riding Tío's bicycle with Isabel following on a rope. We pass a man pulling a wagon with a white dog in it. Behind him is that silent viejo who lost a duel and also his hand so he must carry the basket balanced on his sombrero. And over there, in the field behind the school, a horse is walking with an egret, matching their steps like old compañeros in an old conversation. In the shadow of the church I see one brother sleeping in a wheelbarrow and the other sleeping on a shovel. And every year at Eastertime comes that same Nazareno with no shoes and no hat dragging his cross down the road going who knows where, passing again and again that same burro on the roadside with a circle of vultures on her like they are at the café drinking micheladas.

I knew all their names once, but not anymore.

. . .

I taste of blood and rust and dying. This mezcal is not agreeing with me. And that itching in my legs, deep in the bones — something is crawling around in there trying to get out and there is no way I can reach it. It is telling me to tear my skin apart and I am trying not to listen.

They are watching now, all of them, to see what I will do, but in their eyes instead of eyes are the little metal covers you see in the sidewalk saying AGUA. These are the signs telling you what is really important, medallions for the saints, por Santa Agua. Breathe her name over and over as I do now — AGUA — Agua — *agua,* and you will know the prayer of death and wanting — living and dying all in one small word — the One Word which is not a word at all but only a sound in the throat.

César is here next to me and his AGUA eyes are the old kind with stars on them. They are glowing red hot. I believe this is the sign of anger.

· · ·

It is coming alive like the jungle in here. We are evaporating in a hot cloud and flies are everywhere, or maybe they were always here, waiting. Other things are coming too and for them it is a feast. But I have only thirst. I am shivering from the heat. The light in the pipe is one star in a black sky and someone is howling at it. Maybe you can hear me.

· · ·

Señor Cacahuate, the peanut man, smiles in the corner with his stick and hat and funny eye. He is showing us the painting, the old one from church of the peanut truck with the words on the side —

LA TENTACIÓN MÁS GRANDE. And up on the ceiling in that lonely cloud is the hand of God reaching down. All this time Señor Cacahuate reads the words "La Tentación Más Grande — La Tentación Más Grande," over and over, until I understand that yes, the temptation is too great and this is why He takes the peanuts.

All but one — the one He does not want.

. . .

I am awake now and it is better, talking to you. When I get out I will show you my country — César's country. We can drive the Apache to the coast and see the frigate birds with scissor tails hang still in the air, the clouds racing by above them, and the secret spot south of Puerto where I saw the pelican king with his medallion. Even gringos saw it so it must be real, taking photos as he flew away, chain swinging. And maybe las tortugas. Two days it takes them to make love. I have seen this with my own eyes — just floating and floating like we had all the time — water and sky with only the two of us between. And the babies so sweet and small and sad — perfect in your hand. But into the ocean they must go, and there is nothing more sweet or small or sad than a baby tortuga facing the ocean for the first time.

All the others managed to get out, why not me?

. . .

Yes, I know. I can see you there. You're taller in person and even more beautiful. Is it the light or my eyes? Your hands and face just floating there. Are you here for the judgment? Are you looking for your son? I've said too much already. How did you get in?

The same way they got out. Everyone but me. And now I know why.

Yes, I traveled to the pyramid. I climbed the steps one by one. My feet were wet from the blood — the stones so slippery I had to use my own two hands, fingers in the cracks. I will never forget the sound — and that plane with all those faces in the windows, looking without seeing.

My ears are ringing — humming.

I can hear the organ grinder, but I can't see the monkey.

. . .

There is a page missing from the codex, but I have found it on this wall that wraps around us like the belly of an animal. In the place of words is a jaguar, and in the place of spots are drops of water saying in a thousand different ways, as clear as any voice, for everything that lives, water is the one true thing.

Someday this missing page will be painted where everyone can see it, and there, we will see ourselves reflected —

a jaguar
a water truck
a loaf of bread
a bag of seeds
green shoots pushing through the ground
small black birds escaping
one last bird remaining
a list of questions

Was he too big, or the wrong shape?
Was he too bad, or the wrong color?
Is he waiting for something? Or someone?

And the corn that has been growing all this time.

. . .

Are you the thing you want most, or its opposite? If I want nothing more than water, is it because I am water? Or because I have
none? If I want nothing more than love, is it because I am love?
Do we always want more of what made us? Is what we are what
we need?

Maybe I can give you these. Maybe this is why you've come. After
all this time.

I understand now that all water is holy and that we are made to
drink and to love another. I love you. I do. That is what these words
are. But is it because you are here, a being in the universe receiving
these messages? Or because I hope you are? Is it only because I want
to be saved? And to be saved — to be permitted to live — to drink
and to love — is what I want more than anything besides a pool of
clear water. I know this question is a circle, a deep round pool, and
I am drowning in the answer.

Whose white hands are these? I don't know.

Only that when she holds me the pain is not so much.

All things are mine since I am His
How can I keep from singing?

. . .

There is a breathing in the pipe. Is it you? When you are what I need now more than anything but water. And that same dry sound — the sound of dying. All my water deep inside me now. Only the pipe and what it says.

Its breath — coming and going, in and out. The tank alive now after all, full of us and what we are. A sound from deep in the throat.

Like some stories my abuelo told me.

It's on top of us. Hands. Feet. Paws. Soft pats and the scratching of claws so loud inside my skull. The itch in the bone I cannot reach. The blades in my back. More breathing in the pipe and the paws again, trying to get in — the sound the heart makes beating in the body — so close I can almost touch it. Claws and teeth, a stone blade catching on the bone.

What this creature is wanting.

Saying.

No. All of us are gone.

. . . in this world so much letting go.

Always and forever.

Ya terminé . . .

Ringing —
   a ringing
   a ringing in my ears
           but no answer

Epilogue

Partial transcript of an interview conducted by John Bernard (*Pima County Monitor*) with wildlife managers Ted Harvey and Calvin Wills, Arizona Game and Fish Department.

April 11, 2007

JB: So, how did you find them?

TH: Well, it wasn't us, it was A2 — we call him Alvin —

CW: Rhymes with Calvin.

TH: He's our latest, must have just come across. We've only had a collar on this guy for about a week, trying to figure if he's a transient or if he's going to stay and make a go of it. The males are typically moving quite a bit so when they stop for more than a day it'll mean one of three things: he's sick, he's shot or he's made a kill. Only other possibility is he's found a mate, but that's not likely this far north. Hasn't been a female sighted in Arizona since the sixties —

CW: That's what you call a dry spell.

TH: But we worry when the signal stops moving because it's tough out there — all kinds of people willing to shoot a jaguar. There's narcos would love to have one of these guys on their wall and there's a lot of ranchers have a NIMBY attitude toward any kind of predator. You know, "shoot, shovel and shut up." Indians might have some reasons of their own, but I can't speak —

JB: So, you found them when?

CW: He's wanting to know about the truck, Ted. Sorry. With us it's all about the cats.

TH: I'm sure you know illegals are a dime a dozen out here. They're trashing the desert like you wouldn't believe and it's very disruptive to our work, especially when you're dealing with something as shy as a jaguar. Mostly, we try to work around them.

CW: So I was checking for signal that morning — Easter — and Ted was late coming from church. I picked up Alvin's signal right away, checked the GPS and saw he'd been in that spot more than twenty-four hours so we packed up the gear and went. The nearest road is two miles away so we parked the truck and walked in. We had our packs, radios, camera, GPS, a rifle with tranquilizer darts, and Ted's carrying a sidearm 'cause you never know who you're going to meet out there these days. That area — Altar Valley — is wide open semi-arid desert; you've got ocotillo and mesquite, some barrel cactus and saguaro, but it's pretty fast going. That's why it's a highway for illegals, and with all that foot traffic it gets harder to track an animal. Lots of tire tracks too, lately. A mile or so in — we're maybe a mile north of the border now — we spot a little grove of ironwood and paloverde in a low spot off to the southeast. Looks like a wash. There must be some decent water underground because the trees are old and there's a couple of good-size saguaros, so now we're pretty sure we found our cat. We head over that way and when we're about two hundred meters out we get down and check his signal again. He's still there, hasn't moved at all. It's a good place to lay up, cooler in there, so we're thinking he must have a kill, a nice javelina or something. There's a little breeze out of the east so he won't be winding us, and we creep up on him, belly-crawling —

JB: And the truck?

TH: Almost there, chief. Anyhow, I saw it first — the vehicle — and I told Cal to hold up. Said we got company, smugglers for sure, but you can't tell if it's drugs or people. Makes a difference, safety-wise. If it's mota you're trying to save your life, and if it's tonks you're probably going to have to save theirs. Now, you got 'em both together sometimes.

CW: Hell, these days you can get shot by one of your own.

TH: Happened more than once, I'm sure. Either way, we can't figure what Alvin's doing. Did someone shoot him and dump his collar? Is the vehicle abandoned? Nothing's making sense. So we move in a little closer, but it's still as death in there. Not a sound, just doves and quail. Well, we don't want to be ambushed, but at the same time, you been out here a while you can kind of *feel* if you're alone or not. And this one here is feeling pretty darn lonely.

CW: We get to fifty meters out — close — and we can see the truck back there in the trees. It's some kind of tank truck — old — not the kind of thing you usually find out here. There's writing on the side — looks like graffiti, but the vegetation's too thick to make it out. You can see how they'd miss it from the air. Anyhow, we're hoping it's our cat in there so we move around to the west, downwind, and when we're thirty meters out, that's when we start smelling it. A jaguar'll eat damn near anything if he's hungry enough, and now Ted and me, we're going the same place with this — we're thinking Alvin's on some carrion. Corriente steers'll hide out in places like this, maybe antelope, but so will a Mex, and with that truck there, well, you can imagine what we're thinking. In twenty years I've seen a lot out here, and a lot of changes, but this would be a first. I loaded a dart and Ted's got his Glock in case there's something more than Alvin in there, and we shout then, calling Alvin's name 'cause we're wanting him to move now.

TH: Nothing happening so I throw a handful of rocks. Well, that rousts him up and he's not a happy kitty — he's growling.

Usually, if you spook them they'll just take off and you won't know where they went, but you can tell this guy doesn't want to move. He's definitely got something in there and he ain't sharing. We stand up so he can see us, see we're bigger than him, and we walk in like that, noisy and close together. You can really smell the meat now, like roadkill and outhouse mixed together, and we can hear movement by the back of the truck. It's Alvin and he's growling, just low and steady.

CW: I've got the tranquilizer ready and we're skirting around to the south, looking for an opening, and there he is in the wash. He's standing in the bare sand by the back of the truck. Looks like a water truck; you can see the pipes there just above Alvin's head. Well, Alvin isn't budging and I said to Ted, "I guess he thinks that truck is his." We're looking all around for the carcass because we know it's somewhere close, but there's nothing — not under the truck, not anywhere. It's weird.

TH: I was thinking it must be further back in the trees or maybe he drug it up in the branches, but that's a leopard trick; *onca* doesn't normally do that.

CW: It's in the wash we see the first fresh man tracks mixed in with Alvin's; not old — no more than a few days. Looks like two guys and they're heading south, beating it back to Mexico. Hell of a place for engine trouble. We're not worried about narcos anymore because no Mexican's gonna stick around with this guy. We're maybe fifteen meters off now and I'm waving my arms trying to get him to go. But you kind of hate to, because how often do you get this close to a jaguar? Not often, I'll tell you that.

TH: Heck, never, unless he's dead or you dart him.

CW: And he sure won't just stand there like Alvin is. I'm
wondering if he isn't sick. Rabid maybe. So I took a knee
then and sighted the rifle, but I'm saying, "Let's just watch
him a minute." Well, the way he's pacing back and forth,
glaring at us and growling, he sure doesn't *look* sick. He looks
mad! And I said to Ted, "I do believe old Alvin's giving us
the stink-eye." It was the first time we'd seen him since we
collared him, and he is a specimen — healthy like you read
about. You see him out there in all those pale browns and
greens and him so bright and vivid, the spots jumping off his
body. It's like a piece of the jungle landed in the desert, like
the jaguar is more alive than everything around him — even
you. Hard to explain if you haven't seen it yourself. Isn't that
right, Ted? Ted was taking pictures like a Jap tourist.

TH: I got so many it's like a movie. Here, take a look. Right, that
button there.

JB: Wow. He's beautiful. And big. Jesus, look at those teeth.

TH: Most powerful bite, pound for pound, of any cat. Crush your
skull. That's how they kill, you know — right through the
brain.

JB: Amazing. OK, and that's his collar there.

CW: We watched him for a couple minutes like that.

TH: Which is forever by cat standards.

CW: It was a long time, and we notice that every now and then he'll wave his nose around by the pipes, especially the one on the left — that one with the elbow there.

TH: He's scenting something for sure, and I'm saying to Cal, "Oh Lordy, you think that's what we're smelling?" And then, my goodness, well, we kind of knew, you know — there's people in there. Judging by the smell we're too late, but we have to check it out, so now we got to get Alvin moving.

CW: I didn't want to dart him if I didn't have to, so I jumped up and yelled at him and he backed into the thicket. Not far.

TH: Look at this one — you can just see him there. See his eye?

JB: It's like it's glowing.

TH: Yeah, they're spooky that way.

CW: Well, then Ted and me moved in there together, yelling some more, and that got him. He was gone.

TH: But hard to say how far. *Onca*'s not the kind to attack a man — kid, maybe, but nothing's normal here, so we kept our guard up, threw some more rocks, but it seemed like he'd cleared out for the time being.

CW: So now I'm saying, "Hola! Anybody there? Qui es aquí!" Well, I know my Spanish is lousy, but there's nothing coming back. I'm still keeping an eye out for Alvin, and Ted goes in to check that pipe.

TH: I'm telling you, I about lost my breakfast. Smell was that bad. Make your eyes water. So I catch my breath and try knocking on the tank with a rock. Sounded pretty empty but hard to say for sure, so I put my ear to it. Nobody home, but just to be safe, I hold my nose and give a listen to that pipe —

CW: And that's when he says, "Jesus in Heaven, there's somebody in there. I can hear him breathing."

Acknowledgments

This book was a collaborative and often serendipitous process that would never have begun had not my beloved wife, Nora, moved our family to Oaxaca for a year in 2009. I am deeply grateful to her and to the many people we encountered, Mexicano and expat alike, who made us feel welcome in one of the most beautiful, compelling and troubled places I have ever been. *The Jaguar's Children* is as much a token of my gratitude to Oaxaca and those who illuminated it as it is the realization of a lifelong dream.

Among those who made Oaxaca especially vivid are Niels Barmeyer, Miguel Batista, Katie Fellman, Aldo González, Carlos Hernández, John Kemner, Steve Lafler, Lapiztola, Cathey López, Mercedes López-Zschaemisch, Serena Makofsky, Linda Martin, Eric Mindling, Jorge Pinzón, Nina Pozzi, Jane Robison, David Sandler, Angélica Vásquez Cruz, Gracia Vásquez Olivera, Heather VerWys and Lauren Waits. Special thanks to Larry Cooper, Kara Hartzler, Saúl Orozco, Melanie Thon and Susana Valdivia for their careful reading, and to David Riker, not only for reading twice, but for his deep understanding of the place and the process.

Foremost among many sources were *The Devil's Highway,* by Luis Alberto Urrea, and "Exodus," by Charles Bowden. The excerpt from W. J. McGee's "Desert Thirst as Disease" is reproduced courtesy of *Journal of the Southwest.* For their contributions to my understanding of corn, its history, economy and genetics, I am indebted to

Professors Michael Blake, George Haughn, and Andrew Riseman of the University of British Columbia, and to Timothy Wise of Tufts University's Global Development and Environmental Institute.

Thanks to Richard Grant for sharing "the skeleton key to Mexico," Janet Chávez Santiago for advice on Zapotec translation, and especially to Annita and the late Tom Harlan for taking me down El Camino del Diablo.

My deepest gratitude goes to Beatrice Monti della Corte von Rezzori and the Santa Maddalena Foundation for granting me the space and time to write a first draft in the most idyllic surroundings I could imagine, and to Sonny Mehta and Louise Dennys for their belief that I belonged there. Ted Hodgkinson, Miguel Syjuco and Evie Wyld were delightful companions in that dreamtime.

I also want to thank my agent, Stuart Krichevsky, for handling my transition to first-person Zapotec fiction so gracefully, and for his unwavering enthusiasm throughout.

Finally, I am indebted to my editors, Louise Dennys and Amanda Lewis at Knopf Canada and Jenna Johnson at Houghton Mifflin Harcourt, for seeing the jaguar in its best light.

Mil gracias, amigos.